W. R. BURNETT was born in Springfield, Ohio, in 1899. Between the ages of ten and twelve he wrote some "very bad short stories," and then completely lost interest in writing and took up sports while he attended East High in Columbus and Miami Military Institute in Germantown, Ohio. He left Ohio State University in his sophomore year and drifted from job to job, finally settling down as a statistician for the Ohio Bureau of Workmen's Compensation, where he stayed for six years. Once again he began reading—everything he could get his hands on—and writing. "I had an extremely hard time getting started," he later said. "I had no one to advise me and learned to write by trial and error. My job with the state kept me from starving."

After six years and five novels, several plays, and a large number of short stories, he gave up his job and went to Chicago and then California, where he continued to write novels as well as many screenplays. Among his best known works are *Little Caesar*, *High Sierra*, and *The Asphalt Jungle*.

OTTO PENZLER, series editor of Quill Mysterious Classics, owns The Mysterious Bookshop in New York City. He is the publisher of The Mysterious Press and *The Armchair Detective* Magazine. Mr. Penzler co-authored, with Chris Steinbrunner, the *Encyclopedia of Mystery and Detection*, for which he received the Edgar Allan Poe Award from the Mystery Writers of America.

THE ASPHALT JUNGLE

W. R. BURNETT

A Quill Mysterious Classic

Series Editor:
OTTO PENZLER

Quill
New York ● 1984

Library of Congress Catalog Card Number: 84-60103

ISBN: 0-688-03126-9

Printed in the United States of America

First Morrow Edition

1 2 3 4 5 6 7 8 9 10

BOOK DESIGN BY RICHARD ORIOLO

· 1 ·

Lou Farbstein, middle-aged but still referred to as the bright boy of the *World* (and bright boy he had actually been twenty years back), neither liked nor disliked Police Commissioner Theo J. Hardy, the new power in the city. He regarded him as a rather weird phenomenon, wrote about him often with curious impartiality, and greatly influenced the opinion of the press generally by his sharp but fair pronouncements. Much of what he wrote stuck. For instance, when he referred to the Commissioner as a "Harold Ickes type character," the other reporters realized at once the aptness of the phrase and began to make an exception of the sharp-featured, countrified ex-judge when they wrote their frequent excoriations of the corrupt gentry managing the now shaky City Administration. Owing to Farbstein's clarifying phrase, they perceived that Hardy was honest, able, hard-working, and with plenty guts; they also saw that he was extremely irritable, a little vindictive, and at times—ridiculous.

For some weeks after Hardy had taken over, the reporters had considered him a mere front—a lay figure, humdrum and respectable, behind which the thieves and connivers of the City Hall intended to continue to carry on their denounced malfeasance. Now they knew better. Hardy was the City Administration's one hope, and the politicians stood trembling in the background. If Hardy could not save them, they would all be voted out at the next city election, their enemies and ill-wishers would be in power, and they themselves would be in danger of indictment and conviction, or at least public disgrace.

Bulley, the Mayor, had gradually faded into insignificance. Curtis, Chairman of the Board of Supervisors, was on a highly publicized vacation in California, taking a "well-earned rest," as Farbstein wrote in the *World*, bringing appreciative snickers from those who were in the know. And Dolph Franc, the formidable Chief of Police, was all smiles and sweetness, in contrast to his former cynical ill-humor, and in public kept referring to Commissioner Hardy as "my great little boss."

Nevertheless, the newspapers continued attacking the Administration with non-partisan unanimity—especially the Police Department—and Hardy, no longer able to ignore the blasts and now thoroughly aroused, had sent out invitations to a press conference, to be held at night in his battered and dingy office in the Old City Building.

The reporters sat around smoking their own cigarettes and grumbling. What kind of a lousy conference was this? No free liquor. Not even common courtesy. The harness-bull secretary in the outer office had looked at them as if they were a group about to be shoved into the show-up line.

Only Farbstein was unperturbed. Like Diogenes, he'd been looking for an honest man for a long time, and he had begun to feel that the flame in his lantern would sputter out before he found him. But, though the flame had shortened almost to nothing, here he was at last. Hardy! It wasn't necessary to like him. In fact, it was impossible. But you could respect him, and to Farbstein—at this juncture in his life—that was everything.

He sat listening calmly while the men about him yapped and raved. In spite of all their exterior toughness and cynicism, they were good solid guys, fathers and taxpayers. They'd see the light in all its unaccustomed brightness soon.

A sudden silence fell when the Commissioner walked in. It was a cold night and he was wearing a heavy ulster, old-fashioned rubbers, and a battered, sweat-stained hat, pulled down almost to his eyes.

He did not flash a politician smile on them, or shake hands all around, or get out the cigars and the whisky, or make some touching reference to his poor wife waiting at home or to his charming, and politically valuable, little grandson. He merely pulled off his hat, sat down at his desk still wearing his overcoat, and stared at them hard with his cold, inquisitorial gray eyes. They could see he was sore as hell and hated their guts. It was refreshing.

After a moment, without preliminaries, he began to make a speech.

"I've called you here," he said, "not to soft-soap you and tell you what smart and wonderful guys you are—you hear enough of that, I think. Neither am I going to ask you to lay off. I'm just going to tell you the facts of life and then leave it up to you.

"You say the Police Department is corrupt. You say the bunco squad works with the con men. You say the police are taking a fortune from syndicated prostitution—and rousting around and making their arrest records from the unsyndicated and lone-wolf prostitutes. You say the racket squad allows big-time racketmen to live here for a consideration, and then kicks around and persecutes the little local boys. You say in spite of the laws that bookies are operating all over the place and that a lot of police officers are getting rich on protection money . . .

"Shall I go on?"

Hardy glanced about him sharply, his thin lips set in a harsh line. Nobody said anything.

"All right. I guess that's enough for a starter. Now first I want to say this. I'm not denying that corruption exists in the Police Department. In fact, there is quite a lot of it— more than I can run down and punish in a few months. But there are also many honest men on the force, high and low, and you're making it mighty tough for them to hold their heads up. According to you, every man in a city police uniform is a louse and a stench in the nostrils of you high-minded, blameless, extremely honest gentlemen of the press."

There was considerable squirming in the Commissioner's office, and Farbstein smiled to himself.

"What is your basis for comparison?" Hardy demanded. "Name something that has no corruption in it."

"Mother's love," said Hillis of the *Sun*, and there was a brief titter.

"I deny that emphatically," said Farbstein. "Ever hear of a character called Freud?"

"I'm not going to labor the point," said Hardy. "But you men are criticizing the Police Department as if it alone, in a pure world, suffered from corruption. All human institutions are fallible—even the newspaper business, I'm afraid, hard as that may be for you crusading gentlemen to believe. All attacks and crusades of this kind are alike in the way I'm speaking about—the basis for comparison. The prize-fighting game is lousy and crooked—one of your favorite crusades. But in comparison with *what?*"

"Commissioner Hardy," said Kelso of the *Examiner*, "this sounds to me like sophistry, and I didn't expect it from you."

Hardy laughed shortly.

"Poaching on your preserves, eh? Well, be patient with me. I've got a point to make."

Hardy took out a stogie-type cigar, lit it, and puffed thoughtfully on it. An acrid odor of burning weeds made the newspapermen grimace and draw back from the Commissioner.

There was a long silence, then without another word the Commissioner leaned forward and switched on the special radio on his desk. In a moment, police calls began to pour into the little office without cessation—police calls from all corners of the huge, sprawling metropolitan area.

The reporters listened in silence, shifting about uneasily as the calls continued to come in, one after another, overlapping—from Camden Square, from Leamington, Italian Hill, Polishtown, South River, even from the great suburban areas where the tame and respectable people lived—hundreds of calls of all descriptions, a sordid, appalling, relentless stream.

"I assume, gentlemen," said Hardy, "that, being newspapermen, you know the codes. But in case some of you don't . . . I'll translate for a moment." Then he picked up the calls as they came in: *A drunk lying in the gutter. Another drunk—disorderly. An attempted attack—foiled. A market robbery. Another drunk. A three-car accident, calling for a police ambulance. Drunk. A domestic quarrel—man cut with a butcher knife. A stolen car. An attempted attack— girl injured, ambulance needed. Store robbery—one suspect caught. A drunken brawl at a dance hall. Two drunks. A hit-and-run victim—little boy. Two-car accident—one car over an embankment. A traffic jam on the Parkway—big fight, riot call. A drunk. Another drunk—trying to enter house. Attack reported by girl thrown out of car. Drunk . . . Another drunk. Suspicious character—probably peeping Tom. Drunk . . . drunk . . .*

Hardy's voice trailed off, but the calls went on and on and on until some of the reporters were standing, leaning on the Commissioner's desk, so they could hear better. Farbstein smoked in peace, smiling to himself, scarcely listening.

The Commissioner left the radio on for so long that finally Hillis, wincing a little, asked him to turn it off, which he did with a shrug a short while later.

"And all this proves?" asked Hillis, who knew damned well what it proved.

"It seems obvious," said Hardy. "The Police Department has many problems. Its activity, as I think even you gentlemen will admit, is not confined to shaking down prostitutes or taking graft from gambling. It is performing a public service, and doing damned well at it. You listened to the calls for maybe twenty minutes, say half an hour. They go round the clock, day after day after day, including Sundays and holidays."

Hillis, argumentative by nature, could think of nothing

to say, but merely compressed his lips and pulled out a cigarette.

"I'm all through now, gentlemen—except for this," Hardy went on. "You heard the calls and are able to make your own deductions. But I don't think they will be as radical as mine. The worst police force in the world is better than no police force. And ours is far from the worst—no matter what you may believe. Take the police off the streets for forty-eight hours, and nobody would be safe, neither on the street, nor in his place of business, nor in his home. There wouldn't be an easy moment for women or children. We'd be back in the jungle . . .

"All I ask is, give these facts a little thought before you write your next article damning and undermining the Police Department."

The reporters were dismissed, and filed out thoughtfully to the nearest bar—that is, all but Farbstein. He hurried home to his flat in an apartment building halfway up a steep slope in Leamington, and in spite of the protests of his harried wife, he locked himself in his room to write what turned out to be a much-praised and widely quoted article, which was featured on the editorial page of the *World*, dealing with the intricate workings of, and the dangers faced by, the Police Department, with a bow here and there to Commissioner Hardy, who had succeeded in giving Farbstein a new perspective on the city where he'd spent most of his forty-five years.

He even feared it a little now and felt it to be somewhat sinister as he stood looking down on it from a view window in his clothes closet of a workroom.

• 2 •

A dark, blustery night had settled down like a cowl over the huge, sprawling Midwestern City by the river. A mistlike rain blew between the tall buildings at intervals, wetting the streets and pavements and turning them into black, fun-house mirrors that reflected in grotesque distortions the street lights and neon signs.

The big downtown bridges arched off across the wide, black river into the void, the far shore blotted out by the misty rain; and gusts of wind, carrying stray newspapers, blew up the almost deserted boulevards, whistling faintly along the building fronts and moaning at the intersections. Empty surface cars, and buses with misted windows, trundled slowly through the downtown section. Except for taxis and prowl cars, there was no traffic.

River Boulevard, wide as a plaza and with its parkways and arched, orange street lights stretching off into the misty horizon in diminishing perspective, was as deserted as if a plague had swept the streets clean. The traffic lights changed with automatic precision, but there were no cars to heed or disobey them. Far down the boulevard, in the supper-club section of the city, elaborately glittering neon signs flashed off and on to emptiness. The night city, like a wound-up toy, went about its business with mechanical efficiency, regardless of man.

Finally the wind died down and the rain began to fall steadily all over the huge city: on the stacks of the steel plants in Polishtown; on the millionaires' mansions in River-dale; on the hilly regions of Tecumseh Slope, with its little Italian groceries and restaurants; on the massed tenement apartments along the upper river, where all the windows had been dark for hours and men would start awake cursing as the alarm clocks blasted at five a.m.; on the fanned-out suburban areas to the north and east, where all the little houses and the little lawns looked alike; and finally on the dark and unsavory reaches of Camden Square and its en-virons, the immense downtown slum beyond the river, where there was at least one bar at every intersection, prowl cars by the dozens, and harness bulls working in pairs.

A taxi pulled up at a dark store front near Camden Square, and the driver turned to speak to his fare.

"You sure you know where you're going, buddy?"

His fare nodded, then got out and paid him, giving him a good-sized tip, which made the driver feel kindly disposed toward the dumpy, middle-aged little man who had sat in dead silence all during the long ride up from the bus terminal.

"It's none of my business, partner," the driver persisted, "but this is a rough neighborhood." The fare merely cleared his throat. "There's the number you're looking for. But it's dark. Want me to wait?"

The fare shook his head.

"Okay," said the driver, not too anxious to be sitting all alone on Camden Boulevard West at two a.m. "But take a tip. Don't go parading around here with a suitcase. Some of these young punks would clip you for it—just to get a clean shirt."

The fare had moved away by now and was looking for a buzzer near the door of the dark store front. The taxi drove off slowly, the driver looking back.

After a while the fare heard a movement inside the dark store, then the door, which was on a chain, was opened a few inches.

"Yeah?" came a cautious, gruff voice.

"Joe Cool told me to come here," said the fare. "I want to see Cobby."

"Joe Cool's in clink."

"That's right. I just came from there. Got out this afternoon."

The fare had a slight, foreign accent of some kind, and the man at the door tried to get a look at him in the dim glow from the street light at the corner.

"Cobby's getting tired of you guys that fell putting the bite on him. He ain't no national bank."

"I'm not looking for any stake. I got a proposition for him—a big one."

"How do *I* know that?"

"Go tell Cobby."

There was a long hesitation; then the fare heard the faint

clank of a chain, and the door was opened enough for him to squeeze through.

"You wait here," said the doorman, bolting the door and putting the chain back in place; then he turned and started for a door at the back, where a crack of light showed. On the way he called over his shoulder: "You better be legit, pal. Cobby's been having trouble lately and he ain't so easy to get along with." There was a pause, then he added as he opened the back door: "Not that he *ever* was!"

The fare put down his suitcase and lighted a fat cigar as he waited. He sighed quietly to himself and did not seem at all perturbed by his reception.

In a few minutes the door in the back opened, throwing a canted triangle of light out into the dark storeroom, and the doorman's arm motioned for the fare to follow.

The fare found himself in a narrow, lighted corridor filled with the smell of stale tobacco smoke. Beyond him was the wide, receding back of the doorman. There were several doors in the corridor, and behind them the fare could hear the rumble of voices and the clink of poker chips.

The doorman halted at the last door, then turned to take a look at the fare, who had stopped just beyond him. The doorman was an ex-wrestler with a broken nose and a pair of cauliflower ears. His eyes were small and piggish, and his thick, everted lips seemed swollen. His blond hair had been clipped and looked like gold wire under the garish light of the unshaded bulb. He stared at the fare in moody silence, not able to place him.

The fare was a short man, not over five feet five, with wide, sloping shoulders and the faint suggestion of a paunch: he looked soft and fat and pale. His face was partly shaded by an incongruous Homburg hat, and a pair of thick-lensed glasses hid his eyes. His plump face was completely expressionless. He wore a little clipped black mustache, which somehow didn't seem to go with the rest of him. He looked as enigmatic to the doorman as a clothing dummy, and about as human.

Before the doorman had completed his scrutiny, the door banged open from within and a little ferret of a man in shirt sleeves bounded out and yapped impatiently: "Well, goddamit—where is he?"

Then he turned and saw the plump little man who stood there in patient silence grasping his suitcase and puffing on his cigar.

"All right. Make it fast. I'm a busy man. What do you want?"

"Let me introduce myself," said the plump little man, taking the cigar from his mouth with a graceful movement of his small, womanish white hand. "Maybe you know me . . ."

"I never seen you before," yapped Cobby, dancing on his toes with impatience. "Come on. Come on. What is it?"

"I mean, maybe you've heard of me. The Professor? Herr Doktor, maybe?"

Cobby's mouth dropped open, and he stared in astonishment with his hard, squinting blue eyes, which were much too close together.

"You mean . . . you're Riemenschneider?" The man nodded. "Well . . . why the hell didn't you say so? Come on in."

Cobby turned and glared at the doorman, then bounded back into the little office at the end of the corridor. Although he was in his middle forties, he moved around like an impatient high-school kid, always nervous, always geared up, always irritable.

Riemenschneider took off his Homburg and followed.

The top of his head, completely bald, shone like well-varnished wood and was ringed round with a mat of coarse, curly black hair, which he wore a little long, like a musician.

Cobby, glancing at him again as he entered the office, thought to himself: "He's a weirdy, all right." But a guy you had to respect. How many guys ever pulled off a hundred-G swindle? It took stuff. "Sit down, Doc," he said. "Take a load off your feet. Drink?"

Riemenschneider sat down and settled his suitcase beside him.

"Nothing to drink. I got out of the habit in the Walls. That's all it is—habit." He pulled back his lips in what was intended for a smile, but his face remained expressionless.

Cobby danced around and poured himself a long, straight one.

"Here's to the drink habit," he said. "It's the only habit I got that don't keep me in trouble all the time. What's on your mind, Doc?"

"You remember Joe Cool?"

"Sure. He did fine till he started packing heat. Then he killed a guy. All I say is, if you pack heat, you got to know what you're doing. You're either a heavy or you're not. Joe wasn't. Got out of his class like a selling plater in a stake race." Cobby danced about his desk for a moment. "Remember Joe? I'll say I do. Best thief in the city till he fell."

"I bunked with him the last two years," Riemenschneider explained quietly. "He might have a chance with the parole board if he had a strong fix going outside for him. He got life, but that could mean ten years."

"It's rough now," said Cobby, "since that bad beef over Lefty Wyatt. The parole board sprung him, and two days later he blasted Johnny Abate—right down the street from here. It was the only reason he wanted out."

"I know. But I thought maybe Mr. Emmerich . . ." Riemenschneider began, then paused as Cobby stiffened and stared at him sharply with his hard, squinting eyes.

"What do you know about Mr. Emmerich?" he demanded.

"Listen, Cobb. Why shouldn't we be friendly? Trust each other? Joe Cool turned his biggest proposition over to me—plans and all—providing I'd try to get the fix put in for him."

"What kind of proposition? And for how much?" Cobby yapped suddenly.

"Half a million dollars."

Cobby swallowed painfully, stared at Riemenschneider
for a long moment, then poured himself another drink with
shaking hand. This was the McCoy. When the Herr Doktor
talked big money, he wasn't talking through his hat. He
was a very, very big operator when he could manage to stay
out of the clink. Bigger than Joe Cool even—and that was
big enough.

"Doc—excuse me a minute," said Cobby. Then he danced
out the door and shut it behind him.

Riemenschneider yawned widely, then tapped his mouth
with an affected gesture of politeness.

He felt very comfortable and at ease. Thank God for Joe
Cool! Otherwise . . . well, it would have been pretty rugged
coming out of prison broke and homeless. Now he was
set . . . expenses paid while they fixed up the deal; then maybe the final score, the big last one they all dreamed about.
Mexico for him . . . Mexico City, where a man could live
like a king with a hundred thousand in cold American cash.

Puffing on his cigar, he let his imagination leap as it
pleased. Young girls! Dark, dusky, sultry young Mexican
girls . . . and nothing to do all day long under the hot Southern
sun but chase them. Very pleasant. Very pleasant indeed.

For a moment his pale, slack, fat face looked almost
human, then it resumed its usual dummylike blankness as
the door opened. Riemenschneider glanced up, expecting
Cobby, who, he felt sure, was out trying to contact Mr.
Alonzo Emmerich by phone. But it wasn't Cobby at all,
nor was it the doorman.

A tall, rawboned, dark-faced man of indeterminate age
was standing in the doorway, looking down at him with
mild surprise. Riemenschneider felt a sudden prickling in
his scalp and an unpleasant coldness in his hands as the tall
man probed him with his dark eyes. "A bad one," said the
little doctor to himself as he looked up blankly.

Without a word the man started out; but at that moment
Cobby came dancing back.

"Hello, Dix," he said, forcing the tall man back into the
office. "What do you want?"

Dix glanced at Riemenschneider as if his presence were unwelcome, and again the little doctor was aware of a faint but distinctly noticeable feeling of fear.

"It's okay," said Cobby to Dix. "He's a pal."

"It's about the tab," said Dix, and the little doctor noticed a slight accent of some kind. Plain Southern? Texan?

"Short again?" yapped Cobby. "What are you in for?"

"Twenty-three hundred and some," said Dix.

"Okay," said Cobby. "Your tab's good to twenty-five hundred. But for Christ's sake, Dix—either pick a winner or pay me when you get that far."

Something happened to Dix's face, and Cobby moved back a step and the little doctor sat congratulating himself on his acumen. A real bad one.

"I'm not asking favors," said Dix in his low, quiet voice. "I'll go get you the twenty-three hundred right now."

He went out abruptly. Showing marked distress, Cobby danced out after him, pleading: "Dix! Dix! Listen to me," and shutting the door behind him.

Riemenschneider puffed quietly on his cigar, waiting. He was extremely sensitive, although he did not look it; and this unusual sensitivity made him very acute at divining the secret character behind the masks all men wore. Cobby was a fool—sad but true. The doorman was a suspicious but fundamentally good-natured moron, completely harmless unless goaded by some strong-willed individual. This so-called Dix—this big Southerner—was a dangerous man, probably in one of the strong-arm rackets, a potential killer. The little doctor shuddered slightly. There were times, of course, when killing was necessary—for business reasons— and at such times he would not flinch from sanctioning it. But the men who did it . . . keep them at a distance!

Cobby came back swearing loudly and nervously as if to bolster up his courage.

"This man . . . this Dix . . . ." murmured the little doctor.

"Oh, he's an out-of-work heavy—and crazy for horses. My book beats him and beats him, and he keeps coming back for more." Cobby lit a cigarette and shakily poured himself a drink. "He used to be on the big time, or so I hear. God knows how old he is. You can't tell. Never heard what he does for lucre now . . . but he pays me."

Riemenschneider nodded and puffed quietly on his cigar. Cobby came to himself with a slight start.

"Say, Doc . . . I almost forgot on account of that big tramp, Dix. Mr. Emmerich's going to talk to us later tonight. He and his wife are giving a dinner party at his house in town. They know all the swells." Cobby puffed out his puny chest, proud of his acquaintance with a man like Emmerich.

· 3 ·

Dix paused on his way home at a little all-night hamburger joint to get the morning papers and a *Racing Form*. His anger was receding, his pulse was returning to normal, and the deadly chill that usually settled over him when he felt he'd been affronted was gradually leaving his hard, lean body. "Some day he'll go too far," he told himself. "Some day that little mongrel chump will open his mouth once too often."

A cop in a wet rubber poncho was sitting at the counter wolfing down a hamburger. His partner was standing at the magazine rack leafing boredly through a movie magazine. Neither paid any attention to Dix. But Gus, the little fat hunchback who ran the place, looked up and grinned, then came from behind the counter and went to the magazine rack.

"One *Examiner*, one *News*, and a *Form*—right?"

"Right," said Dix, taking the papers and giving Gus a fifty-cent piece as he did every night. But as he started to turn away, Gus departed enough from the regular routine they used when strangers were present to put him on his guard. Instead of saying: "Right you are; and thanks," he made a commonplace remark about the stormy weather and moved his eyes slightly in the direction of the harness bull at the rack.

"Yeah. Some rain," said Dix; then he made a brief gesture of farewell and went out the door.

The cop at the rack turned to Gus.

"He come in here every night the same time?"

"No," said Gus. "Sometimes earlier, sometimes later."

"But always after midnight, eh?"

"Couldn't say. Don't watch the clock."

"Any idea where he hangs out?"

"Nope. Don't even know his name."

"You're sure of that?"

"I just said it." Gus stared sullenly at the cop, then he turned and went back behind the counter and stood in silence while the other cop paid him for the sandwich and coffee.

"You been such a nice boy for a long time, Gus," said the cop at the counter. "That stretch did you a lot of good."

"Gee, thanks," said Gus sarcastically.

"Never mind the cracks. If you were smart you'd get aboard with us, Gus. Where's the percentage fronting for these hoods?"

"What hoods?"

"Like Dix Handley."

"Who's he?"

"Come on, Tom," said the cop at the rack wearily.

"Listen, Gus," said the cop at the counter. "Right off Camden West there's a bunch of so-called night clubs—gyp joints where a lot of people congregate at night—kind of nice people, too. Don't ask me why."

"You know . . . I never was wised up about them joints before," said Gus, sarcastic again.

"These people get boiled, and it's late when they start for home. No parking-attendants—nothing," the cop went on mildly. "And some so-and-so's been sticking 'em up—one here, one there." He jerked his thumb at his partner. "And Randy and I've been getting the business down at Headquarters."

"I'm awfully sorry," said Gus.

"We got a hell of a beat," the cop went on, "and even with the prowl cars, it's like combing the underbrush."

"Or hunting for a needle in a haystack," said Gus. "I just thought that one up."

Randy, the cop at the rack, suddenly lost his temper and hurried over to the counter toward Gus, but the other cop held him back, then went on mildly: "Gus, all I'm saying is, you've got a chance to do us a big favor. Tonight the club-owners over on the Strip got together and they're offering a thousand-dollar reward for the capture of this heist artist. We could split it."

"If I hear anything I'll let you know," said Gus, eying the two cops coldly.

"Come on," said Randy, taking his partner by the arm. "Why waste time with this louse?"

"I think you're cute, too," said Gus.

Randy started for him, but Tom dragged the younger cop away and shoved him toward the door.

"Where do you guys get off trying to make me fink? For what? I did my time," called Gus. "I didn't get a minute off. I'm no parolee—and if you give me any rough stuff I'll buy me a lawyer."

"You'd turn your mother in for five dollars. Don't kid me!" cried Randy over his shoulder as the two cops went out.

Gus stood looking after them for a moment, then he turned and went over to the phone, muttering to himself: "Just think, Gus. If you hadn't been born with that hump on your back, you might've turned out to be a cop. Every cloud has a silver lining." Then he laughed. "I don't know how it is I keep making up these great remarks."

• 4 •

Dix was lying on the bed with his coat off and a bottle of bourbon beside him, studying the *Racing Form* when his phone rang. Swearing under his breath, he let it ring for a while, hoping it would stop; but as it continued, he grabbed it up irritably. It was either Cobby, Italian Gus, or Doll—and he didn't want to talk to any of them; or to anyone else for that matter.

This was the time of night when he liked to be by himself, completely alone and uninterrupted. Outside, the city was dark and quiet; there was no probing sun to hide from, no distracting crowds, none of the fears, regrets, and ambitions of broad day. His little apartment was warm and cozy, a refuge from the world. He could drink in peace, read his newspapers, speculate on what would be happening the next day at race tracks all over the world, and then as the first light of dawn began to show over the dingy rooftops of Camden Square, and the early hush of a new day spread through the still-dark streets of the immense city, he could turn off his light, which would be looking a little pale now as the night waned, and lying back on the bed, he would return to the past: that happy past which seemed like a dream and not a reality—though he'd lived through it; that pleasant time, completely removed from the ugly, inescapable, harsh certainties of the present; that time when no one knew him as "Dixie" or "Dix," or laughed at his Southern accent, or called him "you-all," or got nasty because he owed them twenty-three hundred he fully intended to pay; or took any attitude at all toward him except one of friendliness and respect.

He was a Jamieson, wasn't he? And hadn't his great grandfather imported the first Irish thoroughbred into their home country? And hadn't both his grandfathers fought in the Southern army during the Civil War—one of them with the Morgan Raiders? Okay! So they were just simple people—nothing fancy. No plantation aristocrats! But real folks all the same, salt of the earth!

Dix roused himself and spoke into the phone.

"Gus? Didn't recognize your voice."

"They was combing me, Dix. You better lay off them clubs for a while."

"I need a little dough, Gus."

"I got a grand planted for you. Okay?"

"I need twenty-three hundred, and I need it bad and quick."

Gus whistled, then spoke.

"All the same, lay off the clubs." He told Dix about the reward and about how the cops were getting the push from Headquarters. Then he went on: "I'll talk to Schemer. Hide the heat if you go out, and stay away from the Boulevard at night for a while. The Happiness Boys would just love to grab and frame you."

"Thanks, Gus," said Dix. "But see if you can't dig me up thirteen hundred more. It's a thing I just got to take care of."

"The Schemer might hold still for it. I doubt it. But I'll try. You know him—saving up for the wife and kid. What a guy like him's *doing* with a wife and kid is something else. Oh, by the way. They knocked over Quigley's tonight. Ain't that where Doll works?"

"Yeah," said Dix; then he laughed, a strange sound that chilled Gus at the other end of the line. "It's coming in bunches, looks like."

"Don't get your flag at half-mast, Dix. You still got old Gus."

Dix shook his head and smiled slightly as he hung up. A poor, benighted, fat, greasy, humpbacked, little Italian, and the nearest thing to a gentleman he'd met in thirty years.

He poured himself a straight shot of bourbon and went back to his *Racing Form*. In the East the racing season was slowly drawing to a close; soon the big stables would be shipping to Little Rock, New Orleans, Florida, and California for the winter season; and here he was marooned in this big, dull Midwestern town without a chance of getting away unless he wanted to hit the rods, which was not in his line. Worse than that, he was in hock heavy to a big-mouthed, silly little feist—who dunned you when he wasn't even trying to. And he had to be paid, and fast, and to the last dime!

Some guys you could owe—like Gus; not many, but some. But with a character like Cobby, you just couldn't be in his debt and keep your self-respect.

Dix rustled the pages of the *Racing Form* irritably, slapped them into place. Then, settling himself comfortably, he was just starting to study the entries for Pimlico when his buzzer sounded, and he sat up swearing.

Suddenly he remembered Gus and the cops, and, jumping out of bed quickly, he took a .45 revolver with a sawed-off barrel from under his pillow, hurried to the bureau, jerked a drawer all the way out, fitted the gun into a little wire frame in the back, and replaced the drawer. Then he went to the speaker beside the door.

"Who is it?" he inquired.

"It's me, honey." The husky, feminine voice drifted up from the vestibule, faintly distorted by the speaker, sad, unintentionally mocking—it was just a way she had, some strange quality in her voice that made people turn to look at her when she spoke. Actually she was a very simple-minded dame. Doll! Why couldn't she take a hint? She'd bored and irritated him for a long time now, and he'd shown it more and more openly as time passed.

He pressed the release button, saying nothing; then he opened the door and stood listening to her high heels tapping nervously on the stairs as she ran up, heedless of the clatter she was making.

"Dix," she cried as she saw him standing in the doorway waiting for her at the end of the short, dingy hallway with its dismal night light; then she hurried toward him eagerly, her long, sequin-covered evening dress making a loud rustling. "Sorry to bother you, honey. But . . ."

"Don't talk out here," said Dix, irritably, as he took her by the arm rather roughly and escorted her into his apartment, shutting the door behind him.

Doll took off her short jacket and tossed it onto a chair. She was tall, heavily made, and coarsely pretty. A brunette by nature, her hair had been dyed so many colors that it now was nothing in particular, neither dark, nor red, nor blond—but something in between and very artificial-looking. She was about thirty-five, and there were faint lines of weariness about her mouth and eyes; but she claimed she was twenty-five, and spent most of her time trying to look and act it. The rough side of life was no mystery to her— she'd seen hardly anything else, as she'd been on her own for over twenty years; but she had managed to keep herself aloof from the sordid fatalism of her associates, and she had fought a constant, tough, but inconclusive battle against the long, easy slide down into the mire. But the struggle was telling on her, and tonight she felt sad, lonely, and discouraged.

Dix's unsympathetic expression chilled her, and she turned away in some confusion and fumbled in her handbag for a cigarette, stalling, trying to think of something to say.

Dix walked into the bedroom and sat down on the bed, glancing at his spread-out *Racing Form*, itching to get back to it. Why did she have to bother him?

Doll followed him and sat down on a little straight chair by the bureau. She couldn't find any matches and began to scrabble about distractedly in her handbag. Grunting with irritation, Dix lit her cigarette for her. Then he said: "If you're going to smoke, you got to learn to carry matches."

Doll burst suddenly into tears and, bending down, put her hands over her face. Her plump shoulders shook convulsively.

"What are you crying about?" Dix demanded harshly.

"Nothing," said Doll. Then she sobbed for a moment, making a great effort to control herself. Sighing and biting her lip, she looked up at Dix. "I mean . . . everything," she amended. But the remark missed fire—it had a false, self-pitying sound, and she winced inwardly.

Dix's expression did not change. His hard, dark eyes regarded her with utter boredom. There was not a flicker of anything else—not even curiosity. What had she expected? Sympathy? She began to laugh a little hysterically; then she got up and stood for a moment looking at this big, rawboned man with the rugged features, the sunken cheeks, and the air of power in reserve—this outlandish stranger with his mysterious contempt for everybody—herself now included. Sympathy? From Dix?

She put her cigarette in the ash-tray, then walked over to pick up her jacket.

"I'm sorry, Dix," she said. "I don't know what I was thinking about, bothering you this time of night. I'll run along."

Dix cleared his throat and shifted on the bed. Let her go. Get rid of her. Why kid around? But some vague instinct, some unconscious memory of the past, made him rise and walk over to her. The poor trollop was in trouble.

"Gus told me the place got knocked over," he said.

Doll turned to look at him, eagerly studying his harsh, lined face. She was crazy about this big tramp. Why—was no matter. She just was. If only he had a little kindness, a little understanding, in his nature; not much—just a little.

"Quigley lost a big sock horse-gambling," she said, quickly putting down her jacket and coming over to Dix. "When pay-off time came round for the club, he tried to pay in promises. With the vice squad, that won't go."

"Sit down," said Dix with an effort. "Have a drink."

Doll sat down quickly, afraid he'd change his mind. She wanted desperately to throw herself into his arms and be comforted; but she knew that it would bore and irritate him, and bring that chill, blank, inhumane look into his eyes.

"Don't care if I do," she said, forcing herself to laugh as if she didn't have a worry in the world.

·5·

The commissioner had three secretaries—all harness bulls— and the one on duty tonight looked like a German storm trooper, tall, heavily made, and with his white-blond hair disfigured by a butch haircut. Sitting at his desk in the outer office, he tried to appear not only very busy but also very important. From time to time, Farbstein, who had been waiting to see the Commissioner for nearly an hour, would stare at him sardonically, and the big copper, feeling that he was being watched, would move about uncomfortably in his chair and portentously clear his throat.

At intervals a harsh, complaining voice could be heard, rising and falling, behind the door of the Commissioner's private office. Every time it happened, it seemed to nettle the harness-bull secretary, who would shift about, scrape his feet, open and shut desk drawers; and once he even began to whistle a popular tune off-key. But when Farbstein joined in, whistling the "tenor" part, he broke off abruptly and threw the man from the *World* a mean look.

Behind the private-office door the harsh, complaining voice rose to a new pitch and a fist hit a desk with a loud thud. The secretary rose abruptly, squeaking his chair; then he walked to the water-cooler, stamping heavily across the worn and uneven flooring with his thick-soled, cop's shoes.

Farbstein put down the magazine he'd been glancing at and said: "Clear a path, Gauleiter. I think some of the boys are going to get flung out on their fat tails."

The secretary turned.

"What's this 'Gauleiter' business, Farbstein?"

"It's a pet name. It shows I like you."

"My name's Welch. Harry Welch."

"I'll put that down," said Farbstein, pretending to scribble on the edge of the magazine. "Never know when it might come in handy."

"I'm the Commissioner's number-one man," said the secretary, walking heavily back to his desk. "I'm one guy around here he trusts."

"Things must be tough then."

The secretary stared suspiciously at Farbstein for a moment; then he said in an uncertain voice: "Oh, I wouldn't say that."

Farbstein laughed and stood up. He'd heard movements beyond the door of the private office that made him think that the meeting was breaking up, and he wanted to button-hole the Commissioner.

In a moment the door opened, and a pale, solemn-faced group of Police Department brass, all in plain clothes, filed out and crossed the anteroom in gloomy silence. After a short interval the big bull-necked Chief of Police, Dolph Franc, appeared, grinning sheepishly like an overgrown schoolboy who'd been caught in some disgraceful act. His face stiffened at the sight of Farbstein, who'd been belaboring him for years; then, remembering, he stretched his sullen face into a smile of almost laughable falseness.

"Hello, Farbstein," he said. "How's tricks?"

"I might ask you the same," said Farbstein, jerking his thumb toward the Commissioner's office.

Franc laughed hollowly, shrugged, and followed the others out into the corridor.

Just as the Commissioner appeared in the doorway, the phone in the outer office rang and Welch grabbed it up at once.

The Commissioner stared silently at Farbstein, waiting. His hat was pulled low, his overcoat collar turned up. His small gray eyes glinted angrily behind his glasses.

"Commissioner Hardy's office," said Welch. "Oh, yes, Mrs. Hardy. He's . . ."

"I've left," snapped the Commissioner.

Welch reddened slightly.

"Yes, ma'am," he said into the phone, "he's just left. Just this minute, ma'am. Oh, I wouldn't fib to you, ma'am . . ."

Farbstein snickered, and the big harness bull turned redder than before, and after a few more embarrassed but reassuring phrases he hung up hurriedly, missing the hook twice.

"I'll get your car right away, sir," he said, grabbing up his cap.

But Farbstein interposed.

"How about me driving you home, Commissioner?"

"It's out of your way."

"Give us a little chance to talk, and it won't take up any of your time. You've got to ride home, anyway."

"All right," said Hardy ungraciously; then he gestured good-bye indifferently to Officer Welch and went out into the cold corridor, where the fall wind was whistling along the floor in numbing gusts.

Farbstein clicked his heels and snapped a Continental bow at Welch; then he followed the Commissioner out into the corridor.

They walked to the elevator in silence.

They drove through the cold, damp, sleeping city shrunk into their coats. It was drizzling, and an arctic wind was blowing off the river.

". . . full article devoted to you, Commissioner," Farbstein was saying. "You know, biographical. The works! The Old Man's behind you a hundred per cent, and he wants everybody to know it. We'll send some of the boys out to your house. Get some nice pictures. Maybe you holding your little grandson. The Old Man's hot for you, I'm telling you. He's ready to back you for Mayor at the next election . . ."

"I'm against articles like that," said Hardy. "That's for actors."

Farbstein turned to look at the Commissioner. He was both startled and pleased.

"You mean you've got no political ambitions?"

"I've got no ambitions at all. I'm just sick and tired of this town's crime record. And I'm going to do something about it."

"No article then?"

"No article."

There was a short silence as Farbstein turned off from River Boulevard onto Lower Locust Road, a third-rate residential street where the Commissioner lived in a ramshackle frame house built in the eighties. It was painted white and had gables, unexpected little balconies and porches, and old-fashioned scrollwork.

"It would be a big Sunday feature," said Farbstein, still trying conscientiously for Old Man Gresham's sake. "Attract a lot of attention. Of course we can run it whether you say so or not, but with your co-operation . . ."

"I'm against it. But I've got a suggestion. Devote the same space to the new equipment we're installing, the new police school we're setting up."

"That's an idea, Commissioner."

"Talk to Randolph tomorrow."

"Yes, sir."

Farbstein wanted to pat this cantankerous old character on the back and show him how much he admired him; but for once he felt at a loss. How did you begin?

There was a short silence; then the Commissioner demanded: "Did you know that Erwin Riemenschneider was released from State Prison today?"

Farbstein turned and stared at the Commissioner, puzzled.

"Riemenschneider? Who's he?"

Hardy chuckled sardonically.

"All asleep. Everybody asleep. Including the newspapers and the Police Department. One of the most dangerous criminals in the world, and they turn him loose and he disappears. Nobody's got the vaguest line on him."

Farbstein nodded to himself.

"Is that why you were giving the boys such a going over in your office?" Hardy turned and looked at him sharply.

"I could hear a lot of noise through the door."

"Farbstein," said Hardy, "this is all off the record. Understand?"

"Yes, sir. You can trust me."

"I know that. Or I wouldn't be talking. Yes. That's why I was giving them such a going over. I can't look after everything personally. We shouldn't have lost contact with such a man."

"If I hear anything, Commissioner, I'll call you right away."

When the car pulled up at Hardy's house, the Commissioner grunted and cleared his throat for a moment; then he said gruffly: "Come on in, Farbstein. Have a sandwich, cup of coffee. It's a cold night."

"Don't want to put you to any trouble, Commissioner."

"If I didn't want you, wouldn't invite you."

"Okay, Commissioner."

Just as Hardy was putting his key in the lock, the front door was opened from within and they were confronted by Mrs. Hardy, a short, rather stocky middle-aged woman with a thick nose, a pleasant full mouth, and blue-black hair streaked with gray.

"Theo, do you know what time it is?" she cried. Then she saw Farbstein. "Who's this man?"

"He's from the *World*. Come on in," said Hardy, pushing past his wife, who drew back reluctantly.

Uncomfortable under Mrs. Hardy's inquisitive, unfriendly eye, Farbstein pulled off his hat and followed the Commissioner into the big, shadowy hallway. In a room beyond, he could see a cheerful fire burning in a tall, old-fashioned fireplace.

Mrs. Hardy shut the door, then turned to her husband, ready to protest, but he said firmly: "Mr. Farbstein is not here on business. He's a guest. I invited him in for a bite to eat."

Mrs. Hardy smiled at once.

"Why, glad to have you, Mr. Farbstein. Go in the library with Theo. I've got some supper ready."

She left at once, and Hardy turned to look after her with an indulgent smile.

"Don't mind her," he said, smiling; "she spends all her time trying to look after me."

He seemed relaxed now, all his defenses down, at peace with the world. Farbstein followed him thoughtfully into the living-room. He envied the Commissioner his happy home. Not that his own home wasn't happy in its way. But Frieda was no Mrs. Hardy. She was too much like Farbstein himself: witty, nervous, moody.

Oh, well!

· 6 ·

Thick, dark clouds were moving slowly in from the north now, traveling so low that they grazed the tops of the tall buildings downtown, and in a little while the rain began to fall in sheets, almost blotting out the lights and filling the silent night city with the steady, monotonous crash of a heavy downpour.

But in a small apartment at the foot of Tecumseh Slope, in a mediocre but respectable little suburb: Leamington—on the fringe of Italian Hill but not part of it—a family of three slept on peacefully, oblivious of the violent assault of the rain. Louis Bellini, better known as Schemer, his young wife, and their year-old son.

Louis and his wife were lying in a big double bed about a foot apart and with their backs to each other, both snoring faintly and easily; and in a crib a few feet away Louis, Jr. smiled at the dream running through his little head and raised his tiny, fat, clenched fist in a vague, happy gesture. The windows were all closed because of the early-evening drizzle, and now the heavy rain was beating at the panes and splashing on the sills.

All about the happy family lay their possessions, sleepless but patient, waiting for dawn and the activity of a new day.

The phone rang in the hall, beyond the closed door, and both Louis and his wife stirred uneasily, and the baby made a faint cooing sound. The phone rang and rang in the deserted hallway, and finally Louis rolled over on his back, then sat up. Maria was stirring, too. Louis now heard the tremendous rage of the elements just outside the bedroom windows.

"Jeez!" he said; "listen to that rain."

"Louis, please don't say 'jeez,' " Maria murmured sleepily; then she sat up and began to rub her eyes. "The phone, Louis," she cried, now wide-awake; then she jumped quickly out of bed and moved toward the crib. "I hope it don't wake the little man. I had a hard time getting him to sleep tonight.'' Then as Louis yawned widely and scratched his head, she snapped at him: ''Get it, Louis. Get it.''

When Maria, the best of women, spoke to him like that, he knew it was time to get busy. Ordinarily she was very patient with him and put up in silence with his inability to rouse himself from sleep with any degree of speed.

He hurried out into the hallway and switched on a night light, shivering a little at the damp wind blowing under the front door; then he picked up the phone.

''Yeah?''

''I thought you was dead. What gives?''

It was Gus! Louis wrinkled up his thin, rather handsome aquiline face and pulled in exasperation at his thick, curly black hair.

''Gus—my God! Must be four o'clock . . . !''

''I keep forgetting you live like a square nowadays. How's the bambino?''

''Fine, fine,'' cried Louis, his anger mounting. ''What the hell you want, Gus?''

''Did I interrupt something?'' Gus demanded with a dirty laugh.

Louis was outraged. For Gus even to mention such a thing in regard to Maria . . . !

''You dirty-minded . . .'' he began.

But Gus cut him off. ''All in fun, buster. You're married, ain't you? And it's legal now.''

Louis fumed at the phone and wagged his head from side to side. Gus was a goodhearted guy, no doubt about it, but he never seemed to get the idea how Louis felt about his wife, Maria. Always these dirty remarks—okay in a poolroom, maybe, where young punks were always talking about the neighborhood tramps, but completely out of line with a settled married couple who had a fat, healthy, and beautiful son.

''Shut your talk, Gus,'' he said. ''Or I'll hang up.''

''Okay, Father,'' said Gus. ''Listen. Can you dig up thirteen hundred for me right away? And I mean by noon tomorrow.''

"Are you crazy?" Louis fumed even more vehemently now. In the old unregenerate days before he'd met Maria, he'd been a spender, throwing his money around like a Texas millionaire. Now he scrimped and saved, thinking about Maria and his son. What would the boys say if they knew he had nearly forty thousand dollars put away in three different safety-deposit boxes?

"Look, buster. I need it, and for a good cause."

"What's the cause?"

"Dix," said Gus, shortly.

There was a brief silence as Louis swallowed and considered. Personally he did not like Dix and was more than a little afraid of him. But Gus, who hated practically everybody, including his old lady and his two brothers, thought Dix was a hundred per cent and was always trying to look after him, help him out. Funny setup!

A rather pathetic note now crept into Louis's voice.

"I'd like to help. You know that, Gus. But I got mouths to feed, rent to pay—all that stuff. I'm not saying I haven't got it, understand? I'm saying I need it for my family."

"You and your family!" said Gus angrily. "Just wait. Some day Maria will turn into a fat Italian mama; and Junior, when he gets to be sixteen, will be telling you where you come off and what a stupid, silly old bastard you are. Why don't you wake up?"

Louis turned pale with anger and his hands shook slightly.

"You're a scum—that's what you are, Gus. A low-down scum to talk to me like that."

"Aw, shove your money," cried Gus. "Some day I'll go to your funeral, and there you'll be—the richest guy in the cemetery." He slammed up the receiver with a crash.

Louis winced away from the sound, sat looking at the telephone for a moment, then slowly and thoughtfully hung up. This was no good—no damn good at all! Gus had everybody's ear in the whole city. He was A number 1 with all the big boys, who considered him a hundred per cent "right." He knew enough about what went on in the vicinity of Camden Square and the Strip to blow a whole administration out of the City Hall, and yet never a peep. He'd done a full hard stretch in the Walls rather than implicate anybody else on the caper. Besides . . . Dix was a bad boy. An ugly enemy.

Louis sat shivering in the little, damp hallway, painfully torn between antagonistic loyalties, worried about the future, sick at heart.

The door opened, and Maria, plump and pretty in her voluminous, figured nightgown, stood looking at him. Her face showed concern.

"Louis, baby," she said, "don't sit there like that. You'll take your death of cold."

Louis laughed suddenly, showing his even white teeth. All at once the world had become a happy place again.

"Come here, baby," he said, holding out his arms.

She looked at him suspiciously, putting her head on one side; then she giggled and said: "Oh, no you don't. None of your tricks. It's too late, Louis. It'll soon be morning, and . . ."

"Why, Maria—I'm surprised at you," he said, bursting out laughing and pulling her down on his lap.

"I mean it, baby," she cried, struggling.

"Okay, okay," said Louis. "Just wanted to hold you for a minute. Any harm in that?"

Suddenly Maria blew into his neck, making him start and writhe; then she leaped off his lap and ran to the door. Louis was just rising to follow her when the phone rang again.

Louis grimaced and looked at Maria as much as to say: "What! Again!" Nevertheless, a certain hope sprang up in his heart. Maybe Gus was sorry he'd acted the way he had. He reached for the phone, and Maria went back into the bedroom shrugging. She was used to late calls.

It was Gus all right.

"Look, meathead," Gus said in his rough voice, "no use us being sore at each other. . . ."

Louis felt light as air. Good old Gus! After all, they'd gone to the old Tenth Ward School together and had fought side by side in the battles with the tough Irish from Minton Hill Parochial.

"That's right," he said. "I was just getting ready to call you back."

"You mean about the money?"

Louis winced and fought a silent internal battle.

"Yes, Gus. I . . . I guess I can make it all right."

"You're a pal," cried Gus. "And Dix's word's as good as his bond. I know. Bring it in about noon, eh, boy?"

"Right you are, Gus."

"Good. And kiss the bambino for Uncle Gus; and tell Maria hello. She's a sweet kid."

Louis's elation drained slowly out of him as he hung up the phone. What was he so happy about? He'd just been clipped for thirteen hundred. And Dix? Well, he was a struggling down-and-outer, no matter how hard he tried to hide it. Maybe his word was good. If Gus said so, it must be. All the same, with the best will in the world, a guy couldn't pay if he didn't have it.

Shivering, he hurried back into the bedroom. Maria was in bed. He paused a moment before he turned out the hall light and shut the door. Maria looked so lovely with her dark hair all over the pillow. She opened her eyes slowly and gazed at him.

"I was asleep," she murmured.

"Shut your eyes again then," said Louis tenderly. "Sleep . . . sleep . . ."

Her eyes closed again. He switched off the hall light, shut the bedroom door, and got carefully back into bed. He lay for a moment shivering; then his body began to get warm and he turned his head to watch the rain slashing at the windows. Here he was safe.

Just as he was dropping off to sleep, an unpleasant thought began to nag at him! She was so innocent of wrong, it was a shame to fool her and lie to her. But on the other hand, why burden her with his worries and problems? Some day maybe . . . things would go wrong, he'd get pulled in, and

then she'd have to know the truth. But maybe that was soon
enough. Or maybe his luck would hold. He'd never fallen . . .
had no record.

He was an expert trouble-shooter for a big electrical-
appliance store. As a matter of fact, he made pretty good
money at it; certainly enough to explain his modest way of
life, and it gave him an excellent front. The money he made
in other ways, he stashed. Even Maria knew nothing about
the safety-deposit boxes, though they were jointly held in
case of a bad beef; and he'd had to go to considerable
trouble, including forgery, to effect that.

Anyway, how could he approach Maria to tell her? It
would take long careful preparation, and even then she
wouldn't be able to take it in, believe it.

Louis began to drift into sleep, but at that moment his
small son made a brief coughing sound that brought Louis
broad-awake at once, in spite of his constitutional lethargy,
and he slipped out of bed and hurried over to the crib.

The damned kid was laughing in his sleep.

• 7 •

The windshield-wiper broke down just as they reached Emmerich's "cottage" hideaway on the river. It had been a
tough, nerve-racking drive through the pelting rain, and
Cobby's teeth were chattering and he was aching for a big
long pull of whisky. But the Herr Doktor had been unperturbed throughout, even when Cobby's roadster skidded on
the curve beyond the Riverdale drugstore and just barely
missed a light-pole.

They saw Emmerich's big, shiny Cadillac parked before
the entrance as they ran for the shelter of the porch.

A politely smiling big man in a chauffeur's uniform let
them in and took their hats and coats. In the living-room
faint rumba music was coming over the radio. Riemen-

schneider looked about him with interest. The one-story "cottage" was quite large and covered a good deal of ground; four bedrooms, maybe, and the whole place was richly furnished, smelling of money.

"This guy does all right for himself, eh, Doc?" exclaimed Cobby; then he bragged: "I been up here lots of times. Me and Emmerich—we're like that." He held up crossed fingers just as the lawyer stepped out into the hallway from a comfortable-looking cardroom, where they could see a fire dancing in a little wall fireplace.

Cobby's attitude changed at once. He looked embarrassed.

"Mr. Emmerich," he said, "this is the man I was telling you about."

Riemenschneider bowed slightly. Mr. Emmerich was apparently a wealthy man and one of the powers of this earth. The little doctor worshipped only three things: wealth, power, and young girls. When Emmerich said nothing, he bowed again—lower, this time.

Cobby eyed him sideways with contempt. These goddamn foreigners!

Emmerich was a big man in his fifties. His iron-gray hair was thick and curly, his shoulders broad, his chest deep. He looked in good trim except for a slight sagging of the flesh around his jowls. The dinner coat he was wearing was a very expensive one, beautifully tailored; and Riemenschneider did not miss it. He had a real eye for sumptuousness of any kind, though he preferred to spend his own money on women.

Emmerich's racket was boyishness. He smiled and moved and gestured like an adolescent. Yet his gray eyes were sad and wary with faint brown pouches under them, and from time to time he sighed unconsciously as if from world weariness. Among other things, he had been for years a top-notch criminal lawyer; and although his public reputation was more than a little shady, and in his long and successful career he'd made many enemies and engineered many off-color deals, he was an expert skater on thin ice and so far had managed to skirt the edge of disaster.

He looked, talked, and breathed money; and the little doctor muttered to himself: "What a front man!" as he studied this almost legendary character he'd heard so much about in the Walls.

And yet . . . the little doctor was somewhat troubled. He noted the weariness, the anxiety to make an impression, the false joviality. What was worrying this big, successful man? Something, he was positive. Certainly not money! It might be love—sex. At fifty odd, that could be more dangerous than anything else. The little doctor probed in silence as they sat by the cheerful fire in the cardroom.

"I don't know if I can do anything for Joe or not," Emmerich was saying. "The parole board is getting tougher and tougher. Besides, I couldn't even start proceedings before another eighteen months."

"He knows that, sir," said Riemenschneider, bowing slightly.

Cobby gnawed on his cigar, sipped his whisky, and silently hated the little doctor for his fawning manner, although he himself felt far from at ease. Something about Emmerich always made him jumpy and dissatisfied. It was as if in sudden and intermittent flashes of insight Cobby saw that he—Charles Cobb, biggest nonsyndicate bookie in the city—compared to the well-known lawyer, didn't really amount to anything at all. This was hard for his ego to take.

Emmerich cleared his throat impressively and lighted one of his huge Cuban cigars, which were made specially for him and cost a buck fifty apiece.

"I notice you have a slight accent," he said politely to the little doctor. "German?" Then when he got a smiling nod, he went on: "The reason I asked, my grandfather was born in Germany—Berlin."

"Ah, a Berliner! Very nice," said Riemenschneider. "I know Berlin very well. No more Berlin, though."

"And a goddamned good thing!" cried Cobby, suddenly; then, at a look from Emmerich, he made an effort to get back into his shell like a frightened turtle.

"My grandfather was rotten-egged on the street here during World War I," said Emmerich. Then he laughed. "And I was across with the A.E.F."

"The world is like that today," said the little doctor. "Even worse now. But the Germans . . . they are no longer the dogs to beat. They are beaten. Now it's the Russians."

"You can say that again," said Cobby, coming out of his shell. This time Emmerich ignored him.

Polite conversation was now at an end, the little doctor realized. The great man was ready for business.

"Now about this proposition of Joe's," he began, smiling tentatively. "Cobby named some outrageous figure over the phone to me—something like half a million dollars. Now of course I didn't believe it, but . . ."

"It's true," said Riemenschneider. "Maybe even more, sir."

Emmerich's forehead grew suddenly red, and the hand holding the big cigar trembled slightly.

"But this is fantastic . . . !"

"Pelletier and Company," said the little doctor mildly. "Biggest jewelers in the state. And with a record of never in forty years having a robbery. They have gone to sleep. For amateurs, an impossible task. For professionals, nothing."

"You make it sound very easy," said Emmerich, lowering his eyes in order to mask his eagerness, and forcing a skeptical smile.

The little doctor shrugged and raised his hands in an expansive gesture. "Really," he said quietly, "you must believe me; with the right personnel it's like taking pennies from a blind newsboy."

Emmerich jumped up and began to pace the floor; then he turned and studied the little doctor's pale, fat, expressionless face for a moment before he spoke.

"My friend," he said solemnly, "to hear the boys tell it, all takes are easy. Then, a few weeks later I'm trying to get them out of jail. Something always slips—especially with the big ones."

"Mr. Emmerich, please. Perhaps you know my reputation," said Riemenschneider modestly. "I have engineered some very big coups. Considering everything, I've served very little time. If I'd saved my money instead of throwing it around, I'd be a rich man now—without a care in the world. Take my word for it. If I didn't know this was a ripe plum ready to fall, do you think I'd be willing to start operating at once? I just came out of prison.'' He smiled and again made an expansive gesture; then he took some papers from his inside coat pocket and went on: ''In my hands I have a plan worth—shall we say?—fifty thousand dollars on the open market. Everything is here, from the observed routine of the personnel of Pelletier's to the type of locks on the doors, the age and condition of the main safe, and the complete police routine of the district. Of course, we may have to do a little checking—as the plan is some years old. But not much, Mr. Emmerich. Not much.''

Emmerich sat down, crossed his legs, and, puffing on his big cigar, tried to appear at ease—tried to give the impression that he was a judicious businessman listening to a proposition that bored him slightly.

''What are the main problems?'' he asked after a moment.

''For the time being,'' said Riemenschneider, ''we'll put the actual execution aside—that I'll guarantee. The main problems are: first, money; second, personnel.''

''No trouble about *operating* money,'' Cobby put in suddenly; then he turned to the lawyer. ''Eh, Mr. Emmerich?''

''That remains to be seen.''

''Then,'' said Riemenschneider, ''we must come to some agreement on the division of the take. This is how my friend Joe Cool sees it. One third to you, Mr. Emmerich, with the proviso that you furnish expense money and work for Joe's parole. One third for Joe, to be held in trust.'' The little doctor smiled deprecatingly and bowed slightly in Emmerich's direction. ''And last, but I hope not least, one third for myself—as manager of the enterprise.''

''What about the helpers?'' asked Cobby.

''We guarantee them a settled amount,'' the little doctor explained. ''They have no part in the division of the take. They merely follow out orders, and then we pay them off like house-painters. They will be told nothing about the size of the take. In fact, it would be a good idea to minimize it. Sometimes men get greedy.'' The little doctor chuckled good-naturedly.

"So far, so good," said Emmerich mildly. "How many men do you need?"

"Well," said Riemenschneider, "we need a top-notch driver—in case of trouble. We need an expert toolman. And then, as always—sad to say—we need a hooligan."

"A hooligan . . . ?" queried Emmerich.

"Strong-arm guy," Cobby translated; and then he went on with a certain amount of pedantry: "A blaster. Heat-packer. Gunman."

"A driver is not so hard to get," said Riemenschneider. "No problem. Joe has already suggested a toolman—Louis Bellini. You know him?"

Emmerich searched his memory, but Cobby cut in at once.

"Know him well. He's a hundred per cent. One of the sharpest boys in this man's town."

"Ah!" exclaimed the little doctor with a note of gratification in his voice. "Him, we pay well. Maybe twenty-five thousand dollars."

Emmerich flinched inwardly and, to hide it, turned and tossed his cigar into the fireplace. Could he manage it without letting anyone know what a desperate financial state he was in? He began to sweat a little, and his hands grew cold.

"With the hooligan," said Riemenschneider, "we must go slow. That is always the danger. Too many of these fellows are drug addicts. They get greedy and scream about the take after it's made. Or they hound you later, claim you've cheated them. They are a no-good lot or they wouldn't be hooligans. Violence is a form of stupidity, and it's all they know."

"Very true," said Emmerich, somewhat impressed with this fat, blank-faced, rather inhuman-looking little German. "Very true indeed. In my profession it's one of the first things you learn—about your clients, I mean."

The little doctor bowed slightly as an acknowledgment of the slightly different tone the great lawyer was taking with him.

"One last thing," said Emmerich after a pause. "How is the jewelry to be handled?"

"Ah!" said the little doctor, "the very nub of the question, sir. Three months ago it would have been no problem at all. But unfortunately, Lefty Wyatt—a hooligan, by the way—saw fit to put several bullets in the best fence in the whole Middle West. Too bad. I knew Johnny Abate very well. Did business with him many years ago."

Emmerich rose and began to pace as before. His eagerness was increasing, and he could hardly contain himself.

"I was just thinking," he began, speaking in a voice that sounded a bit unnatural, even to himself. "Perhaps I could . . . I mean, myself . . . I could . . . ."

Cobby and Riemenschneider stared at the lawyer in astonishment.

"But, Mr. Emmerich," cried Cobby. "You? A fence? It don't sound right, Mr. Emmerich."

"No, perhaps not," said Emmerich, quickly. "The thing is, the proposition sounds so good. Yes, I'll admit it. It sounds wonderful. And . . . well, I don't want to see it go wrong for a mere matter of . . . ."

He broke off suddenly and turned to stare into the fire. God! He'd have to compose himself. He mustn't let these men realize how desperate he was—how willing to clutch at straws. And come to think of it, what the hell had been in his mind when he'd suggested that he act as fence? How could he—possibly? Where would the huge sum of money necessary to swing the full deal come from? Was it that he was merely itching to get his hands on a fortune in jewelry? Was he really considering double-crossing these men?

Cobby was merely surprised by this strange turn of events. But Riemenschneider was a little worried and for the moment felt a certain distrust of this big, handsome, plausible man, who dressed so richly and was surrounded with all the evidence of great wealth. Why, in this "cottage"—a mere hideaway—the furnishings alone must be worth nearly fifty thousand dollars.

Emmerich made up his mind suddenly and turned toward them. His hands were cold as ice, and his stomach felt painfully constricted. What he was about to say was costing him a great effort. But it had to be said. This little German was far from a fool. Smiling easily, he spoke.

"What I was just saying, I suppose, sounded a little foolish. Every man should stick to his own trade. Will you see what you can find out about a fence, Cobb?"

"Sure, Mr. Emmerich, sure," said Cobby, grinning, reassured.

But Riemenschneider was wondering, and sat rubbing his hand over his plump chin. This quick about-face! Did the great lawyer realize he'd made what might be called a blunder? The little doctor couldn't make up his mind.

There was a brief silence, and they all listened to the rain, which was beating at the windows with renewed fury.

Cobby turned to the little doctor.

"He ain't said it in so many words yet," said the bookie, grinning, "but the deal's in. Eh, Mr. Emmerich?"

Emmerich nodded solemnly and took out a fresh cigar.

"If it can be managed." He turned to Riemenschneider. "How much cash money do we need to swing it? And does this cash come off the top?"

"We need roughly fifty thousand dollars to operate," said the little doctor. "And of course it comes off the top, sir. The three shares are each thirty-three and a third per cent of the net."

"Good." Emmerich turned, stared into the fire, and thoughtfully lit his cigar. He intended to get the fifty grand if he had to steal it from somebody or blackmail one of his lay clients—blackmail not being healthy with the underworld; or . . . he could think of nothing else for the moment. But this was no time for caution. Wouldn't these men be astonished if they knew that at the present time he didn't have two thousand dollars cash to his name? And that he owed the Federal Government nearly a hundred and twenty-five thousand dollars in back taxes?

Emmerich made a sudden movement as a thought struck him. What an ass he was being! Why not handle the jewelry himself—not only handle it, disappear with it? Why had he backed down? Wouldn't he ever learn to follow his impulses? They were always right—always!

Why kid himself? He was at the end of his rope. His present course could end in nothing but disaster—and weak, pusillanimous disaster at that: bankruptcy—the sort of thing that happened every day to softies. Why not risk a real disaster—death! He'd always been a gambler. Why not take the ultimate gamble?

He turned and looked at the two men. He felt strong and composed now.

"Boys," he said, "I've been thinking. One false link and we fail. Since Johnny Abate's death there isn't a fence in the district big enough to handle this deal. That is if I understand you right," he added, turning to the little doctor. "You mean, I believe, that what we take will be worth half a million to us. Not actual value, because in no case would a fence give us more than fifty per cent."

"That's right, sir," said Riemenschneider, beginning to wonder if after all Emmerich might not be on the absolute level. "You are quite right."

"Very well then. Let me see what I can do before you try to find a fence, Cobb. News of a deal like this travels fast."

"That is very true, sir," said Riemenschneider, having more and more respect for the lawyer.

"I realize it was wrong of me to think of handling it," Emmerich went on smoothly. "Personally, I mean. But I know some very big men, who might not be averse to a deal like this if properly approached." Emmerich laughed good-naturedly. "Very respectable men, I might add. A few days one way or another doesn't matter, does it?"

"Not at all," said Riemenschneider. Then he bowed deprecatingly and spread out his hands in a gesture of appealing sadness. "Except for one thing, Mr. Emmerich. I dislike to mention it, but I've just come from prison, and I . . ."

Emmerich laughed good-naturedly again and clapped Riemenschneider on the shoulder.

"Don't worry about that, my friend. Cobb will advance you anything you need—find you a place to stay, look after you. Anything you like. Right, Cobb? And it all goes on the expense sheet."

"You bet your life," said Cobby, delighted at the smile Emmerich gave him, and the friendly look.

"And now—what do you say we call it a night? I really ought to get *some* sleep."

Riemenschneider and Cobby rose quickly—dismissed.

"You've been very kind, sir," said the little doctor, making his most elaborate bow.

Cobby grinned easily, not even annoyed now by the German's foreign ways. The great Mr. Emmerich had used him familiarly, unmistakably showing their intimacy to a stranger. Cobby's uneasy ego had been soothed for the time being.

Mr. Emmerich even shook hands with them and showed them to the door, where he said in parting: "Don't worry about the operating money. It's no problem at all. But give me a few days in regard to handling the jewelry. If I can't swing it, I'll call for help."

He smiled pleasantly as they went out into the pouring rain, and made an excessively friendly half salute of farewell; but as soon as the door closed, his smile changed to a look of concentration, and he walked slowly back toward the cardroom, deep in thought.

Suddenly an idea struck him, and he hurried to the phone and dialed a number. After a long wait a sleepy and resentful voice said: "Hello. Brannom speaking."

"Bob? Emmerich. What kind of reputation have I got for not collecting what's owed me?"

"Are you crazy, Mr. Emmerich?"

"Answer my question."

"You are known—if you'll excuse the expression—as a patsy, a quick push, a big softie; and all I can say is, it's a good thing you're not a dame."

"I've got over a hundred thousand dollars on my books. I've been too generous to too many people. I want you to collect it—and right away."

"Are you drunk?"

"You're a private detective, aren't you?—to be polite about it. In other words, a no-good, chiseling, low-down thug. Do you want the job or don't you?"

"Very much indeed, dear. Usual percentage?"

"Maybe more—if you work fast."

"Maybe don't buy baby no shoes."

"I didn't know you knew any babies who wore shoes."

"All right—pants."

"The remark still stands."

"Christ, we're funny for this time of the morning. Do I use polite methods or do I begin to kill people by nine tomorrow?"

"Use the methods called for in each individual case. All I want is results."

"What you figuring to do—skip town with a sixteen-year-old girl? Make it fourteen. The sixteen-year-olds are too smart."

Emmerich started, bit his lips in irritation, then spoke sharply.

"I should have let the District Attorney send you up. He had the goods on you. For an assistant D.A., you were mighty careless."

"What do you expect—gratitude?"

"Yes. I ought to get *something* for my trouble."

"My God! Don't tell me you want me to dun myself!" Then in an altered voice, as if speaking to someone at his end of the line, Brannom said: "Roll over, honey. That's the girl." Then to Emmerich: "My dog is so cute."

"That's more than I can say for you. Now get busy, Bob. And if you want to know the reason, I'll tell you. Uncle Sam and his revenuers—they want money."

"Wait! Wait!" cried Brannom. "Don't hang up. How about that 'maybe' business? You got me so confused with your brilliant repartee and ripostes, Mr. Emmerich."

"Two per cent up."

"It's better than four of a kind against a straight flush. Good night."

Emmerich hung up, rose, then stood for a moment wondering if he'd made a mistake. He realized that he was jittery and that perhaps his judgment was not so good as usual. No doubt about it—this assault on his debtors would cause a stir in certain circles of the city, and there would be gossip, speculation, repercussions. Suddenly he smiled to himself and, leaving the cardroom, he walked back toward the living-room. All such thinking was futile now. There was no future to worry about; at least no future that had any connection with the city and his former life. He was going to cut himself adrift—and soon. Let them talk and speculate!

The radio was still playing softly in the living-room. A red-haired girl was lying asleep on one of the big couches, an opened movie magazine on the floor beside her. Emmerich paused and stood looking down at her for some time with marked indifference. Then he shrugged and went toward the back of the house.

He found Frank, the chauffeur, sitting at a table in the kitchen, drinking a bottle of beer and reading a morning newspaper. He started to rise, but Emmerich waved him back into his seat; then he went to the refrigerator, got himself a bottle of beer, opened it, and sat at the table with the chauffeur.

"Frank, when you finish your beer, call Mrs. Emmerich. Tell her I'm going to be held up. Not to worry about me."

"Okay, Mr. Emmerich."

They drank in silence for a while; then Emmerich said: "Some compensations in being a criminal lawyer. A man can keep any kind of hours and get away with it."

Frank laughed shortly; then he finished his beer, rose, and went to the phone in the servants' quarters. Emmerich heard the vague rumble of his voice as he talked on the

phone, but he paid no attention. He was thinking about the
red-haired girl. She'd cost him a fortune. He'd furnished
this cottage for her; he'd given her money by the handfuls;
he'd sent checks to her mother and several other relatives;
he'd bought her a car, a mink coat, a diamond bracelet.
And now he was sitting here drinking his beer and wondering
why in the hell he had done it. She was a doll—no doubt
about it—with beautiful hair and a lovely body, but, on
close acquaintance, a lazy, ignorant, mercenary trollop.

"It took me nearly a year and maybe a hundred thousand
dollars to find it out," said Emmerich with a sigh. Then he
finished his beer and got up just as Frank came back into
the kitchen.

"I talked to Mrs. Emmerich's new maid. Mrs. Emmerich's asleep," said Frank.

"Good," said the lawyer. Then he started back for the
living-room, but turned. "Take the car into the office ga-
rage, Frank, if you want to. I won't need you till noon
tomorrow."

"How about me sleeping here, sir? It's still raining, and
maybe the road's flooded."

"Okay, Frank. Suit yourself."

"Thanks," called Frank as Emmerich went out; then he
picked up his paper again. He felt very sad about things in
general and Mr. and Mrs. Emmerich in particular. They
were nice to him and paid him well and didn't work him
too hard. But look at them! Emmerich, old enough to be a
grandfather, with a young red-haired girl—and a bum at
that. What did he think he was doing? And Mrs. Emmerich—sick, bored, lonely!

Frank groaned, rustled his paper, and told himself for the
hundredth time that he'd never marry—no matter what!

On his way back to the living-room Emmerich suddenly
remembered how frantic his wife used to be when he was
out late; how she worried, fumed, and fretted. Why, once
she'd even sent the police out to look for him. Now . . .
well . . . time passes, things change, emotions die down!

And that brought him back again to Angela, the red-haired

girl. Christ, what a name for her! He should have left her where he found her. One rainy day he'd ducked into a smart little downtown restaurant for a quick lunch. It was off his usual beat and he'd never been in it before. Angela seated him. She was a politely smiling, efficient hostess, minding her own business. But every man in the room, young and old, was eying her. And it was not only the flaming red hair: she was slenderly but voluptuously made; and there was something about her walk—something lazy, careless, and insolently assured—that it was impossible to ignore.

"Okay," said Emmerich, crossing the living-room and sitting down in a big chair near the couch where Angela was lying. "So now I got her. I carried her off—the big hero, envied by all entire males. Well . . . ?"

In any case, she'd soon be back in the restaurant.

Angela opened her eyes slowly, then turned to look at him. Her eyes were a yellowish brown—very unusual—and her lashes were long, curved, and black.

"What's the idea—sitting there staring at me, Uncle Lon?"

Uncle Lon! What a gag! And there'd been a time when he'd got a terrific boot out of it. Now it seemed merely grotesque.

"You'd better get some rest, darling," she said hurriedly before he could speak. "You've been looking awfully tired lately—working too hard."

Emmerich smiled and nodded wearily. What a comedy! There was no mistaking the anxiety in her voice. She was taking the offensive at once, trying to evade him, put him off—keep him out of her bed tonight without really making an issue of it. After all, as far as she knew, he was still loaded with what the boys vulgarly referred to as moo!

"You're right," he said. "Soon as I smoke another cigar I'm going to get some shut-eye. Why don't you go to bed, baby?"

Angela jumped up quickly and came over to him.

"I'm dead. But I'd sit up ten hours more for you it you wanted me to. Here! Let me do that."

Emmerich was untying his shoes. Angela knelt down in

front of him and in a few moments had his shoes off. Then she rose quickly and, leaning over him, kissed him on the top of his head.

"See you at breakfast," said Angela, smiling sweetly; then, before he could say anything, she went on: "I had the market send over salt mackerel for you—best grade they could find. I know you love it for breakfast."

"Thanks, baby," said Emmerich with an effort.

Angela threw him a kiss and hurried down the hall and into her bedroom, shutting the door soundlessly and locking it.

Emmerich stretched out his sock feet, lit a big Cuban cigar, and sat staring into space. The rain had begun to slacken, and a heavy silence throbbed through the living-room. Emmerich was not used to being alone and he began to feel a little jumpy. Suddenly he realized that he was not enjoying his cigar, and this puzzled and worried him. Cigars soothed him when all else failed.

He put the cigar in an ash-tray, leaned his head back, shut his eyes, and tried to relax. For a moment he drifted into sleep then he woke with a start. He felt trapped, and began to sweat. What was it?

The big gamble—that was it! It had struck him all at once when he was half asleep. It was no longer a matter of dollars and cents now, but of life and death.

Emmerich groaned.

"My God! I'm tired!" he exclaimed aloud, and the metal base of the lamp beside him vibrated slightly to the sound of his voice like a faint, sinister echo.

· 8 ·

It was just a few minutes before noon when Gus came out of his little cubbyhole of a bunkroom at the back of his hamburger joint. He felt groggy with sleep and irritable, and did not even say good morning to his helper, Mike Miklos, a big foggy-eyed Greek who always seemed blankly oblivious of what was going on around him and yet never missed a thing.

A couple of hustlers from the poolroom across the street were eating at the counter; and a truck-driver was standing at the magazine rack, chewing away lustily at a king-size hamburger and stealing a look at the half-naked girls pictured in a movie magazine he had no intention of buying.

Gus threw him a hostile look, grunted when one of the hustlers said hello; then hitching up his sagging pants, he went to the door to take a look at the weather. He'd fallen asleep to the sound of rain battering a tin roof in the alley behind his joint; but now the day was clear, and weak sunshine was spreading out through the streets and alleys of the Camden Square district.

Gus opened the door and sniffed the air, grimacing as if he preferred tobacco smoke and underdone hamburger; then he looked to see if Terry was on time—and sure enough he was. Near the storage mailbox, ten or twelve feet down the pavement from Gus's All Night, a big, tough-looking black alley cat with vicious yellow eyes was sitting, obviously at peace with the world and afraid of nothing, calmly washing himself.

"You, Terry—you big bum," called Gus, his fat ugly face breaking out into a wide, pleasant grin. "Looking for the handout, eh?" Terry answered with a sharp cry, then rose and walked over to Gus. "What a panhandler!" said Gus. "Knows how to live without work. Knows how to get all the nooky he wants, too. Smart cat. Come on in."

Gus went back into the place, and Terry followed him, walking stiffly with great dignity and carrying his tail high.

Big Mike looked down at the cat with pleasure but merely grinned. The truck-driver glanced up from his close study of female anatomy and was annoyed.

"What's a big dirty cat doing in an eating-place?" he

demanded. "Sonsabitching cats. I run over one every time I get a chance. People feeding cats when some kids ain't got enough to eat."

Big Mike groaned slightly and went quickly to the far end of the counter. The hustlers didn't even look up from their food. But Gus picked up the cat, put him on the counter, and began to hand-feed him raw hamburger, which he ate daintily.

"You going to buy that magazine?" Gus asked quietly.

The truck-driver laughed.

"Why should I? I seen all the dames in it already. Why? Want to make something of it?"

Mike groaned again, turned his back, and began to polish already-polished glasses.

"Little off your beat, ain't you, buster?" asked Gus.

"How do you mean, fatty?"

"I mean you ain't a Camden Square boy. You're just passing through—only not fast enough."

Gus came around the counter with a speed that surprised even Mike, seized the truck-driver by the arm, whirled him around, grabbed the seat of his pants, jerked it up tight till the fellow was on his tiptoes, then Spanish-walked him swiftly across the little place and out the front door. Giving the flabbergasted driver a push, he cried: "And don't come back. And if I ever see you running over a cat I'll kick your teeth out."

The driver stood staring at Gus, gradually recovering from his surprise but unable to make up his mind whether to clout the little hunchback or beat a dignified retreat. One of the hustlers laughed inside the joint, and that seemed to unsettle him.

"I'd take you apart if you were a foot taller and straightened out a little," he barked, getting very red in the face.

But as he made no move to come back, Gus stepped across toward him, carrying his hands low, his face livid. Most of the time he forgot about that hump on his back, forgot he wasn't like other people. He didn't like to be reminded.

But somebody laid a placating hand on Gus's arm, and

as he turned, the driver moved off with feigned reluctance toward his pick-up truck, looking back belligerently over his shoulder.

"Gus! What's with you so early in the day?"

Gus glared; then the color began to return to his heavy face, and he managed a smile.

"Schemer! I was wondering if you'd show—or if maybe the bambino had a toothache."

"What's the matter—wouldn't he pay?" Louis Bellini jerked a thumb in the direction of the truck-driver, who was now climbing into his truck.

"Terry didn't like him," said Gus, laughing. "So I flang him out."

Louis grinned and followed Gus back into the hamburger joint. Big Mike was now hand-feeding Terry, whose purrs sounded like the distant rumble of a motorboat.

"Hi, Terry," said Louis. Then he went behind the counter and walked with Gus to the bunkroom beyond.

Gus closed the door, then turned to Louis.

"Did you bring the moo?"

Louis nodded, swallowed, struggled with himself for a moment, then pulled out a big roll with a rubber band around it and handed it to Gus, who stuffed it uncounted into his shirt pocket and chuckled at the wry face Louis was making.

"Okay, laugh," said Louis, nettled. "But that's a lot of cash right now."

"Sure. Sure it is, Schemer," cried Gus, putting his arm around Louis and hugging him with the strength of a heavy-weight wrestler till Louis felt that his ribs were going to crack, and finally managed to extricate himself. "I love you for it," Gus added.

"If it was for you, Gus, I'd never give it a second thought. But this Dix guy—bad medicine."

"No," said Gus. "A hundred per cent. You think maybe I don't know about those things?"

"You ought to. You've got the rep: But you might be wrong."

"If I'm wrong, I'll pay you myself. You got my mitt on it."

Louis evaded the outstretched hand.

"Okay," he said quickly. "I'll take your word for it. I need these fingers of mine in my business."

Gus laughed. Then a sudden thought struck him.

"Say—heard anything?"

"How do you mean?"

"A big boy blew in from the Walls last night."

"I was home all evening. I don't hear things, anyway—unless somebody needs me."

"I got a pal down at Cobby's: Timmons, you know—the old wrestler. Well, a big boy blew in. Something about a deal."

"Could be," said Louis indifferently.

There was a brief pause; then Gus had another thought.

"Say—had your lunch?"

"No," said Louis. "I came right over from the shop."

"How about a nice double hamburger? The best. I got a hundred pounds triple A—hid, I mean."

"Hid?"

"Yeah. For my friends, and for me and Mike and Terry. For guys I don't like—cops, and jerks like that truck-driver—I give horse meat." Gus bent down to laugh, slapping his thigh. "Know the Happiness Boys—the harness bulls from the Strip? Always in trying to pump me. They're going to start whinnying and kicking up their hind feet before I'm through."

Louis leaned against the wall to laugh. Gus roared, beating the door with his fist and startling some new customers who'd just come in from the street.

Louis continued to laugh. There were tears in his eyes, and he bent down to hold his sides. Gus had a faint rush of emotion. This was his pal. His old Schemer Louis, who had gradually drifted away from the boys since he'd met that cute, respectable little Italian girl Maria. Why, Gus hadn't seen Louis laugh like that for over two years.

But in the old days he'd always been laughing. Slim, handsome, sharp-witted Louis, with his tailor-made clothes, his smile, and his little black book packed with the best telephone numbers in the district. Elegant little Louis—the irresponsible dance-hall Casanova!

Now look at him, with the worry wrinkle between his eyebrows, the sober clothes, the responsible air—tight as a country banker and thinking about nothing but his family.

Yet here he was laughing—as in the old days.

Gus remembered a fight he'd had with one of the dance-hall bums who insisted Louis was using his telephone numbers for business purposes—that he was, in short, a M'Gimp. Louis, of all people! Gus recalled with satisfaction how he'd knocked the guy's teeth loose.

Suddenly Gus came to himself, sobered.

"Say—what am I thinking about! I got to call Dix."

The smile left Louis's face immediately, and he was back in character—worried Louis, with mouths to feed.

· 9 ·

Lying on his face, Dix was sleeping heavily in spite of the sunshine streaming in through his bedroom windows and the traffic noises, very distinct in the rain-washed air, rising from the eastern end of busy Camden Boulevard West.

He was dreaming, and in his dreams he was not the big, lanky, harsh-faced man with the sunken cheeks and the coldly blank dark eyes. He was a slender boy, maybe thirteen; and his big, gangling grandfather, a former Morgan Raider, had just lifted him up onto the back of a tall black colt, which was sweating with fear and cussedness, prancing and sidling, waiting its chance to pitch the young rider into a fence. He was badly scared, his stomach had dropped away, and he was sweating as heavily as the colt, but his boyish mouth was grim and his face was expressionless. Just as his grandfather turned the colt loose, he got a quick look at his father, who was leaning against a fence, holding his sides and laughing. In a flash young William Tuttle

understood (in his dreams he was never known as Dix): he'd
been bragging what a wonderful rider he was, and his father
and grandfather had put up a job on him.

But in a little while they were laughing on the wrong
sides of their mouths. The colt ran away with him, tried to
scrape him off against trees, buck-jumped and pitched; but
half an hour later young William Tuttle rode the colt back
to the Jamieson place, tame as a cat, staggering with fatigue,
and completely mastered. And that night, when he was
going up the stairs to bed, his grandfather said: "He's a
real Jamieson, that boy."

It was a very pleasant dream, and Dix often dreamed it—
or something like it.

The facts, however, were a little different. The big black
colt had pitched him into a fence on the first buck, and his
father had prodded him with his foot and said: "Maybe that
will teach you not to be such a goddamned braggart."

Dix turned over on his back and sighed. The snow was
falling lightly over the cornfield—first snow of the year.
He and Lou Sally went out to gather pumpkins for Hallow-
een. It was toward evening and dark; thin smoke was rising
straight up from the farmhouse chimney. The sky was the
color of slate, and a big, rayless red autumn sun was going
down just beyond a rise in the flat farm land. Big, fat orange-
colored pumpkins were scattered all over the field among
the tall corn shocks. They bent down to cut one from the
thick stem of the vine. All about them in the light fall of
snow were the minute tracks of the little field mice. . . .

A bell was ringing, a bell he couldn't make out. Then an
alien feminine voice began to speak . . . and suddenly the
pleasant, safe field disappeared . . . and Dix was awake
and staring at the sunshine flooding in from Camden Square.
He groaned and rubbed his eyes, shrinking from the neces-
sity of facing the new day.

Somebody was talking on the phone in the next room—
Doll! He'd forgotten all about her.

Groaning again, he reached down, picked up a bottle that

was on the floor beside his bed, and took a long pull. Then he lay back and let the warmth of the whisky get to him.

Doll hung up, then came and stood in the doorway. In a timid voice she said: "Honey . . . it was a fellow named Gus. He says you can come over any time. He's got something for you."

"Thanks," said Dix shortly; but a sudden elation was warming him more than the whisky. Now he could tell Cobby off, shove twenty-three hundred in bills into his smug kisser—watch him crawl. He turned to look at Doll, who was still hanging around the doorway. She was fully dressed in her hostess gown, which seemed sordidly cheap and shoddy in broad daylight. She had her coarse, dyed hair wound up anyhow, and she looked pretty old and tired. Dix turned his face away from her.

"Your breakfast's coming right up, honey," said Doll with forced cheerfulness. Then she went on: "God, this place is a mess! Needs a good thorough cleaning—stinks, even. Dix, you need somebody to look after you. How can you stand to live like this?"

Dames! Always on the pitch—always trying to move in. He looked out the window and said nothing. In a moment Doll turned away and hurried out to the stove, where Dix's eggs were cooking. She'd gone out to get them herself when she could find nothing in the larder but some bread and coffee. People had stared at her in the little Italian market down the street because of her carelessly wound-up hair and her startling dress. But she was far beyond worrying about such nonsense as that. Let 'em stare! Dix had to eat!

· 10 ·

Terry was still on the counter when Dix got to Gus's place. A taxi-driver, gnawing on a hamburger (grade B, as he was known in the district and fairly well liked), kept watching the big yellow-eyed alley cat with something like fear. Terry turned with a mewing cry as Dix came up to the counter. Dix roughed him up a bit, and Terry, growling in his throat and flattening his ears, struck at Dix with his right front paw, a series of short, deft jabs like a good fighter.

"Look at him go," said Gus, beaming.

And the taxi-driver laughed appreciatively, trying to get in good with strange little Gus and his big, tough-looking hick friend.

But they both ignored him and went back into the bunk-room, where Gus took a roll of bills from his pocket and handed it over.

"It's all there, Dix. Twenty-three hundred. Schemer came through, and I added the plant."

"Okay," said Dix indifferently. "Now I think I'll drop down and see a friend of mine on business."

"Cobby, maybe?" asked Gus, grinning; then as Dix said nothing but merely stared at him harshly, he went on: "It was only a guess. Sue me. Anyway, if it *is* Cobby, you won't find him. I seen him go past in his car just after I called you."

Dix rubbed a powerful, big-knuckled hand across his chin and considered.

"He's a damned little feist, that man!" he said at last. "A yellow dog!"

"It ain't as bad as it sounds," said Gus, placatingly. "He's nervous. You're A 1 with him, Dix. How many guys can you think of offhand around the Square with credit up to twenty-five hundred?"

"Don't like his manner," said Dix. "Damn him and his credit!"

Gus shrugged and let it go. Dix was beyond him. His ways were not Gus's ways. Sometimes his ideas and re-actions seemed grotesque. All the same, he was a right one, and to Gus that was the prime qualification. Only two kinds of people in the world: right and wrong—and most of 'em were wrong, dead wrong. Gus knew hundreds of men, but there were only three he'd make book on: Mike Miklos, Louis Bellini, and Dix Handley—or whatever his real name was!

After a moment, Gus inquired: "Heard anything?"

"No. Why?"

"Big guy blew in from the Walls last night. Looked Cobby right up. Timmons said something about a deal."

Dix considered, then said: "Yeah. I think I saw him. I was in talking to Cobby. Little fat fellow—foreigner of some kind."

Gus asked many questions, trying to prod Dix's memory and stimulate his meager descriptive powers. Finally, Gus's face lit up.

"I got it. It's Riemenschneider. The Squarehead. A really big guy. Pulled a hundred-G take once."

Dix made no comment, lost in thoughts of what he was going to say to Cobby. He didn't care how big Riemenschneider was. It was nothing to him.

After a while Mike Miklos brought them back some coffee and grinned with deep pleasure when Dix patted him on the back.

· 11 ·

It was late in the afternoon before Dix was able to run Cobby down. The bookie made an abortive effort to duck into one of the cardrooms when he saw Dix coming down the corridor—a purely instinctive and involuntary movement, as all day long he'd been rehearsing what he was going to say to the big Southerner when he turned up with the money he owed. Dix was a puzzle to Cobby, and yet he was astute enough to feel pretty sure that after the brief but ugly wrangle of the night before, Dix would get the money some way— any way!—and pay him off. Why was Dix so touchy? Where did he come off, blowing a fuse merely because Cobby had

suggested that when he got to the top figure of his credit—
twenty-five hundred—not bad: a real favor!—it might be a
good idea to get the money on the line. Business was business. "Why, by God," Cobby kept telling himself, "you'd
think he was a gentleman or something, like Mr. Emmerich!
Not a knocked-out heister, maybe hitting filling-stations or
even rolling drunks." How could Cobby know that a gambling debt was a point of honor with Dix? A point of honor?
With Dix? The mere idea—if it had occurred to him—would
have sent Cobby off into bursts of sardonic laughter. How
silly can you get?

"Hello, Dix," said Cobby, jigging about nervously. "Was
hoping you'd turn up. Come on in my office. Have a drink."

Without waiting for Dix to speak, Cobby turned quickly,
hurried into his office, and with his back to Dix, who followed him leisurely, he took from his desk a bottle of the
best grade Scotch and two glasses.

"Don't bother with your hospitality," said Dix harshly;
and Cobby turned, bottle in hand, looking startled but trying
to smile. "Here's your money," Dix went on, and tossed
onto Cobby's desk a thick roll of bills bound with a rubber
band. The roll skidded across the shiny desk top, hung for
a moment on the edge, then fell to the floor.

"I wasn't boning you, Dix," said Cobby in an aggrieved
voice. "I was only saying . . ."

But Dix broke in violently.

"Showing off is what you were doing. Trying to make
me look small in front of a little man I never saw before."

"No, no!" cried Cobby, badly frightened by the cold,
harsh light in Dix's eyes. "You got it all wrong! Okay,
Dix. Maybe I shouldn't have said anything, but . . ."

"Did I ever welch?"

"No, Dix. Of course you didn't. Haven't you got credit
with me up to twenty-five hundred? Listen, do you think . . ."

"If I never welched, why bone me—and in front of a
stranger!"

"I tell you I wasn't boning you," cried Cobby, all mixed
up now and stammering. "I . . . I don't know what I was

thinking of, Dix. I guess I was just looking for something to say. You know how it is.''

"No," said Dix slowly. "I *don't* know how it is."

Cobby put his hand on Dix's arm and looked up at him pleadingly. This was serious. To have a hooligan like Dix for an enemy was about the worst thing that could happen to a guy.

"Listen, Dix. These things come up. Please overlook it. Maybe I had a slight load on. Maybe I was thinking about something else. Don't you ever make a mistake?''

Dix hesitated and slowly rubbed his big hand over his face. All feeling of satisfaction had left him. Cobby was such small prey—no more guts than a little white mouse!

Cobby noticed the hesitation and began to take heart.

"Here," he said. "How about a drink? Best you can buy, Dix. I save it for my very special friends.''

"I don't drink Scotch," said Dix with a certain amount of contempt. "Got some bourbon in the joint?''

"Sure, sure," cried Cobby, hopping about agilely, extracting a bottle from another drawer, and talking rapidly as he did so. "Dix, I said I was hoping you'd turn up, and I meant it. I ran into a kid who used to work for me. He's over south of town now, working in a big lay-off joint, and he's been cleaning up, betting along with the money his bosses lay off. There's a big syndicate operating through the books in the state, and when there's a fix going, the lay-off parlor gets the overflow. The kid's going to tip me off, and I'm going to wire my bets to a Cleveland lay-off joint I know about. What I was thinking is, every time the kid tips me off, I'll let you know, Dix. Money from home. Money from home . . . !''

Dix poured himself a big drink and drank it in silence; then he poured himself another and stood holding the glass up to the light, admiring the color of the whisky.

"That whisky," he said, as if to himself, "is made in my home state. We got the best water in the country. That's what makes all our liquor fit to drink.''

"Best whisky I ever tasted," Cobby agreed quickly, taking an unusually big slug and drinking it greedily, then smacking his lips.

"About this lay-off business," said Dix. "Why me?"

"Why not?" cried Cobby. "You're a pal and a good customer. I'd like to see you on the right end of the betting for once."

Dix studied Cobby for so long that the little bookie got very nervous and self-conscious and in a moment started to jig about, look for a book of matches, pour another drink— anything to keep from standing still and meeting Dix's steady, hard, dark gaze.

Finally Dix relaxed. Bending down, he picked up the roll of bills from the floor and handed it to Cobby, who took it gingerly, wanting to refuse but afraid to.

"Okay," said Dix. "I'll take you up on that."

"Fine, fine!" cried Cobby, beginning to breathe freely for the first time since Dix's arrival. "Now that's settled, how about another drink?"

Dix nodded, and Cobby, quickly stuffing the roll into his pocket, poured the whisky for him with a flourish and even laid a hand timidly on the big man's shoulder for a moment.

Just as Dix raised his glass, there was a faint, almost deprecatory knock at the door; then the little doctor put his head in.

Cobby grinned with relief.

"It's Doc," he cried. "Come on in. Meet a friend of mine—Dix Handley."

The little doctor smiled and bowed and offered Dix a small, plump, womanish hand, which was cold and moist to the touch. Dix dropped it at once. Neither one mentioned anything about seeing the other before. They merely stood staring at each other.

Cobby poured the little doctor a drink from the bottle of Scotch; then he said: "Dix is one of my best customers. A hundred per cent. With him I never worry. Word's as good as his bond."

Dix knew that Cobby was laying it on pretty thick, trying to make it up to him, and yet he was pleased. Pulling up a chair, he took off his hat, put it on Cobby's desk, and relaxed.

Wanting to be sociable, the little doctor took the drink offered him, though he didn't want it, and also sat down. Delighted, Cobby joined them. He'd known Dix for a long time but he'd never seen him before without his hat. Somehow it made them seem more intimate. And besides, hatless, Dix looked almost like another man and not nearly so formidable. His thick dark hair, almost as coarse as an animal's pelt, was carefully brushed and conventionally parted on the side. His forehead was rather high and somehow reassuringly ordinary. Without his corny-looking hat, the brim of which was too wide, Dix seemed as smoothly human as anybody Cobby could think of.

"This is Erwin Riemenschneider, Dix," said Cobby. "You've heard of him, I guess."

"Yeah," said Dix; then conversationally: "I figure you're a German."

"My father was, sir," said the little doctor, speaking to Dix with marked respect because the big outlander obviously had a rare and admirable quality—ruthlessness, a form of power. "My mother was a Dalmatian, and I was born in Spalato—but I suppose I'm a German. At least, I spent a lot of time there. I even saw the inside of Moabit." He chuckled slightly as if to himself.

"Where's that?" asked Cobby.

"A Berlin prison," said the little doctor. "Very gloomy. I didn't stay long."

"I been in Germany," said Dix.

"Yes?" said the little doctor, surprised. "What part of Germany?"

"I was stationed in Coblenz."

"Oh. You were in the World War."

"Yeah," said Dix; then he grunted, intending this sound for a laugh. "World War I."

The little doctor started slightly; then he carefully studied Dix's face.

"That was thirty years ago," he said.

"Yeah," said Dix; then he rose, put his glass on the desk,

picked up his hat, and nodded to both of the men. "I got to go. See you, maybe."

He went out, shutting the door behind him, ignoring their good-byes.

Dix's abrupt leave-taking startled Cobby and the little doctor into silence, and they sat staring off before them. It was as if Dix had suddenly become embarrassed by the fact that for a few moments he'd relaxed, like other men, and engaged in a fruitless conversation—at least that was the impression Riemenschneider had got. He was very thoughtful. Maybe he had jumped to conclusions too fast about this big, farmerish man at their first meeting. He looked very ruthless—yes; he looked like a bigtime heister—a heavy, always ready to blast; and yet there was something else—something the little doctor couldn't quite express to himself. Something dependable, was it? No, no! That was hardly the word with a man of this character. Something . . . strong? Responsible? The little doctor gave it up, and yet he felt unaccountably drawn to Dix.

Cobby brought him round with a question.

"How was the girl Costa got you? Okay?"

Riemenschneider shrugged inconclusively and wagged his head.

"Very professional. A little cold-hearted mercenary girl. But what does one expect?" He paused and studied Cobby for a moment, wondering if he should tell him what was on his mind. Finally he decided to speak. It might be important. "I find these expensive girls very useful at times. They meet a lot of people and they always talk."

"Yeah?" said Cobby, alert at once. "What did she have to say?"

"Well," said the little doctor, "she was bragging about all the important men she knew in town—clients; they always brag. So—you mustn't be offended now—I worked around the conversation to Mr. Emmerich."

"Emmerich!" cried Cobby, jumping up and jigging about. "Now look here, Riemenschneider . . ."

The little doctor waved his hands and smiled placatingly.

"Wait. Think a minute. She doesn't know who I am. And what I asked her will slip that empty mind of hers in five minutes."

"That ain't what I mean!" cried Cobby.

"Listen to me. There is half a million dollars at stake. All right. I know he is your patron . . . I know all that. I know you will probably go and tell him I've been inquiring. But . . . this little girl told me that he's been ruining himself for a red-headed non-professional! He used to be quite a client."

"Mr. Emmerich?" laughed Cobby. "Ruining himself? Are you crazy?"

"I'm a stranger in town. I've got a big deal to handle. I only ask for information."

Cobby chewed on his lips and pranced about. Here was a pretty go!

"Also," the little doctor went on, "I got to thinking about Joe Cool—he's in for life. It's the only chance he's got."

Gradually Cobby calmed down. Maybe you couldn't blame the little guy after all.

"Look, my friend," said Cobby with deep conviction, "if Mr. Emmerich is ruined, then I want to be ruined the same way. I'll underwrite him myself. Why, the whole idea is so goddamned silly . . . !" Cobby paused to laugh. "Doc, whose word would you take in a case like this—some meat-headed tart's? Or mine?"

"Yours, naturally," said the little doctor at once, and yet he was far from convinced, in spite of the fact that he himself had exaggerated to Cobby what the call girl had told him. He remembered his impressions of the night before: Emmerich did not seem to him like the calm, solid, astute man he'd been hearing so much about from Joe Cool. He decided to bide his time. At least he'd found out one thing. If Emmerich was not on the level, Cobby knew nothing about it.

"Let's have another drink," said Cobby, "and forget this nonsense."

His men had never seen Police Captain Rieger in such a state before, and they sat trying not to look at him, fearful and appalled. His right-hand man, Police Lieutenant "Tip" Collins, a jaunty Irishman, was the most deeply affected and sat twisting his cap in his hands, sweating profusely.

Rieger had been talking on the phone to Commissioner Hardy for nearly half an hour. His big, harsh face was parchment-pale and beaded with sweat. From time to time he reached out a shaking hand for a cigarette, which Tip Collins immediately jumped up to light.

Was this the end of the world? To the coppers it seemed like it. How else could they explain what was happening before their eyes? John Rieger, for years the undisputed tyrant of the Camden Square district, visibly quaking, hopelessly abject.

"Yes, I know, Commissioner," Rieger protested feebly, "but . . ." That was as far as he got; in fact, it was as far as he had got all during the conversation.

Finally it was over. Rieger hung up slowly, like a condemned man whose reprieve has just been denied; then he began to look about him foggily, as if the world had receded and was now once more slowly coming back into focus.

Suddenly he jumped up and shouted in a loud, hysterical voice: "Get Dietrich! Find Dietrich!"

There was an embarrassed silence, and Tip Collins stood up awkwardly. His mouth worked but no words came out.

"Well . . . goddamn it!" Rieger screamed, "hasn't anybody got anything to say?"

"Excuse me, Captain," said Tip, hoarsely, "but Sergeant Dietrich—he's gone duck-hunting. . . ."

Rieger glared at Tip viciously; then he grabbed up a desk calendar and flung it against the wall. The coppers all sat in silence watching the leaves flutter down.

"You . . . you said it was okay, sir," stammered Tip. "I asked you. Remember?"

Rieger pulled out a cigarette, turned away to avoid the match Tip produced at once, lit it himself, puffed on it for a moment, then nodded slowly and sadly. Finally he sank down into his chair and said in a gruff, unhappy voice: "Boys, I'm sorry. I want to apologize for this childish exhibition."

Somewhat relieved, but still jittery because of another unaccustomed switch—an apology—from Rieger!—the coppers all jumped up and began talking at once, but Rieger waved them to silence.

"Boys, we've got to produce. There is no way to kid that four-eyed little son-of-a-bitch in the City Building. Now I don't mean you got to go out and haul in Riemenschneider. Hardy's hipped on the subject. The Squarehead may be in New York, or San Francisco, or New Orleans. Who the hell knows? But we got to clear up those club robberies. Somebody's got to figure an angle." He turned to Collins. "Tip— get hold of Dietrich. Keep at it if it takes you all night. I want him back."

"Yes, sir," said Tip; then he turned and rushed out hastily, as if Dietrich, a fugitive, had just left on the fly and had to be run down in a foot race.

Rieger swiveled round in his chair and sat staring thoughtfully at a big, flat-faced plain-clothes man who stood grinning uneasily.

"Janocheck," said Rieger, and the big man drew himself up like a soldier.

"Yes, Captain."

"I want you to go right over to the Camden West district and bear down on the team that's working tonight." He turned to another dick. "Who are they, LeFevre?"

LeFevre raised his hand and coughed behind it. He was in a panic. Still suffering from a feeling of insecurity due to the sorry spectacle his chief had just made of himself, he couldn't remember anything for the moment, hardly his own name.

"Well, uh . . . uh . . ." he stammered as Rieger stared at him impatiently. Then it came to him, and he heaved a sigh of relief. "Tom Mattison and Randy Cook, Captain."

"Ah!" said Rieger, pleased. "An old-timer and a rookie."
He turned to Janocheck. "Give 'em hell. Make it strong!
Scare the pants off of 'em. Tell 'em I said if they don't
produce, I'll have 'em transferred to Shinetown."

"Yes, sir," said Janocheck; then he turned and walked
out of the office, the boards creaking under his weight.

"The rest of you stick around," said Rieger abruptly;
then he turned to his desk, dismissing them.

They filed out silently into the anteroom. One of them,
Carlson, had a sick wife and two kids with colds, and he
had already received permission from Tip Collins to go
home whenever he felt like it, but he said nothing about
this to the Captain. They'd just have to get along the best
way they could.

As soon as he was alone, Rieger put in a telephone call
to his old friend the Chief of Police. He and Dolph Franc
had been rookies together and had kept up their friendship
through all the vicissitudes of promotions and police politics.
Rieger wanted to talk over the Commissioner with Dolph,
who hated the stiff-faced little man and could be very amus-
ing on the subject. Rieger felt that such a conversation at
this point would soothe his ruffled feelings.

Instead, he got a rude surprise. Dolph immediately began
swearing at him over the phone, told him that his district
had the worst record of any in the town and that if something
wasn't done about it pretty quick, there would be some
changes made.

"And after this," yelled Dolph, "don't call me in the
middle of the night." Then he banged up the receiver with
a crash.

Rieger jumped up immediately and began to pace the
floor.

"Dietrich—that big fathead!" he bellowed to the walls.
"Duck-hunting—for Christ's sake!"

· 13 ·

It was nearly a week before Cobby heard from Emmerich. The lawyer's voice sounded smooth, reassuring, and genial, and Cobby sighed with relief. He'd been getting jumpy over the delay, and even the calm little doctor had begun to show signs of restlessness. And yet . . . what was Emmerich saying over the phone? Some kind of double talk that Cobby, with the best will in the world, couldn't quite unscramble. No trouble about the operating money—no trouble at all. Nothing to worry about there. But the man who was to finance and handle the actual deal after the business was concluded . . . well, Emmerich had contacted him of course; but by phone, as he was temporarily out of town; and naturally a delicate problem like this couldn't really be talked out and settled unless the principals were face to face. It took managing, finagling . . . and time—above all, time. But that didn't mean there were any hitches; Cobby mustn't think that. All was running smoothly . . . and with any luck in the world within a few days . . .

Emmerich went on and on!

With his thin face screwed up, Cobby listened intently at the phone and tried to make some coherent sense out of this flood of words, which were delivered in such a way that they *must* mean something—and yet, what? Was the deal on? Off? Settled, all but a few details? Could they start getting the crew ready? Should they stand by?

And at last when the lawyer insisted on ringing off, in spite of Cobby's stammered pleas for clarification, Cobby was as bewildered as a conscientious voter trying to make some sense out of campaign oratory.

Worst of all, he turned from the phone just in time to face Riemenschneider, who had knocked delicately, as was his way, and then had come in.

Cobby looked at him in silence for a moment; then, made uncomfortable by the little doctor's mild but probing gaze, he decided to speak.

"That was Mr. Emmerich." Cobby swallowed hard before he continued, and turned to light a cigar, avoiding Riemenschneider's eyes. "Looks okay. He . . . he's got a big conference on tonight. Going to call me tomorrow."

"Good!" said the little doctor. "I'm glad to hear it. Naturally I'd rather Mr. Emmerich handled it, because that is the way Joe wanted it. But I was getting worried, and I've been looking around a little. Just in case, you understand," he added with a deprecatory smile, though his small dark eyes, looking vague and distorted because of the thick lenses of his glasses, regarded Cobby with unwinking shrewdness.

"Looking around?" Cobby demanded. "How do you mean?"

"Well," said Riemenschneider, spreading out his hands in an apologetic gesture, "I'm responsible for this deal. I've got to see it through. If there are any hitches with Mr. Emmerich . . ."

"But there won't be," cried Cobby impatiently.

"I'm delighted to hear it," said the little doctor; then he began to improvise rapidly. "But for your information, there's a new man in town. He's got plenty of money and plenty of fix—so I hear. If, by any chance, Mr. Emmerich might not be able to swing it . . . well, we've got some place to go—I think."

"Now look here, Riemenschneider," cried Cobby, exciting himself and trying to shout down his own qualms, "I'm telling you, everything's okay. You've already talked to Mr. Emmerich. You can't back down now."

"But I have no intention of it," said the little doctor blandly. "I'm only exploring possibilities."

Suddenly at a loss for words, Cobby began to jig about unhappily, and his nervousness grew as the little doctor sat smoking in silence, apparently at ease, and even looking somewhat sleepy, as if his intention was to sit and doze in this chair the rest of the evening. Cobby wanted to be rid of him.

He turned with a slight leer and said: "Did you see Costa tonight?"

Riemenschneider started slightly; then he pulled out his watch and looked at it.

"No," he said. "But he told me to call him. Is there another phone where I can . . ."

Cobby smiled to himself. Why the delicacy? The little doctor was a regular mink—a different girl every night since he'd been staying with Cobby. Of course, the guy had done quite a stretch in the Walls, but on the other hand, he was probably fifty years old or better—hard to tell with him, like Dix. Cobby shook his head and observed to himself: "I'm glad liquor's my weakness."

"The back cardroom, Doc," said Cobby. "It's empty right now."

Riemenschneider smiled quietly to himself and left. Cobby waited till he heard the door shut; then he ducked out to a drugstore, where he could call Emmerich without worrying about the little doctor's scratching on the door, then popping in.

Emmerich was pacing nervously up and down the book-lined study of his town house when the phone rang. He grabbed it up at once, eagerly, waited for a moment to see if anybody was going to lift a receiver at one of the extensions; then reassured, he answered it.

"Hate to bother you, Mr. Emmerich," came Cobby's voice. "But . . ."

At first Emmerich showed marked impatience as he listened. He'd been expecting another call, and to find that fool Cobby on the other end of the line was an unpleasant shock. But as Cobby talked on, Emmerich turned pale; then he began to shake with nervousness. He couldn't boot this one—he just couldn't. It would be the end of everything. For the last week he'd been living on nothing but hope.

"But I tell you," he cried, "everything's all right. A job like this can't be managed in a minute. Now, Cobb. I'm counting on you. Keep him in line. It will mean a lot of money to you. I'm going to see that you get a share of this."

Emmerich talked on and on. He was in a state now where he'd promise anybody anything. Why not? He hadn't the faintest intention of keeping any of his promises.

Cobby, stammering, upset, apologized at length, told Emmerich he was just trying to let him know how things were, promised emphatically that he'd keep the German in line, and was still talking when Emmerich hung up.

Evans, the butler, had just tapped at the open door.

"Yes?" cried Emmerich, turning.

Evans hesitated before he spoke, covertly studying his employer, who, with his usually well-combed gray hair on end, looked excessively irritable and ill-tempered. What was happening? Mr. Emmerich had always been so kind and considerate. There wasn't a servant who wouldn't rather work for him than for anyone else in town. But, lately . . . well, Mr. Emmerich was getting quite impossible.

"Dr. Huston will be here in a few minutes to see Mrs. Emmerich."

"Thanks," snapped Emmerich, turning away.

"Pardon me, sir," said Evans, "Mr. Brannom is here. As you were talking on the phone, I put him in the lounge."

The color returned to Emmerich's face. He smiled, and suddenly he was transformed before the puzzled eyes of his butler, who stared, bewildered. Here was the old Mr. Emmerich again. Genial, warm.

"Fine, fine, Evans. Show him in, will you, please?"

"Yes, sir," said Evans; then he turned and went out, telling himself that he'd better have a long talk tonight with Mrs. Emmerich's new maid, Emma. Maybe she'd have some explanation of the unpleasant atmosphere pervading a once-happy household.

Emmerich was mixing a couple of highballs at the little study bar when Evans showed Brannom in, then withdrew.

"For you—it's Scotch. Right?" asked Emmerich jovially, back in his role of happy householder and host.

Brannom nodded moodily and sat down. He was a big young man in his early thirties; broad-shouldered and bulky about the chest, but with long, slim legs. His dark face was both swarthy and tanned, and his hazel eyes had a sad, tough look. He'd run the gamut of jobs through professional football, Provost Marshal's Corps in World War II, City Detective Force, D.A.'s office . . . to private dick—a sordid, melancholy calling unless you were in the top flight, which he was not and never would be.

His reputation was far from good. He was considered not only very tough and dangerous but crooked. Emmerich had saved him from the clink by a great job of defense when his boss, the D.A., had insisted on prosecuting him for putting the bite on the bingo parlors in the river slums south. What few clients he had were obscure citizens who'd read his modest ad in the morning papers: husbands who wanted their wives followed, small operators of one kind or another with bad debts to collect, even a scattering of hardy characters who wanted some enemy beaten up. From time to time Brannom had some exceedingly strange propositions put to him, but none of them promising very much in the way of cash.

Emmerich, none too astute at times in judging character, was not particularly impressed by Brannom one way or another. He couldn't help thinking of him as a young cub, remembering him as an awkward rookie on the Police Force, groping through the political mazes of Headquarters, willing to do what was necessary to get along and be promoted, but very inept in his tactics.

"Good Scotch!" said Brannom, sipping his highball. "Make it yourself?"

"The butler's got a still in the pantry," said Emmerich. "His name's really McTavish."

Neither laughed nor even smiled. They were talking automatically, both lost in their private thoughts.

Emmerich was nervous. If the news was good, why didn't Brannom say something? On the other hand, Brannom was depressed and had a hard lump in his solar plexus. Emmerich's call of a few nights back had given him new hope and new energy. He'd even been counting his commission— which, Lord knows, he needed badly enough.

"Well," said Emmerich, cheerfully, "how about my debtors? Any of them dead yet?"

"Yeah, but they don't know it," said Brannom; then he set his glass down and stared at it for a long time as if hypnotized by its expensive glitter.

Emmerich shifted uneasily, trying to hide his nervousness.

"Are any of them coming through?"

There was a long pause; then finally Brannom forced himself to speak.

"Not a single one of them—yet."

Emmerich jumped up, spilling his drink, and cried: "My God! Why?"

Brannom glanced up at him in surprise. What went here? Emmerich couldn't need the dough this bad!

"Want all the excuses? I've got a bunch of beauts."

Emmerich sat down heavily.

"That bad, eh?"

"Look, my friend," said Brannom, "I can't go around threatening people like these—especially in your name. You're going to have to sue ninety-eight per cent of them. George Laughlin may come through with a couple grand this week— and on the other hand he may not."

Emmerich sat in his chair staring at the floor. He looked old, pale, deflated. A heavy silence invaded the room and a nervous-sounding little French clock on Emmerich's eighteenth-century desk got louder and louder.

"I mean it," said Brannom, studying Emmerich, puzzled, wondering. "You'll have to sue."

"Takes too long," said Emmerich abruptly. "I need money now—this minute."

Brannom laughed coarsely. His laugh was always a shock to people, especially women. Some lucky ones had been warned by it—in time.

"Take it easy," he said. "You know the old man with the whiskers isn't standing at the door with a shotgun. Tax guys can be stalled. Show 'em your list of debtors, tell 'em how things stand there. I'll go to bat for you."

"Oh, shut up!" cried Emmerich, suddenly enraged.

Brannom paled slightly and sat forward in his chair. Resentment was gnawing at him. Maybe he wasn't so big, but nobody talked to him like that—nobody! Not even the Honorable Alonzo D. Emmerich.

"How's that again?" he asked, quietly but harshly.

Emmerich glanced up, saw the mean look in the big ex-dick's narrowed eyes, realized he'd gone too far, and suddenly broke down.

"That's all a gag, Bob," he cried, his voice jumping an octave, sounding hysterical. "All . . . a . . . goddamned, silly, sad, trumped-up gag!"

He put his head in his hands and sat there huddled over, shaken by dry sobs.

Brannom's resentment left him at once. The big boy was in a bad way—no doubt about it. Maybe the red-haired tommy he'd heard about . . . maybe she'd put him over the jumps. Brannom's lip curled slightly with contempt. No man worth his salt ever let a femme put him over the jumps; it was always the other way around.

He picked up Emmerich's drink and shoved it at him roughly.

"Here!" he snapped.

Emmerich looked up, saw the poorly veiled contempt in Brannom's eyes; then he took the glass, finished the drink in one swallow, and got up to pour himself a straight one. His hands were shaking, but all at once his blank despair left him and his mind began to work with nervous rapidity. He had it! Take Brannom in with him—give him a cut. It was silly trying to pull off this hundred-to-one shot alone. Brannom was full of larceny and knew all the angles. He'd jump at the chance. And maybe in an emergency like this, Brannom could figure out a way to raise fifty grand in a few days.

He tossed off the drink, then sat down again. His composed face, his calmness, surprised Brannom, who studied him with open curiosity.

"Bob," said Emmerich, "you are going to get the shock of your life; so go pour yourself a double straight one."

Brannom stared at Emmerich, surprised by the steadiness of his voice; then he obeyed.

Half an hour later Brannom looked like a man who had been hit with a sledge hammer and then propped up so he wouldn't fall.

"Well," Emmerich concluded, "that's the story. You in?"

"I've got to be," said Brannom, beginning to recover a little. "Yeah. I've got no choice when you're playing for those kind of marbles. I've been trying to figure a way to get my hands on some real money all my life. But . . . we may get ourselves killed, my friend."

"I know," said Emmerich quietly.

There was a brief pause; then Brannom said: "How wrong can a guy be! Here I am worrying about your nerve, and you're dreaming up a double cross like this!"

There was another silence. Brannom sat staring at the floor, his brow wrinkled, his eyes lowered. Who could have figured it in a hundred years? Emmerich—of all people. A smooth and unscrupulous operator. But not this!

"Well," said Emmerich, sharply, "what do we do?"

Brannom prodded himself to attention, then spoke with decision.

"We take in Cobby. He can dig up fifty grand without half trying."

Emmerich struck his forehead and groaned. Why hadn't he thought of that? It would have saved him all this anguish. What a fool! Now he had Brannom on his hands. In a moment of desperation he'd made a bad move and an irrevocable one. Brannom was in to the bitter end now, smelling money—big money.

Emmerich nodded, lit one of his Cuban cigars, then sat calmly considering why it had never occurred to him to take Cobby in. Sheer mental blindness? No, he knew it wasn't that. It was because he always thought of Cobby as an underling, a yes man, a dependent, a runner of errands, one who cleaned up after you. Cobby was a prosperous bookie—yes. But it was hard to think of him as a prosperous anything. He was just one of the million—and a little fool to boot. Even if the thought had occurred to him, he might have brushed it aside because of the humiliation involved. Now it didn't matter.

"When you say take Cobby in, Bob, I suppose you mean we borrow the fifty grand from him?"

"What else? If you sprung the double cross on him, his ears would whirl."

"What do we offer him for the use of the money?"

Brannom looked at Emmerich, then laughed.

"Does it matter?"

"I see what you mean. He'll get nothing in any case. But we've got to make the proposition attractive. Suppose we offer him ten thousand dollars and his money back."

"Let's make it twenty," said Brannom. "We can afford to be generous."

"All right," said Emmerich. "It sounds like a good proposition. Twenty thousand for the use of his money for say . . . a week." Emmerich laughed, though shame was faintly nagging at him. "Now about why we need it."

"You leave that to me," said Brannom. "I'll make him dizzy with figures—income-tax demands, outstanding obligations, inability to collect what's owed. The main thing is to persuade him we've really got a big fence to handle the jewelry."

Emmerich nodded slowly and puffed on his cigar. In a moment, Brannom raised his glass and said with a laugh: "Well, here's to crime."

Emmerich winced slightly but made no comment.

·14·

Nervous and confused, Cobby's emotions were decidedly mixed as he waited for Riemenschneider and Schemer to arrive. He felt both impatience and dread, and couldn't make up his mind whether he'd been a chump or a sharpie.

In spite of his uncertainty, he still felt a faint remainder
of the glow that had suffused him at Mr. Emmerich's town
house. Why, they'd treated him like a very important fellow—which, of course, he was, though some people didn't
seem to be aware of it. Mr. Emmerich had broken out a
bottle of extra dry Heidsieck (Cobby had never heard of it
before, but that was a minor detail); and this fellow Brannom, a big, tough-looking boy with a bad eye on him, like
Dix, had gone out of his way to be friendly and polite. In
fact, they'd both listened in flatteringly interested silence
while he told them all about the racing-information racket
and its many ramifications. God! He must have talked for
an hour solid, and not one peep out of them. And finally,
when he'd finished, Brannom had said: "Mr. Cobb, I've
always wondered what the angles on that little business are,
and I'm very glad I was able to hear an expert explain it."
Things like that all evening—mighty gratifying.

And yet . . . ?

Why hadn't a guy like Mr. Emmerich, in spite of all his
commitments, his owed back taxes, and so forth, been able
to raise fifty G's fast? It was weird. Why, he had two big
houses full of gorgeous furniture, four cars, maybe half a
dozen servants, and God knows what all! And wasn't twenty
G's for the use of the money foolishly generous? Emmerich
stood to net between a hundred and a hundred and fifty G's
out of the deal, providing it went absolutely as planned. But
what deal, big or small, ever went absolutely as planned?
As a rule you could cut the contemplated profit in half and
still be toward the optimistic side.

And yet? It was sort of pleasing to be taken into the
confidence of a guy like Mr. Emmerich. He was a real big
boy—class.

"Oh, well," said Cobby, aloud. "As long as I make my
profit, what do I care?"

But another thought struck him, and he turned to look
out the window of his little apartment, which was near the
top of the Slope and commanded a fine view of the immense
Midwestern city, which lay sprawled out below him. Why

keep his participation a secret? Why was it necessary for the crew to think that Emmerich was furnishing the front money? Was this to keep the little doctor from worrying about the fate of Joe Cool? Brannom said merely that it was none of their business who was furnishing the moo, and maybe that was the right angle after all.

The thoughts were coming thick and fast now, jolting him badly, and suddenly he remembered what the call girl had told the little doctor. But . . . Mr. Emmerich . . . ruining himself over a girl—a guy with his assets . . . ? How much could a girl *cost?* Just another malicious whore, popping off to make herself interesting!

Cobby sighed and leaned against the wall beside the window. Maybe he was just a worrier. Maybe he needed a tonic or something. After all, the main point was settled. Both Mr. Emmerich and Brannom had assured him that they had just the right person to handle the jewelry: a big businessman, whose reputation was beyond reproach, and who would pay them immediately on delivery, and who had promised them a much better deal than the fifty per cent contemplated.

"What am I thinking of?" cried Cobby. "Mr. Emmerich's a big man with standing in the town. He couldn't gyp anybody if he wanted to. It would ruin him!"

Cobby sighed again and stood looking down at the city. Far off to the south he could see the bridges with their strings of lights arching off over the black river. A three-quarter moon, the color of a muskmelon, was riding high over the massive, tall buildings of the downtown district, which were stepped like Aztec temples, their ledges faintly colored by the pale moonlight. Several long cloud arms, gray and gauzy, hung motionless above the city in the windless night. Forests of street lights stretched off in all directions, and far to the northeast Cobby could see the furnace-door glow of the steel plant where a night shift was working.

"It gives you the jimmies sometimes looking at it like this," said Cobby, referring to the spread-out city. "You can really see how big it is, and you get to thinking about all the thousands of poor bastards conniving, fighting, bit-

ing, and scratching to make a living." Cobby turned away,
smiling to himself. "And me with a sockful worrying because I'm getting set to clear twenty G's in a few days."

He felt so heartened by this thought that his pulses did
not jump apprehensively when the buzzer sounded, as they
would have ordinarily.

Riemenschneider was the first to arrive. He looked at
Cobby questioningly; then, when the bookie nodded emphatically in answer to his silent inquiry, he smiled but said
nothing, took out a cigar, sat down, and made himself
comfortable.

Cobby sat opposite him.

"I thought it'd be better to meet here—smarter not to
congregate around the joint too much."

"Naturally. Of course," said the German, lighting his
cigar and sighing contentedly. The deal was apparently
working out, and Costa had found him a new girl: a young
waitress just breaking into the professional ranks—very refreshing. "And the fence?"

Cobby explained at some length. Gradually the little doctor's contentment began to leave him, and he felt a dis-
agreeable tautness in his stomach. What was wrong? He
hadn't the faintest notion, and yet some instinct, some animal sixth sense, was trying to warn him. Everything sounded
fine. Maybe . . . too fine?

"This businessman—you don't know him?" he inquired
quietly.

"Of course not," cried Cobby impatiently. "But he's
offering a swell deal—and the dough on the line."

Riemenschneider tried to calm himself. Maybe he was
just nervous as a man was bound to be at the beginning of
a big and potentially dangerous undertaking. Why suspect
a man like Emmerich? He was A 1 with all the boys in the
Walls, and they were not easy to fool.

"Immediate payment, you say? On delivery?"

"Yeah," said Cobby, grinning, a little proud of himself
now. "Great, eh?"

Riemenschneider nodded.

"Immediate money is always best. That way you can pay off and scatter in case of a beef."

Louis Bellini arrived a few minutes later, bringing with him an atmosphere of gloom; his little son had a cold, and Louis was sweating with nervousness and worry.

"If you hadn't made it so strong, Cobby," he said, "I'd have asked for a postponement." He explained about his son at considerable length, and Cobby listened in bored but polite silence. Schemer was a top-notch hand. If you got him to come in, seventy-five per cent of your operating worries were over. He rated a little indulgence.

Riemenschneider listened politely also, beginning once more to feel at ease. It hadn't taken him two minutes to make up his mind about the slim, handsome, young Italian. He was all right—it was obvious.

At last Louis stopped talking and looked about him with some embarrassment.

"I guess I'm boring you guys. Sorry. What's the pitch?"

Louis kept his eyes lowered and showed no emotion as he listened to Cobby, but a great excitement was rising within him. This was a big one—a real big one: the kind you dreamed about!

"Well?" Cobby demanded, grinning, as he concluded.

"Sounds okay," said Louis, still showing no excitement. "Can be done, I guess—with the right management."

There was a brief silence; then Riemenschneider glanced up at Cobby as if for permission to speak, and said: "You understand, Bellini, that it is costing us a lot of money to finance it, and the money has to be split several ways. We offer you a flat guarantee—half down, half when the job's done. Of course, you have to gamble to a certain extent, but . . ."

"Flat guarantee's okay with me," said Louis. "I got bit twice on percentage. I'll take thirty thousand, half down."

He expected the ceiling to fall, but nothing much happened. The little doctor merely shifted his cigar from one corner of his mouth to another, and Cobby jigged about a bit, as was his way, but didn't seem particularly disturbed. Louis realized he was warm on price.

After a short discussion they finally compromised on twenty-five thousand dollars, fifteen thousand down.

They shook hands all around, and the little doctor smiled benignly and waved a hand at Cobby.

"There's your paymaster," he said.

Cobby swallowed hard and began to sweat as he counted out the fifteen thousand to Louis. But actually he was feeling pretty good about the whole thing. It was comforting and reassuring to have a guy like Bellini come in with so little fuss. Obviously everything looked okay to him, and he was far from a fool.

"I got to be getting home," said Louis, quickly pocketing the money. Then he added rather proudly: "Maria, my wife, is worried as hell over that punk kid we got."

"One more thing," said the little doctor, "then you can run along to your family—and I must say I envy you." Riemenschneider, of course, was just being polite. He'd been married twice, and besides, as a young man, had lived for varying periods with many women; he had at least half a dozen children scattered over four countries. They meant no more to him than kittens mean to a tomcat. All the same, Louis's obvious simplicity of mind pleased and reassured him. "The hooligan!" the little doctor went on. "That's a problem."

"Yeah," said Louis. "Always a problem. I'd suggest Gus Minisi, except he's the best driver in town—if you need a driver."

"We do indeed," said the little doctor. Then he turned to Cobby. "What about this Gus?"

"Hundred per cent," affirmed Cobby quickly, not only because he wanted to please Louis, but because he was well aware of Gus's standing in Camden Square.

"Now about the hooligan," the little doctor persisted. "If we settle on your Gus to drive—and that's very important—have you any suggestions?"

There was a pause; then Cobby said: "I know a very tough hood, but I haven't seen him for some time. Red Traynor."

"Drug addict," said Louis, shaking his head emphatically. "Last time I heard, he was taking the cure. The load he'd gradually got up to was getting too expensive. He was just working for his vice."

Riemenschneider laughed shortly and shrugged.

"A lot of us do that," he said in a melancholy voice; then: "We rule him out."

"What about Timmons?" asked Cobby hesitatingly, avoiding Louis's sharp eye. He could get Timmons for peanuts, and he was not only very tough but faithful as a mongrel dog—though not quite so bright.

"You must be kidding!" said Louis in disgust.

"Timmons?" queried the little doctor blankly; then his eyes showed a flash of remembrance. "Oh, no! Impossible! A mechanical man would be better." He thought for a moment, looked from Louis to Cobby, hesitated, then said: "You understand, I'm a stranger here and do not know as much as you gentlemen, but what about this Southerner? This Dix?"

There was a shocked silence, and Louis and Cobby glanced quickly at each other. The little doctor studied the two men carefully before he went on.

"I have only seen him twice—talked to him once. But I must say he impressed me as a very determined man—and far from stupid, unlike your Timmons, whose head is almost as thick as his lips."

Still neither Cobby nor Louis spoke. Although they were both a little befuddled, the suggestion was sinking in as not quite so preposterous as it had sounded at first. Besides, they were both personally involved with Dix. He owed Louis money—thirteen hundred hard-earned dollars, to be exact. And Cobby was anxious to do him a favor to keep in his good graces.

"Well," said Cobby, glancing covertly at Louis, "he's not big-time, far from it—but I hear he used to be."

"We all get down on our luck," said Riemenschneider.

"At least he's not on the junk," said Louis. "Frankly, I don't like the guy. But I never saw a hooligan I *did* like. They're like left-handed pitchers—all with a screw loose. Tell you one thing—Gus Minisi thinks he's tops. Gus'll go all the way for him."

"Well," said Cobby, "it's pretty hard to argue with Gus. If he don't know, who does?"

"They make a good team," said Louis, a little worried as the contemplated choice of Dix began to change from a dubious thing to a near certainty; but he was determined to insure the return of the thirteen hundred. It belonged to Maria and the kid.

"Well, then . . . ?" said the little doctor, obviously trying to bring the discussion to a close.

But Cobby had a sudden qualm that he couldn't shrug off.

"Look, Doc. We ought to get top-notch men. Like Louis here and Gus. Dix is on the way out—a small-time stick-up guy."

"I'm open to suggestions," said Riemenschneider blandly.

Louis, who had been standing for some time, sat down again. The little doctor lit a fresh cigar and waited. Louis and Cobby sat staring uneasily at the floor, at least pretending to try to think of somebody that was big-time and who could be trusted.

In the silence that followed, the hum of the great city began to be audible: faint, shrill newsboy cries rose from the street far below, taxis hooted on Camden Boulevard West, and they heard the clock in the old Engine House at Five Corners strike two.

· 15 ·

As Dix stood looking out the window, he was thinking: "I'm slipping, that's all. Not the man I used to be," and yet he didn't feel to any marked degree the self-contempt he was trying to force on himself. In the old days, brushing off a boring, importunate dame was routine—hardly worth a second thought. And yet here he was, wanting to be rid of Doll but inwardly making very heavy going of it, though she'd moved in with him uninvited and her very presence was an exceedingly disturbing and alien element, shattering the easy, frictionless life-plan he'd worked out for himself laboriously after years of failure. Time he was rid of her; time he spoke out and got it over with. But . . . he had a real reluctance to say anything, and this puzzled and worried him.

"Dix," called Doll. "Honey . . ."

Dix turned from the bedroom window and went out into the living-room. Doll was sitting at a little table with a steaming coffee pot and two cups in front of her. She was wearing a small, conservative hat and a dark suit. She looked very respectable—even a little dull and ordinary. Dix noticed that there was a small battered traveling-bag on the floor beside her. He made no comment about it, though he felt a slight, puzzling stab of apprehension.

"Here's your coffee. I think I'll have some, too."

Dix sat down and began to sip the coffee offered him. Doll picked up her cup, and they drank for a long time in silence. Finally Doll said: "I found a place."

"Did you?" said Dix, a little startled but showing a blank face.

"Yeah," said Doll. "And I think I got my old job back. Quigley's going to reopen in a couple of nights. He said he thought he could put me back on."

"When did all this happen?"

"Today. While you were gone. You see, I can't live off you forever." Doll lowered her eyes and gave a little shrug; then she raised her coffee cup and drank, but avoided Dix's steady gaze.

She'd beat him to the punch! Dix smiled to himself. Maybe the poor trollop was as fed up with him as he was with her. This was rich! As he raised his coffee cup he studied her from under his eyelids. Come to think of it, maybe it was going to be a little lonesome without her . . . yeah, a little lonesome! But suddenly Dix, disgusted with himself for such softness, set down his coffee cup with a crash. Doll rose half off her chair, and he saw at once that she was emotionally unstrung, extremely nervous, and maybe on the verge of breaking down. He looked away uneasily.

"I was glad to have you," he said in an unnaturally polite voice. "Glad to help out. You don't owe me a thing. Forget it."

Doll regained her composure, finished her coffee, and got up.

"There's my address," she said, indicating a card on the table, "and my telephone number—just in case."

"Okay," said Dix, rising slowly.

He felt considerably disturbed. But . . . wasn't this what he had wanted? And it was all so easy, too—no tears, no fuss, nothing. With Doll out of the way, he could go about his business as usual, a free man.

Feeling excessively awkward, he picked up Doll's traveling-bag and walked with her toward the door. The bag was light as a feather, and it contained all she had in the world.

"Got any moo?" he asked, clearing his throat uneasily.

"Few bucks. Enough," said Doll, keeping her eyes lowered.

Dix fumbled in his vest pocket and came up with a dirty, creased twenty-dollar bill.

"Here," he said, then added almost involuntarily: "And if things don't work out . . ."

Doll pushed the bill away.

"No, Dix," she said. "I'm through bothering you." Then she took the bag quickly from his hand and started to open the door.

But Dix stopped her.

"What you sore about? We're friends, aren't we?"

Doll laughed shortly and studied Dix's dark face, noticing the perplexity in his eyes but misinterpreting it.

"Yeah," she said. "I guess that's what you might call it—friends. I'll get along all right without the twenty, Dix. You may need it."

The phone rang insistently. Dix looked from the phone to Doll, then back again.

"Wait a minute," he said; then he hurried to answer the phone. It had to be either Cobby or Gus, and it was probably Gus, who'd told Dix that afternoon that something was up—something big—and he might call.

Doll put her bag down, took out a cigarette, and began to scrabble nervously through her purse looking for a match.

"Hello," said Dix into the phone, but his eyes were on Doll.

"Dix? Gus. You're in trouble. The Happiness Boys are on their way up to see you, and they got a customer with them. A guy who got stuck up outside one of the clubs—they think maybe he can identify you. I got the tip straight from the horse's mouth. So blow, and blow fast. Come to my place—the alleyway. I got something to talk to you about. For Christ's sake, don't get took! It might cost you ten, twenty thousand dollars."

Dix almost dropped the phone.

"Okay," he said. "Thanks."

Then he hurried over to Doll, who had a scared look on her face. Something about Dix's attitude had warned her.

"Blow fast, honey," he said. "Down through the basement—you know—and out the basement door. Wouldn't do you no good to be picked up here."

"But, Dix," cried Doll, "are you okay?"

"Sure, I'm okay," said Dix harshly. "I got my own way out. Go on. Blow!"

He pushed her out, shut the door after her, and locked it; then he stood for a moment listening to her high heels clattering down the back hall. That big broad just couldn't walk quiet!

Reassured, he hurried into the bedroom, pulled out the dresser drawer, recovered his heavy-caliber, snub-nosed gun, thrust it into his pocket; then he rushed over, opened one

of the windows, and glanced down cautiously. Below his
windows ran an almost rooflike ledge with very little slope
to it. His apartment was on a hill, and the pavement mounted
steeply from front to back. Toward the front of the house
there was a three-story drop from the ledge; but in back the
ledge was only six or seven feet from the sidewalk.

Dix was just stepping out onto the ledge when he remembered something, and, turning, he hurried back to re-
trieve the card Doll had left for him. As he put it in his
pocket, he heard heavy, thick-soled, cops' footsteps in the
outside hallway and smiled contemptuously; then he pulled
off his shoes, moved swiftly to the bedroom window, and
stepped out onto the ledge. Far beyond the hill the huge
city lay spread out below him, all its lights winking in the
still air. A tug moaned on the river, a solo voice against
the vague, rumbling background of night sounds. The steel
plant glowed at the edge of the city horizon like a great
conflagration. Dix felt a sudden dizziness and looked away.

Inside, his buzzer was sounding and echoing through the
now deserted rooms.

Dix, looking resolutely away from the great abyss of the
city, moved quickly down the ledge, paused at the far end
for a moment, then dropped quietly to the street. There
wasn't a soul in sight. Dix took plenty of time putting on
his shoes.

· 16 ·

Gus let Dix into the dim-lit bunkroom without a word, then
motioned for him to wait. Dix felt calm and at ease, and
watched with incurious silence as Gus opened a false door
in the side of the bunkroom and motioned him to follow.

The place beyond was dark as a pit. Dix stumbled, and
paused. In a moment Gus switched on a weak, unshaded,
yellow bulb, and the darkness drew back away from them,

and Dix saw that he was in some kind of storeroom full of cobwebs and dust.

Gus offered him a cigarette, and they lit up.

"First," said Gus, "my info bureau's running true to form." He grinned a little proudly and patted Dix lightly on the back.

"So far, anyway," said Dix, smiling wryly. "They were banging on the door when I left."

"Good. They'll stake out the joint now, waiting for you to come back. Meanwhile, we'll fix the beef. It's a cinch. If we'd been wised up sooner, there wouldn't have been any beef. This complainant runs a big restaurant over in Polishtown. He can be got to. When the cops don't find you, they'll tell him to go home and wait till they pick you up. Cully, the bail-bond guy, knows him. He'll call him at the restaurant tonight—it stays open till two, three o'clock, or until all the Polacks go home. So much for that."

Gus grinned again and puffed on his cigarette. It made him feel great to look after this big rough character of a Dix; and it also showed how smart he was.

"Nice going, Gus," said Dix, gruffly.

"You ain't heard nothing. Louis came by—braced me. Biggest thing in a lifetime coming up—and we're in."

"How big?"

"Half a million—plenty for all."

Dix stiffened slightly. Half a million? He'd never been within yelling distance of a take like that. In his best days a fifty-grand haul had been a huge one, even for a mob of four. His hands began to get cold.

"Somebody must be kidding you," said Dix, crossing his fingers superstitiously and spitting over his left shoulder as he and his brothers used to do on the farm as boys.

"No. It's straight. And the manager himself asked for you—personal. Got sense, that guy."

"The manager?"

"Riemenschneider."

"Him? Yeah, I chewed the fat with the guy the other day at Cobby's."

"Well, you sold him a bill of goods, one way or another. You're the heavy. Me on the crate. Louis on the tool. And the Dutchman going along for the ride—supercargo."

Dix nervously smoked one cigarette after another as Gus talked on; little by little his mind began to wander, and he grew violently irritated with himself because he couldn't focus his attention on what was being said. A picture, and a very unpleasant one, kept recurring: himself shoving Doll out into the dark hallway and slamming the door in her startled face. There'd been a sort of pleading look in her eyes. Where was the poor trollop now, with her battered traveling-bag and her scuffed and run-over street shoes? Tramping what half-lit street, what dark stairway?

"What the Jesus is wrong with me?" Dix asked himself, and Gus saw a spasm of worry cross the big Southerner's face.

"Wait a minute now, Dix," said Gus. "This is a good setup—though I can see you don't think so."

"Who don't think so?" cried Dix.

"Okay, okay," said Gus, puzzled. "But there's more to come. You not only ask for plenty dough—you ask for percentage. Here's the angle. Emmerich's handling it."

Dix came out of his coma at this.

"Emmerich—the big fix?"

"The same. So it's good money—ought to be; and Louis says it's pay on delivery."

A sudden hope began to tug at Dix, the first real hope he'd known for years. If this one went right, maybe he could go back and take a look at the old place—God knows he'd been thinking about it all these years! Yeah, that was it. Once he got his hands on some real dough, he'd go back. He'd always intended to! Let's see . . . how long had it been since he'd gone down the lane for the last time? Nearly twenty-five years—a whole generation; and yet it was all as fresh in his mind as if he'd seen it yesterday.

"Maybe they won't hold still for the percentage," said Dix.

"The manager's for you," said Gus. "They'll hold still."

And Gus was right, in spite of the fact that Louis and Cobby were both feeling somewhat guilty about agreeing to Dix's participation under any circumstances. But they were reassured by the little doctor's evident satisfaction with Dix. After all, Riemenschneider was nobody's fool. And besides, Dix was far from exorbitant in his demands—very reasonable, in fact. Five thousand down, five thousand on completion of job; and three per cent of the net.

If there was trouble and a strong arm was necessary, and if Dix was as competent as he seemed, they were buying his services cheap.

Gus was delighted and showed it plainly now that the deal had been concluded.

The meeting was being held in the filthy little storeroom behind Gus's all-night hamburger joint. Gus had provided boxes for them to sit on, and Cobby, Louis, and Riemenschneider seemed far from at ease and kept shifting about, brushing off their trousers, and looking up with some trepidation at the huge spiders sitting motionless in their webs waiting for their dinners.

Once, while they were in the midst of a rather tangled discussion, a bat flew in under the eaves and blundered crazily around the unshaded yellow bulb till Gus chased it away with a scantling. Cobby and Louis both jumped up nervously and drew back in horror from the bat. The little doctor kept his seat but clapped his hat on and sat huddled in apprehension till the bat was gone.

Dix hardly stirred and sat with his elbows on his knees and his hat dangling, watching with mild amusement Gus's frantic pursuit of the little winged monster.

In the midst of a shocked silence he said: "Bats are sure funny little buggers. Used to catch 'em when I was a boy. Lots of 'em around where I lived. They'd fly out on summer nights and chase the bugs in among the trees. The women used to scream and carry on and grab at their hair—afraid

the bats would nest there. It was sure funny.'' Dix laughed—
a short, ugly, snorting sound, then sat staring down at the
dirt floor, lost in thought.

The other men glanced at one another with some embarrassment. Were they like the screaming women? But Dix
didn't pursue the point.

When the meeting was over and all the plans had been
made, Louis left by the back, hurrying home to Marie and
Louis, Jr.; Cobby left by the front, pausing to buy a scratch
sheet on his way out; but Riemenschneider remained behind
and sat turning his hat in his hand and clearing his throat
nervously. Finally he said to Gus: "Do you mind if I talk
to . . . ah . . . Mr. Handley alone for a few minutes?''

Gus stared, not understanding that the little doctor was
referring to Dix; then he grinned and said: "Help yourself,
Doc; Dix ain't going no place—at least for a couple of
days.''

Riemenschneider had heard all about the beef, and smiled
slightly. Gus turned, looked at Dix a little puzzled, then
went out slowly. Riemenschneider was a hundred per cent
for the big Southerner—that was obvious. But why? "Maybe
he's a mind-reader,'' said Gus to himself as he entered the
bunkroom, where he'd set up an army cot for Dix.

"I can talk to you, I think,'' said the little doctor, smiling
ingratiatingly at Dix.

"Sure.''

Riemenschneider shifted about nervously on his box,
glanced up involuntarily at the spiders above him; then he
took out a couple of cigars and handed Dix one. There was
a silence as they lit up, and the night sounds of Camden
Boulevard West seeped through the flimsy walls of the
storeroom.

"My friend,'' said the little doctor, "what do you know
about Emmerich?''

Dix showed mild surprise.

"I know he's the fix. I know he's big. But I only know
what I hear.''

"I don't exactly trust him,'' said the little doctor. "But

we've got to do business with him. No alternative. I've looked high and low for a big-time fence. None operating that I can find—none big enough for us. Of course, I pretended otherwise with Cobby when I was trying to apply the pressure.''

Dix was scratching his head.

"You sure are surprising me, Doc,'' he said, staring.

"I've got no real proof of anything—it's just a feeling and I may be wrong, but . . . it's up to us to collect. You and me. So I just want you to know how I feel. Everything may go smooth—about the collecting, I mean. I'm not worried about the take. But if it doesn't . . .''

"If he's got it, we'll collect,'' said Dix shortly.

"Good!'' said the little doctor. Then he got up, hesitated, puffed on his cigar thoughtfully for a moment and went on: "As soon as we make the take, we will hurry the stuff over to Emmerich and collect. Cobby's going to talk to him late tonight and make an appointment. Then we will pay off and scatter.''

Dix nodded; then as the little doctor continued to study him, he said: "Don't worry, Doc. We'll collect or bust a gut.''

Riemenschneider laughed suddenly; then he laid his hand lightly on Dix's shoulder, turned, and began to look for the place in the wall where the hidden door was. He had a horror of dust, cobwebs, and insects, and pawed about him gingerly and futilely. In a moment Dix came over and found the door for him.

· 18 ·

Dix was having a hard time sleeping, and he lay on his cot in the middle of the bunkroom staring out the high window above him at a small patch of sky, jeweled with a star. It was a cloudless night, the air thin and clear, and a deep-indigo light seemed to tremble over the housetops.

In the hamburger joint beyond the door he could hear the clatter of dishes, laughter, desultory talk. Occasionally Mike Miklos, who was helping Gus tonight, would burst out singing—very flat, and mangling the words of a popular song with his Greek jargon.

Several times Dix heard Gus tell Mike to shut up, but there was no ill-nature in Gus's voice, and Dix knew that he was only kidding, as he liked the big dependable Greek, and if Gus liked you, you could do no wrong.

Gradually the voices and the clatter faded, and Dix dozed, starting up from time to time, coming to himself, and then noticing with a feeling of pleasure that the star framed in the bunkroom window was still there—only each time a little farther down toward the sill as the earth turned and all the heavenly bodies made their nightly journey from east to west.

Sighing and settling himself comfortably, reassured by the company of the star, Dix lay thinking about home country—blue grass, crows in the woods, mares heavy with foal nuzzling you at the fence corners, good fishing in the creeks and good swimming, good company, too, of an autumn evening when there was frost in the air and a wood fire was jumping on the hearth and a hot toddy tasted better than anything else in the world . . .

Dix sat up with a start and looked about him as if he'd never seen this place before—never heard of it even. He had an uneasy feeling that he had been lifted up in the night by unknown hands and carried to this place of exile, this alien city with its canyons of masonry and its unpredictable and ugly ways—far from home, far from sense and meaning, far from any resting place.

"What's the matter with me?" Dix asked himself, uneasily. "I been away twenty-five years." Swearing to reassure himself, he fumbled around till he found his cigarettes; then he lit one and lay back.

The fog began to lift. He lay watching the framed star, which had now reached the edge of the sill and was slowly beginning to disappear. A bright triangular constellation was showing in the upper right-hand corner of the window now—something else to watch. It had been thirty years since Dix had observed the nightly procession in the heavens—thirty years that now seemed to him like thirty minutes.

He was fully awake now, and the phantoms had fled. But their influence remained. Dix had a blinding desire to go home—to see all that lovely land again, maybe to stay. He felt a sudden and violent hatred of the city that throbbed and pulsated for miles in all directions beyond the thin walls of the bunkroom.

"I'll collect all right," he told himself savagely. "And when I get what's due me, I'll hit for home. That's where I belong—always did belong. I'm like a fish out of water in this lousy place."

He felt easier now and lay smoking in peace. But in a moment, an alien image rose before his eyes—Doll! What about Doll?

"You damn fool!" he said to himself. "Forget about her. You're going home. You can't take her there. She's got big-city dirt all over her."

Finally he went to sleep.

· 19 ·

Emmerich sat in his book-lined study trying to compose himself. He smoked one big cigar after another, played solitaire, tried to read a murder mystery, and even turned on the television for a few minutes and sat staring listlessly at a boring, small-time prizefight.

But it was no use. *This was the night*, and Emmerich was becoming more and more certain that he'd never be able to see it through. He was no criminal. Or was he? What was a criminal after all? A man desperate for money and not too nice about his methods of getting it? Or was he a man with a screw loose, a wack? Or was he merely an unfortunate individual who was unable to play the game according to the rules and tried to improvise as he went along, outraging the conventional players?

Emmerich rose and poured himself a drink. This was silly. He should be ashamed of himself letting such trivial and useless thoughts run through his mind when he should have been concentrating on the business in hand. "Emmerich," he warned himself, "there's a million dollars at stake. Stiffen your spine."

The drink warmed him for a moment, but then all his worries and fears rushed back over him. A few days ago it had all seemed so simple. He was merely taking the biggest gamble of his life—that was all. He stood to win or lose big. Either way his troubles would be over. But he found his flesh to be very weak—in short, he was terribly afraid; and even the thought of bankruptcy—certain now if he hesitated—was far less distressing to him than the blank unknown he felt to be just beyond his doorstep tonight.

Evans knocked softly at the open door, startling him.

"Mr. Brannom is here, sir."

"Thanks," said Emmerich, avoiding Evans's politely inquiring eyes. "Show him in."

Brannom entered the study slowly, glancing back at Evans, then turning to wink at Emmerich.

"He's a creep, that character," he said.

Emmerich shrugged impatiently. Brannom looked like a movie thug tonight. He was wearing a dark-blue serge suit, a dark-blue flannel shirt, and a white tie. Dressed to kill, no doubt.

"What are you made up for?" he asked sourly.

Brannom showed a quick flicker of resentment, then smiled.

"This is my intimidation costume."

"These boys don't intimidate worth a goddamn," said Emmerich. "Anyway, intimidation's not the idea. You'd better go put on your persuasion costume."

"I'll leave that to you," said Brannom insolently; then he sat down uninvited and poured himself a drink. "All set, eh?"

Emmerich nodded.

"They'll be at your place as close to two as possible—probably on the dot."

Brannom nodded, then lifted his glass and said: "Well, here's to crime."

Emmerich turned away impatiently, then started as Evans again knocked softly.

"Goddamn it, Evans!" he cried. "What is it?"

"Sorry to bother you, sir," said Evans, glancing surreptitiously at Brannom. "But Mrs. Emmerich wants to know if you can come up and see her for a few minutes before you go out."

Emmerich showed marked irritation, thoughtfully chewed his lips, frowned dubiously, but gave a brusque nod, and Evans went out.

"I'll be right back," he said to Brannom; then he took a settling pull from his highball, sighing.

"Okay. But first . . . give me something to worry about while you're gone. Who's the hooligan?"

"Somebody I never heard of. A fellow named Dix."

"Outsider?"

"I don't think so."

"Maybe they're getting him cheap. Hope so. Anyway, I don't care how big he is as long as he's dumb. Is he going to deliver?"

"That's the understanding."

"Check."

Emmerich turned and went out.

Brannom finished his drink, then rose, unbuttoned his coat, and tried to work the shoulder holster he was wearing into a more comfortable and inconspicuous position. It contained a big Navy .45, a heavy, bulky weapon with terrific fire power.

Mrs. Emmerich's bedroom was stacked with all the appurtenances of a chronic invalid: three therapeutic lamps, a special reading-light with a bluish daylight bulb that cast a ghastly glow over the bed, and two night tables loaded with bottles, glasses, eyecups, spoons, and other paraphernalia. The room smelled of staleness and medicine.

Emmerich hated his wife's bedroom and always tried to avoid entering it. Tonight he felt less inclined than usual, keyed up as he was and with his mind elsewhere. And yet, for some reason, the sight of his wife sitting up in bed in her ancient, food-stained bed jacket (she wouldn't give it up), and with her horn-rimmed glasses halfway down her nose as she peered dimly at a magazine, gave him a pang, and he felt a sudden pity for this unhappy woman who seemed to spend all her waking hours worrying about things: her health, the house, the servants, the weather, even the state of the world. Luckily she never paid any attention to money, had no charge account of her own, left all such things in her husband's hands.

Although her illnesses were largely imaginary, as several doctors had assured him, she looked pale, debilitated, far from well.

She lowered the magazine, pushed her glasses to their proper position on her nose, then turned and glanced up at him slowly. Her blue eyes had faded in the last ten years and now looked surprisingly pale, almost white. Her thick blond hair was streaked with gray. For years she had dyed it; now she'd given up—a bad sign. It looked coarse, ill cared for, and very unattractive in the bluish light of the reading-lamp.

"Lon, Evans says you're going out."

"Yes, May," said Emmerich with a sigh.

His wife hesitated, then gave an apologetic laugh and lowered her eyes.

"I wish you wouldn't, Lon."

Here was a surprise! She hadn't said a thing like that to him for over ten years. Emmerich studied her, puzzled.

"Why not, May?"

"Lon . . . I'm not feeling well; and when I don't feel well, I get nervous; and when I get nervous, I hate to stay in this big house all by myself."

"But, May . . . Emma's here. You're not alone."

"Emma!" cried Mrs. Emmerich contemptuously. "A lot

she cares about me. Selfish, like all the rest. Thinks of nothing but herself.''

"But I thought you were so crazy about Emma. You told me only two days ago . . ."

"I've found her out since," Mrs. Emmerich broke in. "You wouldn't believe . . . but that's neither here nor there. It's just that I haven't been feeling at all well today. Sometimes I wonder if I'll ever feel well again. . . ."

Emmerich found himself growing impatient once more. Same old tune. Now Emma's usefulness was at an end— like all the rest: the long procession of female servants that had fled through the house in the last ten years. Emmerich forgot that he'd been pitying his wife a moment before. Now all that he felt was irritation.

"It seems to me," he said coldly, "that you can get along very well without me tonight. I don't know what I could do if I stayed but sit and watch you read a magazine."

"We could play cards. Cassino, like we used to."

She had surprised him again. What was it? Did she have a foreknowledge of disaster, a premonition, an intuitive desire to keep him at home? He shrugged off such nonsense.

"Some other night," he said, and as the words passed his lips he suddenly realized that this was the *last* night; there would never be another—not one; he was taking his final look at this dreary bedroom and his sadly changed wife.

Was he a monster? Not in any realistic sense, certainly. She cared nothing for him—hadn't for a good many years. Besides, when his tangled affairs had finally been put back into order, she'd realize quite a bit from the mortgaged properties, the antique furniture, the furs, and the jewels. Anyway, she wouldn't starve.

"Look, May," he said, "I've got to go out tonight—on business. Very important."

"Couldn't it be tomorrow night?" Mrs. Emmerich persisted.

"Of course not. I've got an appointment I must keep." The conventional words echoed in Emmerich's ears and

began to take on a new and sinister meaning. *An appointment
he must keep!*

"Well, if you must," said Mrs. Emmerich, turning her
face away.

Emmerich started off toward the door, but he noticed that
his wife's shoulders were trembling slightly and he paused.

"What the devil, May!" he cried impatiently.

"Oh, it's nothing," she said, with her face still turned
away. "I couldn't sleep last night and I got to thinking about
the old days and how we used to like to stay home and play
cassino, just the two of us."

Emmerich grimaced and ran his hand impatiently through
his thick, curly gray hair. At the moment he was not in the
mood for nostalgic sentiment.

"May, I don't want to sound heartless, but . . ."

"I know, I know," said his wife quickly, turning to look
at him now, her face composed. "Just forget about it, Lon.
It's nonsense—nothing but nonsense. Go ahead. I'll be all
right. Good-bye."

Emmerich turned and went out quickly, softly shutting
the door after him. But his heart was heavy, and doubts and
fears began to assail him. Was he the man for such an
enterprise? Desperation was a sharp and efficient goad but
a shaky staff. Why not call it off? Work out some reasonable
compromise. He could think of something certainly.

But no . . . the thing was started now and must run its
course. He'd just have to abandon himself to destiny.

But . . . couldn't he stay at home, safe and quiet, and
let Brannom take the delivery? Impossible! First, it would
make the thieves suspicious. Second, could he trust
Brannom?

A voice spoke at his elbow, and he started slightly.

"Good evening, Mr. Emmerich."

It was Emma—a plain, rather sly-looking brunette, about
thirty.

"Oh, hello, Emma. Mrs. Emmerich is a little nervous
tonight. You mustn't mind if she gets slightly . . ." Emmerich smiled and made a vague gesture.

Emma stood eying her handsome, gray-haired boss speculatively. She thought he was wonderful, and was always talking about him to her girl friend, boring her. How could he stand that faded, homely, irritable imaginary invalid in the bedroom upstairs!

"I'm used to it," said Emma, smiling slyly. Her air was conspiratorial, and her manner indicated: "We know all about that damn fool you're married to, don't we, Mr. Emmerich?"

He noticed for the first time the bold black eyes. Or was it that she'd never unveiled them before? A self-willed, stormy, maybe even a dangerous, woman, he thought, assailed by a sudden qualm. May would ultimately be left in her hands. But, no! What was he thinking of? May had already made up her mind to sack Emma; he knew the signs. In this instance perhaps a very good idea, Emmerich decided, as he nodded coldly to Emma and went on toward the study without once looking back.

He found Brannom smoking one of his dollar-and-a-half cigars and lounging at his ease with a bottle of Scotch on the coffee table before him.

He discovered all of a sudden that he hated Brannom violently.

"Is the missus okay?" asked Brannom with a marked effort to be polite, straining himself a little, no doubt, Emmerich thought.

"Yes, thanks," said the lawyer, pouring himself a drink.

· 20 ·

Louis was punctual to the dot. He drove up the alley behind the hamburger joint in his neat little Ford coupe, stopped at the bunkroom door, and sounded the horn once, then waited composedly. On a job Louis was coldly efficient, never suffered from nerves, never had to fortify himself with liquor or drugs like so many fellows he knew. He pushed all thought of danger—or failure, for that matter—out of his mind and concentrated on ways and means.

Inside the bunkroom Dix was having a last-minute conversation with Gus, who was saying: "Louis's sure he'll have the burglar alarm solved and the alley door open in five minutes, but we'll give him seven. A couple minutes can seem like a long time on a job, Dix; so don't get impatient."

Dix grimaced as if to say: "Stop wasting words."

The bunkroom door that led to the lunch counter was partly open, and Dix could see Cobby sitting on a stool, pretending to eat a hamburger. His face looked slightly greenish.

Dix jerked a thumb toward him and inquired: "Horse meat?"

"Cobby? No, grade A. What do you think?"

"Well, it's choking him."

"Cobby's a nervous bastard."

"Tell him to go home and hide. One look at him, and a cop would wonder who he'd killed."

Gus laughed, then patted Dix on the back as the big Southerner went out the door into the alley.

Louis opened the car door for Dix, who got in without a word and lit a cigarette. Louis drove out of the alley, angled up to the peak of Wharf Hill, turned off at Camden West, and made for the Pulaski Street Bridge.

While they were crossing the bridge, Dix said: "They're going to give us seven minutes."

Louis laughed shortly.

"We'll be standing waiting."

Dix made no comment and sat looking off across the wide black river, which moved sluggishly southward between its steep cement embankments toward its faraway union with the Mississippi.

There was no moon, but the sky was cloudless and a handful of bright stars, diamond points of bluish light, glittered coldly over the tall buildings on the far shore. The houses along the embankment were almost all dark, but here and there a window showed light and cast golden zigzag reflections onto the shiny black pavement of the river. A slow, damp wind was blowing, carrying a smell of deep water.

Late as it was, traffic was fairly heavy on the big, three-lane bridge. Suddenly a siren wail rose from the darkness of the far shore, and in a moment a prowl car passed them, going back at high speed toward the hilly slums of the Camden Square district.

Neither Dix nor Louis paid any attention to the prowl car.

A little later they reached the end of the bridge, and Louis drove straight down Blackhawk Street, the main thorough-fare of the downtown section of the city. It was very wide and plaza-like, with traffic islands in the middle, the whole place blazing with light. Taxicabs scurried in every direction, looking for fares. Newsboys cried from almost every corner, selling the early editions of the morning papers. Repairmen were working on the trolley line, their big truck blocking one lane of the street, and talking to each other lightheartedly and laughing as if it were broad day.

Car wolves were driving slowly, pausing at the intersections, looking for girls to pick up, and also keeping a wary eye out for the motor cops, who were making a drive on them, due to a sensational murder and a violent newspaper campaign.

A couple of drunks staggered across the street, supporting each other and yelling insults at the drivers of the passing cars.

At one intersection there was a beef of some kind. A prowl car was angled into the curb, and a big fat cop, supported by a couple of motorcycle policemen, seemed to be frisking a bunch of teen-age boys, who weren't taking it quietly.

"Yeah," cried one of them as Louis drove past, "that's what *you* say! I'm minding my own business and you . . ."

Neither Louis nor Dix paid any attention. The voice faded away behind them.

At another intersection, near the financial district, two

men were having a fight, and a girl was trying to separate
them. As Louis drove past, one of the men impatiently
elbowed the girl out of the way, and, losing her balance,
she sat down heavily on the pavement, then began to scream.
Men came running from across the street.

Dix shook his head slowly from side to side but made no
comment.

The scene of the brawl was soon left behind. Now the
streets grew progressively more empty as they skirted the
edge of the financial district; traffic and street lights were
fewer; boulevards seemed to wind off darkly into no place;
and high above towered the huge skyscrapers—floor upon
floor upon floor of masonry, sheer-windowed cliffs showing
not a single light. The narrow streets, cluttered with car
tracks and flanked by the tall buildings, were angular, artificial canyons, ugly, sinister, and deserted. Sounds of the
night city failed to penetrate this area, and yet it did not
seem asleep, but wakeful in a kind of dark, Gothic torpor.

Louis turned up Commerce Street, a narrow thoroughfare
on the far outer edge of the immense financial district, and
they drove for two blocks between the black façades of
wholesale houses, minor office buildings, and plumbing-
and electrical-supply stores.

"Getting close to home," said Louis, jerking his thumb
toward a building on a corner. "That's where I work in the
daytime."

Dix merely grunted. Louis glanced at him, then offered
him a cigarette and they both lit up.

"Look good to you?" asked Louis, who always felt more
than a little uneasy with Dix—so uneasy in fact that his
aplomb would desert him and he'd find himself trying to
make conversation merely in order to dissipate the gloomy
and intimidating silence that seemed to hang like an invisible
cloud around the big Southerner.

"What?" asked Dix, glancing sideways at Louis, whose
presence had as little effect on him as if the Schemer had
been a dummy or a mechanical man. What did Gus see in

him? A slim, finical little guy, always talking about his kid. Other people had kids, too, didn't they?

"The job," said Louis quickly, feeling like a damn fool with his futile chatter.

"Can't tell from here," said Dix, and there was a certain contempt in his voice, as if he were speaking to a boring small boy who was pestering him with questions about why the moon wasn't green.

Louis, always fair-minded, felt that he merited the contempt, but it irritated him just the same. He continued stubbornly: "I doubt if it's as big as they think."

Dix yawned and put a big, powerful hand up to stifle it.

"Time will tell," he said, looking away from Louis and pretending to be studying the deserted buildings.

Louis ground his teeth in annoyance.

"Cobby kind of worries me," he said.

To his surprise Dix laughed, a grating and rather subhuman sound such as you would expect from a contented gorilla.

"He was looking a little green, all right," said Dix. "But then . . . it's not his racket. You get used to your own racket and it don't worry you."

Louis felt better. Dix had condescended to enter into a conversation with him, making Louis's earlier chatter not seem so futile after all.

Commerce Street came to an abrupt dead end as it drew clear of the financial district and skirted Marquette Square, the city's exclusive shopping-center, which was lined with swank shops of all kinds: furriers, perfumers, couturieres, jewelers. The glow of blazing shop fronts and high-powered street lights showed above the dingy darkness of the buildings on Commerce Street.

Louis turned down a side street, and ahead of them was Marquette Square, an island of light. In the middle of it was a huge equestrian statue of some Civil War general or other, who sat in rigid dignity all day and all night, year in, year out, with sword upraised, urging forward a non-

existent army. The statue, white originally, and built for a
simpler and cleaner age, was now streaked with soot and
mottled with pigeon droppings. Nevertheless, it was one of
the city's proudest monuments, and floodlights exaggerated
its size and its ugliness.

Louis turned into a street close to and parallel with the
Square, and drove slowly across an intersection, indicating
a corner shop on the far side of the Square to Dix.

"There's our baby," he said.

Dix saw a monumentally impressive façade, very smart
and modern and blazing with light; tall, narrow, plate-glass
show windows cast back the reflections of the street lights;
a bronze door, twice the height of a man, gave an air of
impregnability to the place.

"Company hasn't been touched in forty years," said Louis.
"That's what makes Cool's idea so smart."

Dix grunted, but good-naturedly this time.

"Yeah," he said.

"In fact," Louis went on, "the Square hasn't been touched
for anything big for over ten years—not since the Belkner
fur store was looted. I guess the lights scare everybody off."

He laughed rather nervously—although he didn't feel at
all nervous—as he avoided the north end of the Square,
ducked down a circuitous side street and pulled up finally
at a parking-lot about a hundred feet behind Pelletier and
Company.

Although it was late and the lights were out and the
parking-attendant had gone home, a few cars were still on
the lot. Around the corner was a huge, all-night movie
theater.

Louis drove into the lot and backed his car into one of
the front stalls, talking to Dix as he did so.

"That Heinie, he's smart. It's just like he said—perfect.
No cops seeing your car, remembering it, wondering what
it's doing where it is. All set?"

"Yeah," said Dix.

They got out of the car and walked back across the lot
to an alley that led them to the rear of Pelletier and Company.

Louis was wearing an overcoat with big, hidden, inside pockets, where he had his tools. He jingled slightly as he walked, and Dix glanced at him in slight surprise, not getting it at first.

The big jewelry store seemed as deserted as a tomb. Two big bulbs, at about the level of the second story, cast a bright pool of light down onto the semi-circular, terrace-like rear entrance. The light bothered Dix a little, and he kept glancing up—he was used to working in the dark. But the light suited Louis's purpose—no torch to worry about or to be seen by prowling coppers.

He went to work at once, his back to Dix, who stood looking up and down the alley.

"Dix," said Louis, "if I happen to make a mistake and set the alarm off, we just go sit in the car and wait for the others. Okay?"

"Unless we get a rumble."

"Yeah," said Louis. "If we get a rumble and the boys don't see the car in the lot, they won't stop."

A heavy footfall sounded in the Square beyond, and Louis glanced around quickly. But Dix's attitude reassured him, and he went back to work. The big Southerner hadn't moved a muscle or made an unnecessary remark, but he was listening intently.

"I'm set, I think," said Louis. "How about it? Shall I wait, or see what happens first?"

"It's two guys," said Dix. "So it can't be cops—as they don't work in pairs here. Go ahead."

But before Louis could try the door they heard voices, and in a moment two men passed at the far end of the alley, silhouetted against the bright lights of the Square.

"Fuzz," said Dix. "Coppers. How come?"

One of the cops laughed and hit the other one on the back; then they disappeared from view.

"Going off duty, looks like," said Dix. "They must have changed their schedule lately. I don't know what else. Go ahead, Louis."

Louis sucked in his breath and hesitated for a moment.

This was the most ticklish part of the whole operation. If he was right, everything was okay. But if he'd made an error of any kind, the burglar alarm would ring loudly in the silences of Marquette Square.

Dix glanced at him impatiently.

"Something wrong?"

"No," said Louis. "Here we go."

Dix waited, heard a slight creak; then the big, massive back door, which looked strong enough to stave off the assaults of a mob, opened inward slowly a few inches.

"Duck soup!" said Louis, laughing a little.

Then he and Dix drew back into the shadows to wait for the little doctor.

"I told you we'd be waiting," said Louis, proud of his skill and trying to draw some word of praise from the big Southerner.

"You sure did!" said Dix, and although he spoke flatly, indifferently, what he said was intended for commendation, and Louis was aware of the fact and very pleased.

"I guess this little German knows what's what about everything," Louis told himself. The plan was perfect, and Dix was working out, acting like a real big-timer in spite of his low rating around Camden Square.

Headlights flashed into the parking-lot, and then went out.

"This is us, I think," said Louis, "and right on the schnoz."

A few moments later they saw the little doctor walking sedately toward them up the alley. All that he needed was a cane to suggest a gentleman out for a stroll. Louis laughed a little.

"A character!" he said.

They stepped out into the light, and as the little doctor started across the terrace, Louis indicated by an expansive gesture that the door was open and Riemenschneider was to enter.

But the little doctor stopped and said: "Sorry, gentlemen. But a big accident happened just beyond the bridge and we were delayed. Three cars ran into each other at an intersection. Several people hurt, maybe killed.''

"Will it be clear going back?" asked Louis.

"Probably. But just to be sure, why don't you take the Erie Street Bridge?"

Louis nodded. He was driving back alone, as Dix was going with the others to make the delivery, and he wanted to be sure of a clear path. As soon as the job was done, he knew he'd have only one thought in mind: how to get back to Maria and Junior as fast and safe as possible.

Turning, the little doctor opened the door and went inside; Dix followed; Louis paused long enough to lock the door behind him. They found themselves in a rather wide corridor without lights but dimly lit, as the walls of it only went up halfway. Above them was all the wide space of Pelletier and Company's big store, faintly glimmering in the glow from the façade lights and from the show windows. They could see long, shadowy galleries above them, reached by winding, decorative metal stairways. They passed along the corridor, their guarded footsteps echoing over the marble floor, and came out into the main showroom, where heavy plate-glass cases glittered dimly in the half light, and rows of angular chairs sat waiting patiently for tomorrow's customers.

At the far end was a huge, spectacular steel screen, covered with big peacock designs in glazed copper, menacing in its metallic splendor in the half light. Beyond it, filling almost half of the wall space, was the Pelletier and Company safe.

Dix looked at it with awe, noting with a kind of dismay how invulnerable it seemed, with its slick, hard steel front, its powerful-looking bolts, wheels, and gadgets.

The little doctor took a small leather bag from under his overcoat, put it in front of the safe; then he pulled up a chair, sat down, and lit a cigar.

Louis began to take tools from his hidden pockets and put them on the floor in front of him; and then in a moment he rose and began to look for an electric plug, using a tiny torch that cast a faint, pin-point light, with little glow or spread to it.

Dix began to move about, and finally went beyond the screen and stood looking out into the big, main showroom. A heavy silence throbbed along the shadowy galleries overhead and through the faintly glimmering aisles and corridors of the main floor; mirrors, showcases, and tall, angular glass and metal ornaments glittered darkly and seemed to move and sway in the pale, dim light, like objects seen under water.

Dix remembered a woman he used to know, a singer who made a lot of money at one time and was always filling her apartment with stuff that looked like the furnishings of Pelletier and Company, only of course on a much smaller scale. He recalled how uneasy he used to be in her apartment, like a man in a monument store, as he once told her; and he also remembered a violent brannigan they'd had because he'd kidded her cruelly one night about her "rust-proof furniture."

Now the silence was broken by the faint whirring of a small electric drill, and Dix stood listening. Suddenly there was a sharp, shrill scream of metal, and he heard Louis swearing matter-of-factly. He'd broken a drill.

In a short while the whirring resumed, shrill and high, and of a sudden it reminded Dix of another sound—a sound he hadn't heard for years—a sound that had accompanied the happiest part of his life. Katydids! Little devils, singing all the summer night while the full moon rose above the hill at the edge of the cornfield, laying a pale-blue drugget over the countryside, the frogs plucked bass strings in the pond where the cattails waved and the bluish witch light of the will-o'-the-wisp flickered over the stagnant water, and cows rubbed their sides against the fences and sometimes lowed plaintively in the darkness as if afraid. Dogs barked from farm to farm, answering one another, and keeping up a wordless conversation far into the night, and freight trains hooted lonesomely at the far edge of the horizon, trailing a long plume of gray smoke streaked underneath with red reflections from the firebox . . .

Of a sudden the drill stopped whirring, and Dix came to himself at once, jolted back to reality by the cessation of sound. There was a long silence, and Dix was beginning to wonder what was wrong, when the little doctor spoke from behind the screen.

"Hear anything, Handley?"

Dix didn't reply, but stood straining his ears and trying to separate from the throbbing, palpable silence surrounding him various vague, unidentifiably faint little pinpricks of sound. Finally he heard it.

"Siren," he said, "coming this way from the direction of the river."

They all stood listening as the sound drew closer; and in a moment they heard other sirens, a lot of them, converging on Marquette Square from all points of the compass.

In the midst of the silence of the store the drill started whirring again, and Dix laughed to himself and felt heartened. All business, this Bellini guy.

"What do you make of it?" asked the little doctor calmly.

"Don't sound good," said Dix.

"How could it be for us?"

"It couldn't unless there's a police fink in the outfit, and who would that be?"

"Any idea?"

The sirens were drawing nearer and nearer, wailing wildly through the canyons of the financial district.

"No," said Dix. "Except maybe somebody might have shot off his mouth to the wrong guy, bragging. Plenty guys brag on a big one, before and after."

The drill continued, piercing the silence of the big shop, as the sirens screamed loudly in various keys in the streets beyond.

"How close are you, Bellini?" called Dix.

"Getting pretty close. Maybe two minutes."

"Something funny about this," said Dix. "Sounds like they got the whole Square covered. Bellini, how about that burglar alarm? Isn't there a central station where any alarm would show on a board?"

"Sure," cried Louis above the noise of the drill. "But I killed it . . . unless I don't know what the hell I'm doing."

The sirens were so loud now that they seemed to fill the whole neighborhood.

"What do we do, Doc?" called Dix. "Name it."

Now the sirens were singing in a lower key as the cars began to slow down.

"What do *you* think?" cried the little doctor, nervous and sweating now, but not out of fear of the police. He had the awful vision of a million-dollar job—the ultimate big one they all dreamed of—gone glimmering, and he hated to be run off the kill by a lot of extraneous sounds, no matter from what source.

"If it's for us," said Dix, "we're close to cooked anyway. Let's take a chance."

The drill had never stopped, and the little doctor spoke somewhat shrilly above it.

"I'm for it." Then he turned to Louis. "How about Gus? Will he hold still?"

"Don't worry about Gus," said Louis.

As the sirens ceased, one by one, Dix caught another sound, which rose higher and higher now. A bell was ringing down the street, violently and insistently.

"What's that bell?" he demanded.

"Holy Mike!" cried Louis. "A burglar alarm! Maybe I started something."

"Funny we didn't hear it before."

"Strange things happen with them gadgets," called Louis; then he said suddenly: "Okay. We're through. Come on, Doc."

The drill stopped whirring, and Dix heard a distant, vague creaking noise as the heavy, well-oiled safe door swung back. There was a long silence except for some faint metallic sounds and low muttering from the safe; then Dix started slightly as another alarm bell started to ring further down the square.

Dix hurried around the screen and went to the open door of the safe.

"Louis," he said, "you sure must have fixed things up. Another bell's going."

Neither Louis nor the little doctor looked up or replied. They were busy dumping diamonds and other stones into the bag. Louis' pin-point torch was burning, and Dix caught dazzling, prismatic gleams from the jewels as they were hastily grabbed up and sacked like so much junk.

"Take a look, Handley," the little doctor called over his shoulder. "See what's happening. We'll be ready to leave in a minute or so." Then a note of triumph came into his voice. "And this is the biggest one yet—the biggest one ever heard of! Wait till you see the papers!"

Dix snorted quietly to himself. This little foreigner, he was okay—really big-time! He moved cautiously to the large front window and, pulling aside a heavy drape a few inches, he stared up the street. The Square seemed to be full of prowl cars, and uniformed policemen were swarming around a big fur store on the corner. Further up the street two prowl cars had just drawn up in front of another big store, and coppers, leaping out, were running across the pavement toward the brilliantly lighted show windows. He watched them for a moment, then hurried back behind the screen.

"They're up the way a block or so," he called. "Busy as one-armed paper-hangers right now. But they'll be combing the whole Square shortly—taking no chances. How we doing?"

"Ready," said the little doctor.

"Let's blow fast," said Dix.

Louis was picking up his tools deftly and stowing them away in his big overcoat. The little doctor picked the bag up, hefted it, then fastened the straps.

"The Du Ponts wouldn't sneer at this load," he said complacently.

"All set," said Louis at last, and they moved swiftly through the glimmering twilight of the big, ornate main room, turned off into the corridor, where it was darker and the outside sounds did not penetrate, and made for the back door.

"I'll go ahead," said Dix. "See if it's okay."

He disappeared around a bend in the corridor, and Louis and Riemenschneider lagged a little, waiting for the word to move out.

"I'll be glad to turn this load over to Emmerich and get our money," said the little doctor. "Then we'll be clear."

"Say," said Louis suddenly, worrying about one thing now, "you suppose maybe the cops might set up road blocks at the bridges? A guy might have to go thirty miles out of his way—and I'm anxious to get home."

"They could. But why? They'll soon find out they're running down a false alarm." The little doctor giggled suddenly.

"Yeah," said Louis, relieved. "Guess you're right, Doc."

Dix moved cautiously toward the door, and he was just getting ready to open it when an elongated shadow fell across the stone terrace outside; then a man appeared, walking briskly. He was headed for the back door of Pelletier and Company—no doubt about it. Dix got a quick picture of him as he came into the pool of light: a husky fellow in his thirties, wearing a private-police uniform—probably hired by the merchants of the Square. In fact, Joe Cool's chart had mentioned a hired watchman. But they'd all ignored it. Private police were nothing to worry about.

Dix waited tense in the shadows. The policeman tried the door, hesitated, tried it again. The second time, Dix noticed that the door gave a little, and he could see that the policeman was slightly suspicious. Louis had carefully locked the door behind them, and yet in disengaging the burglar alarm he had changed in some way the feel of the door to the policeman, who tried it several times every night.

Dix moved back into the corridor, where Louis and the little doctor were waiting.

"Store cop," he said quickly. "May cause us a beef. You better unlock that door, Louis, so I can get this guy before he decides to yell copper."

Louis looked at Dix, startled. Beyond, they could hear the policeman trying the door again.

"Maybe he'll go away," said Louis.

"Do what Handley says," the little doctor broke in sharply.

Louis did not like violence. It was outside his scheme of things. Always these heavies, looking for a chance to belt somebody . . . ! As he moved cautiously and silently toward the door, he felt a sudden cold hatred of Dix and all he stood for—ruthlessness, brutality, lack of pity.

Dix moved silently to the other side of the door, waiting like some predatory animal. Louis stooped, unlocked the door with one swift movement, then jerked it inward, masking himself behind it.

The policeman froze, showed a startled face; then Dix grabbed him by the left arm, pulled him toward him suddenly, and hit him full on the chin with a blow that would have knocked down a full-grown bull. The policeman didn't fall, however, because Dix had hold of him, though he sagged like a sack of grain with a sudden rip in it. Dix hit him twice more, then let go of him.

The little doctor looked on calmly, but Louis was wincing inside and trying not to see what was going on, though it was only a few feet from him.

The policeman, who hadn't uttered a sound, staggered wildly, then fell to the floor with a clash and clatter as if he'd been dropped from the ceiling.

He was wearing a gun in a strapless holster, and when he jerked over onto his side convulsively, the gun butt struck the marble floor and there was a blinding flash, a terrific echoing roar—then black silence.

Dix and the little doctor stared at each other in dismay, appalled by the sudden violence of the sound, but Louis let go of the door and swayed back like a drunk standing on the platform of a moving streetcar, then fell to his knees, groaning.

Dix snapped: "Doc, we got to blow. I'll carry him."

Riemenschneider, hugging the bag under his coat, pulled back the door, and Dix grabbed hold of Louis, jerked him to his feet, and put him over his shoulder. Louis was swearing weakly and protesting that Dix was killing him, but Dix paid no attention.

"You better take the heater, Doc," said Dix. "I got my hands full."

Riemenschneider felt himself flinching, but took the heavy, snub-nosed revolver from Dix without a word.

"Gus has got to get Louis to a doctor," said Dix. "So I'll drive you."

Riemenschneider nodded quickly, for the moment unable to speak; then he hurried out the door, stopped on the terrace, and stood looking up and down the alleyway. Dix came out behind him, carrying Louis, who was no longer protesting and swearing at Dix but was keeping up a steady groaning that got on the little doctor's nerves. It wasn't that he pitied Louis; Riemenschneider was casehardened and had been immune to pity for thirty years; it was that Louis's groans kept reminding him that chance, or whatever you wanted to call it, had played them a dirty trick. This was the kind of thing you never could allow for, no matter how carefully you planned, and the German was very proud of his ability to reason things out coldly and act accordingly.

He felt a growing sense of frustration and futility. Why plan at all? Why not just blunder about impulsively, trusting in God, like the rest of the chumps and hoosiers? You figure everything out down to the last detail, hours and hours of planning, then . . . what? A burglar alarm goes off for no sensible reason—as if merely to point the finger at you; then a gun butt hits the floor by chance; the gun, a senseless hunk of metal, fires of its own accord; and a man is shot!

Fear began to nag at the little doctor, turning his blood cold and making him sickish. Facts he could face, yes— and fight. But blind accident . . . what could you do?

A big, powerful hand reached out and took him by the arm; its crushing grip brought him back to reality.

"Pick up your feet, Doc. You're stumbling," said Dix.

Like a sleepwalker suddenly awakened, the little doctor started and looked about him wildly. They were nearing the parking-lot now, and Gus flashed the car lights briefly. At the end of the alley the little doctor could see the brilliantly lighted Square; the marble general astride his marble horse and with his marble sword raised seemed to be urging on the swarming police, who were now going from shop to shop farther down the Square, trying doors, peering into windows, calling back and forth to one another.

When they got to the parking-lot Gus jumped out of the car and stood waiting for them.

"Gus," sobbed Louis, "you got to get me home. Maria and the kid, they . . ."

"Get him to a doctor," said Dix. "He was shot point-blank."

"Right in the thigh," gasped Louis. "I could feel it traveling up through my leg. I think I got it in the belly, too. Please, Gus . . ."

"I'll take him to that Polack abortionist," said Gus. "He's a good guy."

"But Maria . . . !" gasped Louis as they helped him into his own car.

"I'll call her," said Gus, jumping in beside him.

"I'll do the driving for Doc," said Dix.

"Watch the bridges," said the little doctor. "The net might be out."

Dix turned suddenly. He heard footfalls—a number of people walking near by.

"Give me the heat, Doc," he said sharply.

Riemenschneider handed him the gun, but Gus said: "A show must be over, Dix. People coming from the all-night theater to get their cars. That's a break."

Gus waved a fat, square hand, then started to drive out of the lot. The little doctor and Dix could see Louis crumpled in his seat, leaning forward and gasping as if he was having a hard time getting his breath.

Just as Dix and the little doctor were ready to follow, half a dozen people, men and women, came into the lot, walking slowly, talking about the picture, and laughing lightheartedly. Dix had to wait for them. One of the men

hugged one of the women and tried to kiss her, and, struggling good-naturedly, they stopped in front of Dix's car.
He switched on the lights, and the woman gave a faint
squeal.

"Is that the gentlemanly thing to do, sir?" called the man
in mock protest.

"Sorry, buddy," said Dix. Then as the couple moved
back out of the way, a little chilled by Dix's voice, he drove
past them and headed for the dark, winding side street Louis
had followed on his way in.

They drove in silence for a long time, until the dark
buildings of the financial district began to tower over them,
blotting out the sky; then the little doctor glanced at his
watch in the light from the dash and said: "We're going to
be a little late. Not much though." Dix, intent on driving
in an area not very familiar to him, made no comment. The
German went on: "I'm glad we're going to get rid of this
stuff before we have to cross back over the bridge. When
that watchman comes to, there is going to be plenty heat
on this town."

There was a brief pause; then Dix said: "Okay by me.
I'm blowing."

"Leaving town?"

"Yeah."

"How do I get in touch with you later?" asked Riemenschneider. He knew a good man when he saw one. Mexico
City might not work out. It was always well to be prepared
for eventualities.

"You don't," said Dix.

"Leaving for good? Quitting?"

"It's about time, ain't it?" Dix laughed shortly. "I'm
going home. Haven't seen it for twenty-five years."

The little doctor sighed and paused to light a cigar.

"You'll be back. I'll leave my address with Cobby."

Dix said nothing further, and the German drifted off into
plans for the future. Little by little his confidence was returning to him. Tough, running into so much unnecessary
trouble. But it might have been worse, much worse! He

thought about Mexico City with a stab of pleasure—eight thousand feet up, the air so clear and pure, many first-class clubs and restaurants, a horse track, and girls . . . plenty young girls!

But there were problems too. A man like himself had to be on guard all the time. It might get around he was carrying a big bankroll—and, not knowing who he was, the city wolves might start to gather.

"Handley," he said, "ever been in Mexico City?"

Dix glanced at him in surprise, then returned to his driving.

"Nope. Never been out of the country—except when I went across in the war."

"How would you like to go there—all expenses paid?"

"Sorry, Doc," said Dix laconically. "Not interested."

Riemenschneider sighed and puffed on his cigar in silence. With Dix looking after him things would be so simple!

· 21 ·

"It's after two o'clock," snapped Emmerich, who was pacing up and down impatiently and throwing accusing glances at Brannom as if the private dick were somehow to blame.

Brannom shrugged and poured himself another drink. He was half tight now and felt very self-confident, even reckless. His coat was off, and his dark-blue shirt was open at the neck, the white tie to one side. He had put his shoulder holster away in a drawer and planted the .45 between the cushions on the settee where he was now lounging.

Emmerich had watched this maneuver nervously but had made no comment. A sense of gloomy and inescapable fatality had settled over him hours ago, and he couldn't shake it off.

"Brannom," he said, "you're drinking a hell of a lot."

"I always drink a hell of a lot."

"Sometimes you get drunk. You'd better have your wits about you tonight."

"Half drunk I've got more wits than most people—and more nerve!" he added suddenly. "Why don't you sit down? You're wearing out my Sears-Roebuck Aubusson."

"I don't want any of your insolence," said Emmerich, turning quickly.

"Relax, will you? You're not talking to some cokie client, my friend."

They stared at each other in silence for a moment; then Emmerich turned away and finally sat down, put his elbows on his knees, and rested his chin in his hands. Brannom regarded him with marked distaste; then he insolently tossed down his drink and poured another one.

Live and learn! The great Mr. Emmerich—how he'd fooled the public all these years! Why, tonight he looked like a fat old woman, flabby and pale, with trembling hands and bloodshot eyes. The Big Fix! "Bob," Brannom said to himself, "all these years you've just been suffering from an inferiority complex—that's all that's the matter with you. These Big Boys . . . what have they got? Front—nothing but front. And when that slips . . . !" Brannom laughed curtly and Emmerich turned to look at him.

"Something funny?"

"Oh, I was just thinking about the time my father got run over by a tractor," said Brannom.

Emmerich turned away in disgust and sat staring morosely at the carpet. Suddenly he remembered his wife lying alone in her dreary bedroom, which smelled of disinfectant and mortality, endlessly turning over the pages of magazines, taking medicine, and complaining in a quietly rancorous voice about everything. Was he at fault? Certainly he'd turned away from her many years ago. But . . . maybe she'd driven him away. Who could say? Emmerich felt a sudden rush of despondency and restrained a groan; then he took a firm hold on himself, thinking how this slick ape in the blue shirt would laugh at him if he knew what was running through his mind.

He turned at a sound. Brannom had risen and was listening.

"Mr. Emmerich," he said in a cruel parody of a polite society voice, "I believe our guest is arriving."

Emmerich got up quickly, and they both stood listening.

Outside, Dix had just parked the car, and he and the little doctor were getting out.

"Who lives *here?*" asked Dix, staring distrustfully at the modest little frame house with its tiny strip of lawn and its ragged-looking shrubbery. This poor but genteelly respectable neighborhood made Dix uneasy. "I thought this Emmerich guy was really in the chips."

"Oh, this isn't Emmerich's place," said the little doctor. "But whoever lives here, it's a good idea—the neighborhood and all, I mean. No rumbles in this suburb . . ." His voice trailed off as Dix followed him across the lawn toward the front porch.

Although Riemenschneider spoke calmly and seemed at ease, all of his old doubts and suspicions of Emmerich began to assail him—the delay, the smooth con talk, the abrupt about-faces . . . and yet, considered coldly and rationally, what could Emmerich hope to gain by a double cross?

"It could be just my imagination," the little doctor told himself as he shrugged off his doubts and rang the door bell.

In a moment Emmerich opened the door.

"Good evening," said Riemenschneider.

Emmerich quickly masked his start of surprise at the sight of the little doctor; then he looked beyond him at the tall, rawboned man in the shadows.

"Why, Riemenschneider," cried Emmerich genially, "we didn't expect *you*. This is indeed a pleasure. Come right in."

He stood aside, and the little doctor entered, followed by Dix, who looked about him uneasily, then took off his hat. The little doctor held up the small leather bag, and he was just smiling and opening his mouth to make a remark about it when Brannom stepped into the hallway. Riemenschneider looked him up and down, the smile faded from his face, and doubts again began to nag at him.

"This is Mr. Brannom," said Emmerich, indicating the

private dick. "He's been very helpful to me in regard to
this deal. We've been going round and round. Very big
deal, you know. Takes finagling, managing, and time—
plenty of time."

Dix and Brannom were regarding each other silently,
taking each other's measure. Brannom was taller than Dix
and wider. But Dix didn't think much of him in spite of
that, and looked away in a moment, concentrating on Emmerich, whose nervous joviality puzzled and jarred on him.
Brannom couldn't make Dix out, and kept glancing at him,
noticing the rough, khaki-colored shirt, the cheap, wrinkled
tie, the forty-dollar suit that was too small for him, and the
scuffed, tan shoes.

"They must've bought him cheap," he told himself finally, turning away with a certain amount of contempt.

"Will you follow me, gentlemen?" asked Emmerich
pleasantly. "It's more comfortable in here."

Then he turned to the little doctor and indicated the bag
as if he'd just noticed it for the first time. "Full of Kohi-
noors, I hope."

Dix wondered what the hell this big, handsome guy was
talking about, and turned to Riemenschneider for enlighten-
ment, but the German merely said: "Could be."

They followed Emmerich and Brannom into the living-
room, where they were offered drinks, which they refused.
They even refused to sit down; so Emmerich stood with
them, but Brannom moved over to the settee and finally
established himself in one corner, and Emmerich glanced
at him quickly out of the corner of his eye.

"Well," said the little doctor, speaking matter-of-factly,
"here's the stuff, Mr. Emmerich. Now if you'll be kind
enough to give us the money, we'll be on our way."

"Do you mind if I take a look?" asked Emmerich, clearing his throat nervously.

"But of course not," said the little doctor, unstrapping
the bag. "You're entitled to a look—naturally."

There was a tense silence in the room, and Dix kept eying
Brannom, who was lounging back with his legs crossed and

a cigarette in his fingers, glancing about him as if completely indifferent to what was going on.

Riemenschneider moved over to a little table a few feet from Brannom, cleared a space, then slowly and carefully turned the bag upside down. For what seemed like minutes diamonds, rubies, emeralds, and star sapphires slid down onto the cheap, worn cloth.

Even Dix stared open-mouthed, stunned. Emmerich turned pale, and Brannom, unable any longer to keep up his indifferent role, dropped his cigarette on the carpet and stooped to pick it up.

A heavy silence throbbed in the little room. The men all stared, motionless, at the huge, glittering treasure scattered on the table before them, as if it had suddenly cast a hex on them, turning them to stone.

Finally the little doctor broke the spell. Chuckling nervously, he held the mouth of the bag below the level of the table and began carefully to scoop the gems back into it.

"Convinced?" he inquired.

"Of course. Of course," said Emmerich jovially. "In fact, there never was any doubt in my mind, knowing your reputation, Riemenschneider. A mere matter of curiosity, nothing more."

The little doctor had finished raking in the gems now and was strapping up the bag again.

"Good, good!" he said. "Well, Mr. Emmerich, in that case, it looks like our little deal is about concluded."

There was a brief silence as Emmerich cleared his throat portentously and got ready to speak.

"Gentlemen," he said, "I must say that at this moment I find myself a bit embarrassed."

The German threw a quick look at Dix, whose face showed nothing; then he turned and spoke: "You mean . . . you haven't got the money, Mr. Emmerich?"

"I don't mean anything quite as crude as that," said Emmerich. "I have the money . . . that is, I have the assurance of it, and from a party whose word is as good as an iron-clad contract. No, there's no trouble about the money.

But the sum is a very large one—an almost impossibly large
one, considering present-day conditions and the fact that it
is wanted in cash . . . so a little more time is needed to
raise it . . .''

"Then you *haven't* got it," said Riemenschneider, his
fat, pale face a blank, but his little dark eyes showing a
sudden glitter behind his thick-lensed glasses.

"Riemenschneider," said Emmerich, "I'm somewhat
disappointed in you, a man of your sublety, using such
black-and-white terms. I haven't actually got the currency
here in my hand." Emmerich made an eloquent gesture,
and you could almost hear the judge crying: "Objection
overruled!" Then he went on: "But in the strictest sense of
the word, I actually have the money—promised by an un-
impeachable source. I'm sorry things worked out as they
did. I guess we were all too anxious and moved too fast,
but . . ."

"We moved on your word."

"There you go again, Riemenschneider—black and white.
There are certain intangibles that it is not always possible
to control, as you well know, a man of your experience."

The German started slightly at the mention of intangibles,
remembering all at once the senseless burglar alarms and
the self-firing gun.

Emmerich noted the little doctor's sudden thoughtfulness
and, feeling that he'd gained a point, went on rapidly: "The
money's as good as here. I heard from my source tonight
that it might take a little longer than we thought to raise the
full amount. I would have called you and asked you to
postpone the . . . the business—only for a few nights, you
understand—but by that time it was already too late . . ."

"This is very awkward," said Riemenschneider. "A few
nights may not seem like a very long time to you, Mr.
Emmerich. But to me, carrying around a package like this,
it seems like years. Wait till you see the papers tomorrow.
This is the biggest beat in the history of the city."

"I quite understand," said Emmerich. "And I have a
solution for that." He paused, glanced from Dix to Rie-

menschneider with affectionate familiarity, then went on: "That is, of course, if you boys trust me. If you don't . . . well, then there's nothing I can say except that I'm exceedingly sorry I wasn't able to make a more professional job of this affair." He cleared his throat and, taking out a handkerchief, slowly mopped his brow, eying Dix and the little doctor sadly and resignedly.

There was a brief pause; then Riemenschneider asked: "Mr. Emmerich, what are you trying to say to us?"

"The jewels," said Emmerich, smiling pleasantly. "They're very dangerous for you to carry around. You've just said so."

"You mean we leave them with you?"

"Not if you can think of a better plan. Actually they're no more good to me than they are to you until we're financed. But they're less trouble to me. When the police start looking for them tomorrow, will they call me up or send detectives around to my house?" Emmerich laughed and gestured expansively. "To state it is to laugh. But you . . . doctor! You were just released from prison. I assure you the police aren't going to start looking for petty thieves on a job like this. They're going to look for big-timers, like yourself. And some detective may be smart enough to connect this million-dollar robbery with your release."

Riemenschneider felt cold sweat breaking out on his forehead. He'd been right! It *was* a double cross. But what kind? How?

"Nobody knows I'm in town," he said after a pause.

"Are you sure of that?"

Riemenschneider hesitated, then spoke in a low voice, eying Emmerich coldly.

"No," he said. "Not now."

Dix, bewildered by Emmerich's subtle flow of talk, and almost convinced against his will, was brought up short by a warning note of harshness in the little doctor's voice. He glanced at Riemenschneider, then at Emmerich, whose cheeks had begun to show a touch of pallor.

"Well, there you are!" cried Emmerich, sounding as jovial as before, but actually beginning to lose his nerve under the German's stare. His eloquence deserted him. With a quick gesture of dismissal, he seemed to brush off the whole controversy. "But, of course, as I said, it's up to you. Take the jewels. Have Cobb keep in touch with me. Maybe by the end of the week . . ."

Brannom, who had been forgotten by everybody during the discussion, suddenly spoke harshly.

"You did a great job, Emmerich. But it's not working. So . . ."

They all turned to him at once. He was sitting on the edge of the settee staring hard at Dix and Riemenschneider. In his right hand was the Navy .45. His face was pale, but his heavy jaw was set and he looked grimly determined.

Emmerich was genuinely shocked. Although far from unprepared for this action, he had hoped all along that it would be unnecessary, owing to his own superior eloquence.

"Bob!" he cried involuntarily.

"Back away and keep out of this, Emmerich," said Brannom harshly, never taking his eyes from Dix and the little doctor. "Now you . . . farmer! Get your hands up. Now you . . . Heinie, throw that bag on the floor. Over here by my feet. And be careful how you throw it. I got a pistol-expert medal."

The little doctor glanced sideways at Dix, who, expressionless, was slowly raising his hands.

"What do you say, Dix?"

"He's got no say," cried Brannom. "If he makes a crooked move, he'll never pitch another forkful of manure on the farm."

Dix cleared his throat and spoke hoarsely.

"Toss him the bag, Doc. He's got us."

"You're not as dumb as you look," said Brannom.

There was a brief pause, and the three men could hear Emmerich breathing heavily in the silence. Then Riemenschneider tossed the bag toward Brannom, and at the same time Dix jerked the snub-nosed revolver from the waistband of his trousers and jumped sideways.

Two guns roared, violently shattering the silence of the genteelly respectable little living-room. Emmerich, though not in the line of fire, turned away and fell to his knees. Brannom stared stupidly into space for a moment, then slid slowly to the floor, knelt by the settee in silence as if praying for his sins, then slowly lay down and buried his face in the "Sears-Roebuck Aubusson."

The German turned to look at Dix. The big Southerner had staggered back against the wall and was pressing his left hand to his left side. Riemenschneider saw a long, ragged tear in his coat. Before he could speak, Emmerich, who was kneeling in a corner with his hands pressed to his chest, completely unnerved, cried out: "It's my heart, gentlemen. Another attack! This horrible thing that's happened . . . I'll . . . I'll never survive it. That fool signed my death warrant when he . . . my God! Why did he do such a thing?"

Dix advanced on him slowly.

"You son-of-a-bitch," he shouted. "You smooth-faced, preachifying, double-dealing bastard!"

Inept in violence, staggered by what had happened, Riemenschneider knew he must intervene, but for the moment couldn't force himself into action—his mind busy with the appalling ramifications of this disaster.

"Are you a man?" shouted Dix, moving steadily toward Emmerich, who stared glassy-eyed, wild with panic. "Or a half-woman? Or what? Trying to gyp and double-cross, but with no guts for it. Why didn't you die long ago? What's keeping you alive?"

Emmerich rose suddenly as a strange expression passed over his deathlike face—an expression that made Dix hesitate and stare, an expression compounded of resignation, dignity, and sudden resolution. Color started to come back into his cheeks, and the look of extreme, disintegrating flabbiness began slowly to be modified, until his jaw showed a certain firmness and the lines about his mouth hardened.

He backed a few steps away from Dix, then stood looking at him coldly and without fear.

In a flash, Emmerich had made a startling discovery. When humiliation reached a certain point, death was preferable. He had heard the fact stated many times, in and out of court, sometimes seriously, sometimes ironically. It had always struck him as a preposterous assumption—belonging to another age. *But it was true.*

The German had recovered now. He saw that Emmerich wanted to die; was, in fact, by his attitude of contemptuous indifference, actually goading the big Southerner to kill him. He rushed up to Dix and caught the gun from behind, pushing the barrel slowly down and talking rapidly at the same time.

"Dix—listen to me. He deserves to die. But what about us? We're in trouble—real trouble—and we need help. Don't kill him, Dix. It's too easy an out for him."

Dix stopped struggling, turned and looked at Riemenschneider blankly, then suddenly grimaced and grabbed his side with a groan. The lawyer glanced at the body of Brannom sprawled on the floor by the settee; then he fell down heavily into the one easy chair in the room. The German stood eying him coldly.

There was a prolonged, uneasy silence. Dix shoved the gun back into the waistband of his trousers, moved over to the wall, and stood with his hand pressed to his side, keeping a wary eye on Emmerich.

"He's all yours, Doc," he said. "But what use you're going to make of him, I don't see."

Riemenschneider walked over and retrieved the little bag, which was lying near Brannom's left foot, put it on the table, then turned to Emmerich.

"What did you think you were trying to do, Mr. Emmerich? Are you crazy?"

"I must have been," said Emmerich with an effort. "Trying to get away with a thing like this."

"You're lucky you're alive; that's the truth," said the German, looking at him deeply puzzled. "You're all through, Mr. Emmerich. Washed out. Ruined."

"Wait a minute, Doc," said Dix, coming to himself. "This guy's a witness. He saw me knock off that louse on the floor. You think he wouldn't holler if they turned the heat on him?"

"He's in no position to talk," said the German, dismissing the idea indifferently. Then he turned to Emmerich. "What did you and this man here on the floor intend to do with the jewels?"

"I was desperate," cried Emmerich, breaking out suddenly. "Broke. Facing bankruptcy . . ."

"You!" exclaimed the little doctor in surprise. Then he remembered. That explained it—all his own uneasiness in Emmerich's presence, his doubts and suspicions. He'd sensed the lawyer's inner turmoil. "I know all about desperation," the little doctor went on, smiling slightly as the world came back into a more normal focus, and his thinking in regard to Emmerich changed from puzzlement to something like understanding. "But the jewels? How could you handle them?"

"Leave town. Sell them off a little at a time."

"No good. The police would have been on you after the first sale. These have to be handled by a fence who really knows his business. He places them with jewelers all over the country—right jewelers. It's a business by itself. You acted like an amateur, Mr. Emmerich. For us, you've got to do better."

Emmerich glanced up at the German in surprise.

"Better?"

"You've got to figure a way out for us, Mr. Emmerich. I didn't save your life because I'm a lover of humanity." The German smirked a little at what he considered a fine phrase. "We're in trouble with this satchelful of jewels. If we can't unload it, it's just so much junk. Think and think fast, Mr. Emmerich."

Dix's face showed pain and he kept grabbing his side, but the pain was secondary to his surprise at Riemenschneider's attitude toward Emmerich.

"Look here, Doc," he said, "you're kidding yourself if you think we can deal with this double-crossing bastard here."

"What do we do then?"

"I don't know what we do. Except get out of here. Somebody might have heard the shooting. It's pretty quiet in this neighborhood. This'd be a great time for a rumble!"

"Be patient, Dix."

Riemenschneider stood studying the lawyer, who seemed to be staring vacantly.

"Well, Mr. Emmerich . . . ?"

The lawyer rubbed a shaking hand over his moist brow and considered. Death had confronted him, and he'd faced it down. But that seemed like a long time ago now—ancient history. Life was going on again with all its old worries and responsibilities. He'd only gained a reprieve, not a pardon.

"I have an idea, I think," he said suddenly, sitting up straight. "What about the insurance company?"

"Insurance company?" said the little doctor slowly; then his eyes lighted up. "I know what you mean."

"They might listen to reason. This is a very bad jolt for them, and it's possible they'd be willing to buy them back— no questions asked, for, say as high as thirty per cent of their insured worth."

"How is it to be handled?"

"Doc," cried Dix, "let's blow!"

They ignored him. Emmerich rose and put his cigar in the ash-tray. He felt vaguely hopeful. Could he possibly pull this one out of the fire?

"Say the word," he said, "and I'll start on it tomorrow. But . . . you keep the jewelry."

"You're goddamn right we'll keep it!" Dix broke in.

Emmerich compressed his lips and turned away from Dix's hard gaze. He felt nothing but contempt for the big Southerner now.

"Get busy," said Riemenschneider. "And remember— you might have been lying here dead, with your friend."

Emmerich controlled his face and averted his eyes from Brannom's sprawled body.

"If anything comes up," he said, "I'll get in touch with Cobb."

Riemenschneider nodded. Dix, who was very pale now and leaning against the wall for support, was in too much pain to make any more protests. The hell with it!

Riemenschneider helped him down the hallway, and Emmerich held the door open for them.

Nobody spoke again.

After they'd gone, Emmerich stood listening. He heard the car start and drive off; then, avoiding Brannom's body, he took out his handkerchief and began to wipe off every object in the room that might show fingerprints, and as he went about this job, his mind began to work with nervous rapidity. The police would easily discover his connection with Brannom—it was routine. And he'd never be able to deny that they'd been together tonight—a few rudimentary questions would bring that out. An alibi? Emmerich smiled to himself wryly. After all, maybe he could put Angela to some use—she might yet turn out to be worth all the money he'd spent on her!

It was well past three o'clock when he got home. He let himself in with his latchkey and quietly mounted the stairs. But his wife's door was open, and a bar of light fell across the carpet of the dark second-floor hallway, showing the pattern faintly.

He looked in. Tonight his wife's bedroom did not seem like a place to avoid, but more like a quiet refuge. His wife was sitting up in bed reading a magazine. She turned and stared at him with marked surprise. For years now he'd slipped in without bothering to say good night.

"Well, Lon . . . !" she exclaimed.

"Why aren't you sleeping?"

"I had the light out twice. But I couldn't sleep. What time is it?"

Emmerich hesitated, then pulled out his watch and pretended to study it. "It's nearly two," he said. "Ten of."

"That's pretty late, Lon."

"I know. I was held up. Why don't you try to sleep?"

"I think I will. I feel easier now you're home."

Emmerich patted her hand, then, with a sigh, started for the hallway. He was reluctant to leave, and had a strong desire to sit on the bed and have a long conversation with May, as he'd done in the past—the remote past—when he'd been a struggling young lawyer, working late over an important brief. At the door he turned.

"I've been thinking about what you said tonight. We used to have fun playing cassino, didn't we?"

"Oh, Lon," said his wife, embarrassed, "don't pay any attention to me. You know how I am sometimes."

"No, I mean it. It's an excellent idea. Good night, May."

After he'd gone, Mrs. Emmerich sat for a long time lost in thought. Was Lon drunk? He did look a bit pale and his eyes were bloodshot and he was getting more and more nervous every day! But, no . . . he may have had a few drinks, but he wasn't drunk.

"I wonder where he goes," she mused, "when he stays out so late?"

· 22 ·

Cobby was lying on the hard leather couch in the back cardroom, trying to compose himself. His face was pale and drawn, and from time to time he groaned faintly. He was suffering from shock and fright, and couldn't shake off an irrational feeling that any time now the world would come to an end.

Dix, swearing quietly to himself, had his shirt off, displaying a powerful chest covered with matted black hair. Sitting sideways on a straight chair, he was swabbing his wound with a big hunk of cotton dipped in iodine. His bloody shirt was on the floor beside the couch, and Cobby kept trying not to see it.

The little doctor was sitting at a card table still wearing his overcoat and hat. The bag containing the jewels was on the table in front of him, and he kept sliding it round and round idly.

"Dix," he said, "you had better get in touch with Gus and let him take you to a doctor. Don't be foolish."

"I don't like doctors," said Dix. "I'm getting along all right. The bullet just ripped through my side and went on about its business. Good thing I jumped!"

Cobby began to talk again in a whining, aggrieved voice, and Dix and Riemenschneider glanced at him in irritation. Ever since they'd got in from the job and he'd heard what had happened, he'd been breaking out periodically into long monologues of complaint and self-justification.

"How could I know about Emmerich?" he demanded. "Ask anybody how he stands. They'll tell you he's one of the biggest boys in the city and right as they come. I'm no mind-reader. I was just going along with the act, trying to do the best I could for everybody. And now look! I'm already clipped for thirty grand, and you boys got a load of rocks you can't peddle without blowing things up . . . a couple of guys have been shot and . . ."

"Aw, shut up!" cried Dix.

Cobby, who wanted to talk on and on endlessly, not only to relieve the oppression he felt in his chest, but also to protect himself, turned away with a groan and clamped his mouth shut.

"You should have told us you were furnishing the money," said Riemenschneider. "It would have made us suspicious, and we would have looked into things further."

"I know. I know," said Cobby, contritely. "But that Emmerich . . . he can talk a guy into anything." He turned suddenly and pointed a shaking finger at Dix and Riemenschneider. "Look at you guys. He throws a double cross at you, and what happens? He's still in. You're still working with him."

"This is different," said the little doctor. "Right now we've got no choice."

"It was Doc's idea," Dix broke in. "And he's stuck with it."

Cobby groaned, then got up to pour himself a drink; but the sudden movement made him dizzy, and he sat down again and took his head in his hands.

"I must be awful stupid," he said. "Here I am with a good business, money rolling in, and I got to get myself mixed up in a thing like this. I ought to have my head examined."

Dix was standing now, putting his shirt back on. He turned to the bookie. "Come on, Cobby. Quit crying—and get me some bourbon, will you?"

Just as Cobby was rising to get out the whisky bottle, the phone rang, and he answered it.

"Hello. Yeah, this is Cobby. What!"

He yelled so loudly that both Dix and the little doctor started and turned to stare.

"It's Gus," cried Cobby. "Dragnet out. They're combing the district. He wants to talk to you, Dix."

Dix jerked the receiver away from him.

"Gus? Dix."

"Listen careful, pal. I just got Louis home, and I'm leaving his place when I see the coppers. They're knocking over all the joints along Crane Boulevard—mobs of 'em, meat wagons and all. They'll be hitting Camden West shortly. Now look. I already called Eddie Donato. He's got a grocery down near the river—116 Front Street. Got that? Okay. You and the Doc better get down there as fast as possible. Eddie'll leave the side door unlocked—that's on Guerand Street. Just walk in and climb the stairs. Eddie's got a place where you can stay. Hole up till you hear from me. Boy, this is rough!"

"Thanks, Gus. How's Louis?"

"Not so good, and what a cock-and-bull story I had to give his missus. Say, I couldn't get hold of the Polish doctor. He got in a bad jam and blew. I had to take Louis to a guy named Halsey—he's a new one in from Chi. I guess he's okay. Anyway, I didn't have no time to argue. Blow now, Dix." Dix was just getting ready to hang up when Gus remembered something. "Wait, Dix. Did you leave my car in the alley behind the joint?"

"Yeah."

"Good. Now listen. You guys will be safer if you walk to Eddie's. Go by way of the Old Market. You can cover at least three blocks without having to worry about anybody. When you get beyond the Market it's a waltz. The neighborhood where Eddie lives is clear. Cops never bother it. So long."

Dix hung up.

"Come on, Doc," he said. "Let's get out of here."

Riemenschneider picked up the bag and followed Dix, who was struggling into his coat. At the door Dix turned.

"Cobby, we're going to lay low for a while. If you hear anything from Emmerich, tell Gus."

They went out and Dix slammed the door, Cobby wincing at the sound.

"How can things go so wrong?" Cobby asked the walls. "How is it possible?" Then he poured himself a drink and swallowed it quickly, shuddering violently as the raw liquor got to him.

Half an hour later Camden Square was swarming with prowl cars and patrol wagons, and in the back cardroom at Cobby's, Police Sergeant Monk Dietrich, an enormous man with a reputation for brutality, was sitting at his ease, smoking one of Cobby's best cigars and drinking Cobby's Scotch. His uniform coat was unbuttoned, showing a thick woolen undershirt. His cap was tilted back, and sweat beaded his low, corrugated forehead.

"This Timmons guy," he was saying; "I hate to jerk him in, Cobby. But we got to make a showing. Dragnet don't mean a goddamn thing. We can pull 'em in till Christmas, and we won't turn up nothing. The Old Man wants to make a show for the papers. But some fink'll blow this case sky high. Don't quote me." Dietrich's coarse laughter filled the little cardroom and bounced off the walls.

Cobby sat regarding Dietrich with a fixed, ingratiating smile.

"Timmons is a harmless guy," he said, mildly. "Kind of an errand boy. He's not smart enough to roll a drunk even."

"A night in the clink won't hurt him," said Dietrich, holding out his glass for more whisky. "Tomorrow morning he appears at show-up; then we let him go."

Cobby poured the glass full.

"As a favor to me, Dietrich," said Cobby, "let the poor guy alone. You'll scare the pants off him."

"Aw, come on," said Dietrich. "He's a beat-up old hood, and you know it. And he's got about as much scare in him as a telephone pole." Dietrich threw his head back and emptied the glass; then he peered up at Cobby with his shrewd, piggish little eyes. "However . . . since you've always been a good boy—except for running a book, and who the hell cares about that!—tell you what I'll do: I'll turn the old pug loose . . ." Dietrich paused and watched Cobby's slow, relieved smile; then he went on: "Yeah, I'll turn him loose—and take *you* instead!"

Cobby stared in horror, then began to jig about, unable for a moment to bring himself to speak. Dietrich stared at him stolidly. Finally Cobby found his voice.

"Now wait a minute, Dietrich. You can't do that. I'm just a little piddling businessman. Me! In a show-up? Now, look, Dietrich . . ."

Suddenly the big Sergeant of Police threw his head back and roared with laughter. The whole thing struck him as so funny that he gasped and wept and even leaned his head on the table for a moment. Finally he managed to get himself in hand, although his big stomach was still shaking; then he rose, opened the door, and yelled down the corridor: "Hey, Carlson! Throw that crooked-eared bastard in the wagon. We're taking him down."

Then he turned back to Cobby, who had a sickly smile on his face and was pouring himself a drink.

"Funny guy!" said Cobby in an aggrieved voice.

"In this job I got to look for laughs," said Dietrich, grinning. "Say—know a guy called Brannom?"

Cobby managed to keep his face at least tolerably composed.

"Brannom? No. I don't think so."

"You'll read it in the paper tomorrow. One of his neighbors called the station, said they thought they'd heard shooting at his house. People are always calling in, hearing shooting. I think they sit up nights just so they can jam the police switchboards. But this time . . . they weren't kidding. Somebody plugged this character right in the pump. What a night! I wish you could have got a gander at the Commissioner. They got him out of bed, and his hair was all standing on end. He looked like a constipated fighting chicken!" Dietrich roared again and hit the wall with his big, meaty hand.

"Is that what this is all about? One guy getting knocked off?" asked Cobby. "Who was he—the Governor's son, or something?"

"Naw," said Dietrich. "That's incidental. Read your paper tomorrow." He began to button his coat. "Got any more knocked-out characters around here I can pull in so we can make a showing?"

"Nope," said Cobby. "When the sirens started, all the card-players went out the alleyway."

"Then they been took. Okay, Cobby. Don't worry about your punchy friend. He'll be out tomorrow. Give me a couple more of them cigars. They're okay. Takes a bookie to smoke them kind. An honest cop hasn't got a chance."

He snatched the proffered cigars and went out. Cobby heard him tramping heavily down the corridor.

· 23 ·

A short way down the street, in the back of Gus's hamburger joint, the Happiness Boys, aided by a Headquarters dick, were giving Gus a going over.

"I ain't been out of the place," Gus was saying. "Ask Big Mike. Anyway, why don't you guys leave me alone? I been going straight since I did my time, and you know it."

The dick was getting irritated.

"Let's pull him in for the show-up and stop this silly talk."

"Just a minute," said the Camden Square harness bull named Tom; then he turned to Gus and laid a hand on his shoulder. "Look, Gus. Maybe you have been going straight. Okay. In that case, why can't you give us a little help? Like telling us what happened to that friend of yours—that Dix guy."

"I keep telling you he's no friend of mine. Don't know his name—except you say his name's Dix. Don't know where he lives. Nothing. He buys *Racing Forms* here and newspapers. Is that a crime?"

"All right," said Tom to the dick. "Take him."

"Come on, humpy," called the dick.

"Okay, fathead," said Gus.

"Smart guy, eh?" cried the dick, advancing on him. "How'd you like to get your teeth knocked out?"

"I don't want nobody calling me humpy," said Gus. "I was born with this; I didn't grow it myself."

The dick grimaced and turned away.

"Put him in the wagon."

· 24 ·

Maria, Louis's wife, was sitting by the bedroom window with her hands clasped tightly in her lap, trying to compose herself. She was completely bewildered.

Occasionally she looked out the window at the dark city, which a few hours ago had seemed so pleasant and friendly and familiar, and now seemed so alien and hostile.

How could it have happened?

She turned to look at Louis. He was lying on his back, asleep and breathing easily, but his face locked so pale and drawn in the dim glow from the night light, and from time to time he muttered frantically as if in fear.

Now she remembered what her brother Attilio had said. "Louis—he's a wild one; not the fellow for a tame pigeon like you." Her Louis? A wild one? Attilio had always been a big, fat fool.

But why had Louis got into a fight? Louis—who knew better than anybody how to mind his own business. And who was that awful, fat, humpbacked little creature? What had her Louis to do with such a man?

Maria could hear the sirens wailing all up and down the hills, and suddenly she became conscious of the number of them and their persistence.

"Must be a fire," she said aloud. "An awful one."

The thought of fire terrified her, especially now with Louis lying helpless. She rose, opened the window, and leaned out to look. But there was nothing to see except the silent, dark city with its tangled network of streets stretching off in all directions, and its thousands of street lights mere yellow pinpricks in the universal blackness.

Maria felt a sudden fear of the city, quickly drew in her head, and closed the window.

If it wasn't a fire, what was it then?

Louis made a vague sound, and she hurried over to him. He was moving his head slowly on the pillow and muttering unintelligibly in a harsh, unfamiliar voice.

Maria felt alone and defenseless without Louis to depend on. She had a wild desire to make him wake up and talk to her, tell her what to do! She began to cry and wring her hands.

Then . . . she thought about Father Sortino and grew a little calmer. He would know what to do; he always knew. But . . . no! She couldn't do that. Louis did not like priests— he was an infidel! Louis would be very angry if she ran to Father Sortino with her troubles.

Little by little, Maria composed herself. She went over to the crib and stood looking down at Louis, Jr., who was sleeping peacefully with his tiny thumb in his mouth. Then she went back to the chair by the bedroom window and sat down. Sirens were still going, but further away now.

· 25 ·

Cully, the bail-bond guy, had a face like a fox, and coarse reddish hair like a fox's pelt. His eyes were small, bright, and alert, and he had a sharp, Broadway look to him. But as a matter of fact he was from a small town downstate, where he'd run a poolroom. He was an adept chiseler, inured to cutting corners and flirting with illegality, but Mr. Emmerich had him scared. This was too big!

He squirmed in one of Emmerich's big, expensive, red-leather office chairs.

"But . . . did you read the papers?" he demanded in an awed voice.

"Certainly I read the papers, Cully," said Emmerich, puffing calmly on one of his Cuban cigars. "Don't let that bother you. The noise will die down."

"Over a million bucks!" gasped Cully. "Wham! Like that! Pretty big stuff for me."

"Oh, you can find some way to feel them out," said Emmerich soothingly, "without committing yourself. They'd love you. You'd be doing them a big favor. You think the company won't play ball to save maybe six hundred thousand dollars? If you do, you don't know anything about insurance companies."

"Frankly, I'm petrified," said Cully. "I don't know *what* I think. If there'd be any slips . . . !"

"That's my responsibility, Cully. As a matter of fact, I'm just trying to perform a public service. Once the jewels are returned, everything will settle down to normal. Come on, Cully. I always considered you a sharpshooter with plenty of nerve."

"That's what I always considered myself," said Cully.

"But this is World Series stuff—and it begins to look like I'm bush league."

"I just don't believe it."

There was a long pause, and Emmerich sat watching Cully squirm on his chair and pull at his underlip. Finally Cully got to his feet and said: "If I was a man with kids, I wouldn't get mixed up in this. But since I only got a wife . . . I'll see what I can do."

"Good!"

"Now don't get me wrong. If it looks too rough, I'm going to back out."

"All right. Give it a try."

Emmerich rose and walked around his desk, smiling genially. Just as they were shaking hands the dictaphone buzzed. Emmerich frowned slightly, then switched on the key.

"Yes, Miss Thompson."

"Commissioner Hardy would like to see you, Mr. Emmerich."

Emmerich started slightly; then to cover his reaction he cleared his throat, coughed, and said:

"Hold him for one moment, then send him in." He turned immediately to Cully, took him by the arm, and escorted him toward a side door, talking as they went. "Really there's nothing much to this, Cully. No danger certainly. It just looks big, that's all. Give it a circus try. I'm counting on you."

Before he could say good-bye or even blink, Cully found himself in the corridor. The double shuffle? But why? Maybe a hotter prospect? Cully began to worry about losing a big chunk of commission, forgetting all his doubts and fears of a moment ago. By God, he'd prove to Emmerich he was big-time!

The Commissioner's stiff, unruly blond-gray hair was standing up all over his small skull, and he looked like a belligerent porcupine. There were dark circles under his eyes, and his thin lips were set in a grim line. He regarded the bland-looking Emmerich with ill-concealed disfavor.

"Sit down, Commissioner Hardy," said Emmerich politely. "I'm certainly surprised to see you in *my* office. What can I do for you?"

Hardy grunted and sat down; then he barked: "Where were you last night, Emmerich?"

The lawyer, though not taken entirely by surprise, as he'd expected an inquiry, felt a marked inward shock but managed to control his face. Taking plenty of time about it, he settled his chair to suit him, sat down, crossed his legs, and puffed on his cigar.

"First," he said, "why do you want to know? Have you got some special reason for asking?"

"Naturally," snapped Hardy. "A man's been killed. He was working for you."

"I see," said Emmerich. "I presume you mean Brannom. I read it in the paper. Commissioner, if I could help you in any way, I'd be glad to answer your question. But I'm sorry to say I can't. Answering your question might embarrass me to some extent, so . . ."

Hardy rubbed his sharp chin and stared at Emmerich with open dislike. The big phony! The windbag! An educated man who used his brains to circumvent the law. The most noxious type of human being. No excuse for him.

"Oh, you'll answer my question all right, Emmerich," he said. "I've already talked to your servant Evans—and to your wife. Where were you last night?"

Emmerich puffed on his cigar and smiled slightly.

"On advice of counsel," he said, "I've decided to answer. I know I can trust your discretion, Commissioner—though I still find myself a little embarrassed. I was at home till after eleven. Brannom was with me. We were trying to figure out a way to make my debtors pay up. I happen to need a little cash at the moment. I drove Brannom home and left him there. That must have been about eleven thirty."

Hardy waited for Emmerich to go on, but as he showed no signs of it he barked: "Then what? You went back home, I suppose."

"Commissioner," said Emmerich, "you've already told

me that you talked to my wife. She knows I didn't get home till nearly two.''

"Well?''

Emmerich sighed and sadly lowered his eyes.

"Commissioner, as a man in his fifties I hate to make this admission, but a very beautiful red-haired girl happens to be living at my cottage on the river. I went to see her last night after I left Brannom, and I stayed later than I intended. She will confirm this, I think.''

Hardy was staring at the lawyer now with contempt. True to form, this big fourflusher! Leaving his wife alone and fooling around with some little tart young enough to be his granddaughter!

"Perfect alibi, eh?''

Emmerich laughed deprecatingly.

"The truth is always the perfect alibi.''

Hardy jumped up and paced the floor for a moment. His overcoat collar was turned up and he was wearing his old-fashioned rubbers. His spectacles cast back the sunlight as he moved about, and Emmerich, sitting comfortably with his legs crossed, smoking his cigar, thought that he looked like a jittery, overworked corn-country college professor.

"How long has Brannom been working for you?'' asked Hardy at last.

"Few weeks—and being no help, I might add. Would you like a list of my debtors? Maybe it would shame them if you turned up.''

"We know all about your debtors. We went through Brannom's files. He collected three thousand dollars.''

"That's the first I heard of it,'' said Emmerich.

"Well . . . deal with gyps and that's what you get.''

Hardy rubbed his chin, paused thoughtfully; then, abruptly turning, he walked across the big office and went out, calling over his shoulder: "I may want to talk to you again.''

"Any time, Commissioner.''

The door closed softly. After a moment Emmerich rose, went to the window, and stood looking out. His office was on the sixth floor of the Enright Building, and the whole downtown area was spread out before him. It was a fine fall day. The sun was shining brightly but there was a nip in the air. A brisk wind was blowing across the city, and Emmerich could see the flag on the new Post Office Building standing straight out from the tall pole, which was swaying slightly. Traffic was jammed below him as usual, and frantic horns were blasting.

He was surprised how calm he felt. You could only die once, the boys said. But it wasn't true. He could prove it.

· 26 ·

Eddie Donato brought their lunch up to them. He was a short, stocky, dark Sicilian with kinky hair and a mouthful of beautiful white teeth.

"You like spaghetti?" he enquired. "I make it very good. Nice meat sauce. You like?"

"Sure," said Dix. "Put it down. Thanks."

Riemenschneider's stomach was rumbling with hunger, and he pulled up a chair at once.

"Real spaghetti—great," he said. "I ate it by the yard in Naples."

"Naples!" cried Eddie, contemptuously. "They do not know how to make spaghetti in Napoli. They don't know nothing in Napoli. A lousy place!"

"I didn't find it so," said the little doctor mildly as he wound up the spaghetti on a tablespoon, Italian style. "I enjoyed myself there."

"Sure, a foreigner . . . you enjoy yourself there. The Neapolitans—all broke. You can buy what you please. Even girls."

"You're right, my friend," said Riemenschneider.

"Say," Dix broke in, "what size shirt you wear?"

"Me? I wear a fifteen. But I buy a sixteen and a half

because I like lots of room. Same with underwear and pajamas. I always wear pajamas. In the old country, people sleep in underwear—a very dirty habit.''

"How about me buying a couple of shirts from you?"

"Sure, sure!" said Eddie. "What color you like? I got pink, yellow, salmon—very pretty, light blue, purple . . .''

"How about brown or white?"

Eddie shook his head.

"That is no color—brown, white.''

"Okay," said Dix, impatiently. "Anything you like.''

When Eddie had gone, Dix sat down and began to struggle with the spaghetti.

"Goddamn it!" he said finally, dropping spaghetti on his shirt, "I wish I had a T-bone steak.''

· 27 ·

Doll sat on the edge of a lower bunk watching the futile riot with detachment. Females of all shapes and sizes, but most of them fairly young and half a dozen of them punk kids, were milling hysterically around the jammed women's tank, screaming insults, rattling the steel doors, and beating on the bars with tin cups. Violent waves of sound, wild and ear-splitting, rose and fell, echoing harshly along the steel-and-cement corridors of the old prison.

A fat woman with tousled, orange-colored hair and wearing a badly torn pale-blue evening dress, stopped screaming for a moment to stare at Doll.

"Come on, sister," she said belligerently. "Give!"

"Sore throat," said Doll, tapping her neck, wanting no argument.

"Oh, a sissy-pants, eh?" cried the woman. "Come on, I said, give!"

"No kidding," said Doll mildly, "I got a bad throat. Strep, I guess.''

The woman, who was still a little drunk, regarded Doll steadily for a moment, anger and resentment showing in her fat face; but something about Doll's attitude convinced her, and she came over and sat down beside Doll on the ramshackle bunk, which creaked under her weight.

"Hell, ain't it?" said the fat woman. "Here it is two in the afternoon, and we're still in. Should have been out at dawn."

"They'll let us out when they're good and ready," said Doll. "The way the prowls were going last night, every station in town must be full."

"It's that goddamned Commissioner!" said the fat woman. "I seen a picture of him in the paper, and he looks like an old billy goat, only he ain't got any beard! Why can't he let us alone? We got to eat, don't we? What's his beef—that's what I'd like to know. Just because he's all for morality and stuff like that, that don't change the world, does it?"

The riot suddenly died down to a whisper, and both Doll and the fat woman stood up to see what was happening. A turnkey and a couple of women cops had just appeared in the corridor, dragging a fire hose. The turnkey, a mild-looking little man with iron-gray hair, pointed the nozzle at the tank and cried: "You dames want a good sousing? Or are you gonna shut up?"

"We want out," yelled a big, strapping girl with bushy black hair. "What's the idea keeping us here?"

There were shouts of derision and defiance.

"Shut up!" said the turnkey. "Now listen. I'm not going to warn you again. One more outbreak, and I turn this hose on. Then you'll all be a lot cleaner than you've ever been in your life before!"

The big girl with the bushy hair stepped to the bars and in well-chosen language delivered an eloquent speech dealing at some length with the turnkey, his antecedents, and his probable descendants. The other women listened in silence, giggling from time to time.

But the turnkey seemed unmoved. He stood looking at

the girl with patient boredom, and when she had finished, he turned and left the corridor, followed by the two women cops, whose faces showed nothing.

The big girl tried to start the riot going again, but the other women had had enough. They were tired and discouraged and longing for the comforts of bed after such a wild and sleepless night.

The fat woman with the orange hair went over to talk to the big girl, who stood leaning against the bars, looking out into the corridor, her face twisted with anger and frustration.

"I'd like to get my hands on that little bastard," she said to the fat woman. "I'd pull his hair out, one hair at a time."

"Sure, sure, honey," said the fat woman. "I know just how you feel. Say—baby, who you working for?"

"I'm in that clip on Baxter Street."

"The Bandwagon? Listen, you got too much class and stuff for a joint like that."

"It's a beehive, all right. But I'm a stranger here. Just got in last month."

"I'm Belle Anderson," said the fat woman, and the girl's handsome face showed a flash of interest. "You come and see me. It's a dirty shame a kid like you in the Bandwagon— that cheap dive! Come see me now—mind!"

"I sure will, Miss Anderson," said the girl, her whole attitude changing and an ingratiating smile playing about her pretty mouth.

Doll paid no attention to what was going on around her. She sat staring at the dirty cement floor, worrying about the future, which looked hopeless. Why keep on? She'd even lost track of Dix. She'd called him half a dozen times, and once she'd even gone back to his apartment looking for him. Last night, in fact. Nobody knew where he was. He'd just disappeared. The landlady told her his rent for the month was paid up, so she expected him back. But that meant nothing. He'd probably been on the lam since that night when he'd roughly pushed her out the door and slammed it in her face.

Doll had a sudden and violent desire to burst into tears

and ease the pressure of her emotions, but she did not want
to be pitied by this crew of harpies. Lighting a cigarette,
she rose and began to pace up and down in front of the
bunk. Talk buzzed all about her, but she didn't hear a word
that was being said.

· 28 ·

Emmerich was eating his lunch in a little bar-restaurant in
the alley back of the Enright Building. It was a hangout for
downtown business and professional men, and besides there
was usually a sprinkling of horsemen from the Rivermount
Race Track, which was just concluding its fall meet, also
a few big bookies and newspapermen.

Emmerich was sitting with Ben Craven, a rather shady
young lawyer who'd built up quite a practice representing
bookies and other borderline chiselers since World War II,
and Lou Farbstein, Old Man Gresham's pet on the *World*.

Like everybody else in town, they were talking about the
million-dollar robbery of Pelletier and Company.

"The Commissioner'll bust it wide open before the week's
out," said Farbstein. "He's got everybody scared to death
in the Department. They produce on this one, or else! He's
in personal charge and never sleeps, and hardly eats."

"Well, well!" exclaimed Craven, staring at Farbstein.
"A new note from the *World*. You boys been lambasting
the Police Department for ten years."

"Who hasn't? And why not? But we're getting results at
last. Old fuzztop has put a bomb under them."

"Bombs sometimes don't go off," said Emmerich easily,
relishing his thick slab of Kansas City roast beef and his
imported Pilsner.

"He's planting them every place," Farbstein went on.
"Not only under the Department. Wait till you see the first

edition of the *World* this afternoon." A sudden thought struck him, and he glanced at his watch, then called a waiter over. "Will you see if the *World*'s on the street yet—get me one?"

"I think it was an out-of-town job," said Craven. "And the boys who pulled it off are probably in California by now, buying one of the movie studios."

"A million bucks!" mused Farbstein. "Twenty years ago nobody would have believed it. Now it doesn't seem like so much."

"It's not," said Craven, "minus taxes and so forth. Only these boys are in the right business. No taxes."

"I'd still rather be a newspaperman," said Farbstein. "I got ulcers as it is," he added, looking dubiously down at his meager, unappetizing lunch, then over at Emmerich's roast beef and Craven's thick steak and French fries. "It's not so much what you acquire as what you keep, I always say. All is not gold that glitters; and an honest man is the noblest work of God, I keep telling myself, even when my wife wonders what she's going to wear to the employees' dance. It's a mad world, my masters. And I'm the maddest of the lot—sore, I mean. Look at me. Poor but honest, but with ulcers. Look at my boss, Old Man Gresham. He's got a hundred and fifty million bucks—but can he enjoy it? The answer is—yes. He eats like a pig, drinks like a Congressman, and will probably live to be ninety. You know—sometimes I wonder about them copybook maxims."

Emmerich and Craven both burst out laughing. What a character, this Farbstein! He could go on like that for hours and never repeat himself. And yet there was something sad about him, too, as if long ago he'd discovered the limitations of cleverness, but, having no other approach, persisted in it, like a man butting his head against a stone wall. His sharp tongue had earned him many enemies; and his brilliance, many ill-wishers. His lack of success, however, when so much had been expected of him, lost him no friends. Those he had, swore by him. Emmerich was one of them.

He could always go to the lawyer for a small loan without feeling humiliated. There was a certain largeness about Emmerich, and money seemed to mean nothing to him.

"You know," Farbstein went on, "I'd go Communist if it wasn't for my wife. She said to me: 'Why divide up all the money? That would only mean about $4.65 apiece— and we're doing better than that.' Never underrate the power of a woman. They have a logic of their own, which only God can understand!"

The waiter interrupted Farbstein's flow of talk by thrusting a newspaper under his nose. The waiter did not like Farbstein, thought he was a smart aleck. Even if he was a regular customer, to hell with him! Talk, talk, talk!

Farbstein fumbled in his vest pockets for a coin, then said: "Put it on my tab."

Emmerich noticed the waiter's belligerent attitude and interposed: "All on one check when we're through. Paper and all." He handed the waiter a dollar. "There's for your trouble."

"Insolent bastard!" said Farbstein, as the waiter left, and he began to unfold the newspaper. "I don't know what the world's coming to. This lower-class snobbery will undo us yet. Why can't they realize we're human beings like themselves? I suppose, as the new aristocracy, they can't help feeling superior to us, but must they show it so plainly?"

He had the paper unfolded now and passed it across the table for Emmerich and Craven to look at.

Craven merely stared with mild interest, but Emmerich started in spite of himself, then to cover it, took a long pull from his glass of beer.

On the front page was a two-column picture of Erwin Riemenschneider under the caption: Have You Seen This Man?

The story read in part:

. . . Erwin Riemenschneider, arch international criminal, was released from the State Penitentiary on October 15th, and hasn't been seen since. He is wanted for questioning in the sensational million-dollar looting of Pelletier and Company. . . .

. . . if you know this man's whereabouts, or have seen him, communicate at once with Commissioner Theodore J. Hardy, or call your local Precinct Captain. . . .

Emmerich had composed himself now. Looking up from the paper, he spoke indifferently.

"Well?"

"It's a bomb," said Farbstein. "Did you read about the reward? Ten thousand iron men. I'd turn my youngest daughter in for that—except I'm too public-spirited. She'd drive poor old Hardy to drink with her questions. Like . . . why do rabbits have white tails? Can you answer that one?"

"This is a good idea," said Craven.

"Sure," said Farbstein. "And every paper in the city is collaborating. The heat is really on for the little doctor."

"Except he's probably blown already," said Craven. "Or maybe he never was in town."

"One gets you five with Hardy! And the old boy knows his criminals."

Just as Emmerich was paying the check, a bus boy began to page him. Emmerich was wanted on the phone, and he followed the bus boy to a private booth in the back reserved for regular customers only.

An unfamiliar, agitated woman's voice began to shout incoherently at him.

"Wait! Wait!" cried Emmerich. "Take it slow."

"It's Mrs. Cully," the woman cried. "He said I was to call you. I been trying to get you all over town—your home, every place. They arrested my husband." Mrs. Cully now burst into tears and sobbed loudly into the phone. "What has he done, for God's sake, Mr. Emmerich? He's a good man—fine to me, wouldn't hurt nobody if he could help it. You got to get him out, Mr. Emmerich. How can I live if you don't?"

"Okay, okay!" said Emmerich, trying to resist the chill he felt settling over him. "Now take it easy. What happened?"

"They arrested him, that's what happened. I just told you they . . ."

"Who arrested him?"

"The police. A horrible little man was with them. A lawyer or something."

"What was his name?"

"I think his name was . . . Harding."

· 29 ·

The night had come down so swiftly that the Commissioner hadn't turned on the lights in his office yet. He sat in the semi-darkness, his face dimly lit by the glow from the street outside, idly patting his palms together lost in thought. In a few moments his secretary, a uniformed policeman, came in, switched on the lights, and stood waiting.

After a moment, Hardy looked up.

"Well?"

"Mr. Emmerich, sir."

Hardy nodded curtly. In a moment Emmerich came in. He was impressively dressed in a well-cut, double-breasted blue-serge suit, a black Homburg, and black shoes. He had apparently just come from a barber shop, and diffused through Hardy's musty office an odor of bay rum and talcum powder.

"Well, Emmerich . . . ?" snapped Hardy.

"I have a little document here I thought might interest you."

"Yes? What?"

"It's a writ of habeas corpus."

"For Cully, I presume?"

"That's right."

"Who issued it?"

"Judge Dickerson."

Hardy gritted his teeth and swung around sideways on his swivel chair. High and low there were these chiselers, these no-goods . . . from the lowliest harness bulls to the city bench. Thank God there were some honest men too!

He turned back to Emmerich.

"I don't suppose," he said, "that you'd be public-spirited enough to hold off for twenty-four hours with that writ?"

Emmerich laughed.

"Charge him, Hardy—or turn him loose."

"I suppose you know that he approached an agent of the Colonial Insurance Company in regard to . . ."

"That's the agent's story. No corroboration! I feel that you are persecuting my client, Hardy. Everybody's a little hysterical right now about this robbery."

"All right," said Hardy, turning his back on Emmerich. "I'll turn him loose."

Emmerich tossed the writ onto Hardy's desk and went out.

A few hours later Cully and his wife took the night train for Chicago. They had decided, they told relatives and friends, that Cully had been working too hard and needed a rest.

· 30 ·

The Cully business was a triumph for Emmerich, but an empty one. Needing money, he had gambled, not only with his reputation, such as it was, not only with his future, which was problematical anyway, but with his life; and while he'd preserved all three, at least for the time being, he hadn't gained a penny by his desperate shifts and turns. Financially he was right where he'd started.

Worse still, the insurance company's denunciation of Cully had ruined Emmerich's only chance of a profitable disposal of the stolen jewelry. No use to worry any further about it.

Riemenschneider and his big bodyguard could take what action they liked. It was every man for himself now.

After some thought Emmerich had decided to act sensibly and in a conventional manner for once and take advice—expert and respectable advice. All day long the shrewd little lawyer and C.P.A. Angus McDonald had been studying his books. Emmerich knew that McDonald was honest, reliable, and discreet; and he would have consulted him before if it hadn't been for the humiliation involved. For years Emmerich had lived on a tremendous scale—fortunes had rolled in and rolled out, but there had always been plenty. Then . . . trouble! First, he'd got behind on his income-tax payments; then, money had got tight, and he'd found it harder and harder to collect what was owed him; then, he'd gone wild beyond all reason over a worthless young red-haired girl, and to impress her he had thrown money about like an Indian maharaja! All the same he felt that it was a terrible come-down to be forced to call in a penny-pinching, ledger-banging little character to save him from ruin.

They sat in the study, talking. McDonald wasn't at all perturbed about the situation.

"You should have come to me sooner, Mr. Emmerich," he said. "But even so . . . in a month or two I'll have you on the right road; then it's up to you. By mortgages alone I think we can raise close to a hundred thousand dollars. Fifty of this we'll give to the government, and that will keep them quiet for a long time." Emmerich groaned but made no comment; so McDonald went on: "I suggest you sell that place on the river. Values are way up in that district now; if you're lucky, you may get close to eighty-five thousand dollars for that place furnished. I'll consult a couple of real-estate brokers I know. You are carrying far too much insurance—and it's too scattered. Some of it we'll cash in. The rest can be amalgamated into one policy, with retirement features, which you've neglected entirely. As for the money that's owed you, the process may be a slow one, but we'll eventually collect enough of it to represent quite an item . . . ."

In spite of the fact that Emmerich kept telling himself that this was all futile and that his time was short, he felt heartened. Besides, no matter what happened to him now, May would be looked after. McDonald, a rigidly honest little man, would see to that.

In a short while, his business at an end, McDonald rose to leave—he was no man for casual conversation. Emmerich went to the door with him and shook hands. McDonald's hand was hardly bigger than a child's, and cold and dry to the touch.

"Like shaking hands with a lizard," Emmerich told himself as he climbed the stairs to his wife's bedroom.

She looked up with a smile when he entered, and waved at him lightheartedly. She not only had the cards ready on the bed, but she had put on a new bed jacket, a very pretty one of padded pink silk.

They played in silence for a long while, both of them a little shy and self-conscious at this unaccustomed intimacy. Then, remembering, out of what seemed like a terribly remote past, how she loved to win at any card game, he began to cheat in her favor.

In a little while she was laughing triumphantly.

"As a lawyer you may be very brilliant, Lon," she crowed. "But as a cassino-player you have a lot to learn."

Emmerich found himself whistling an old tune.

"Mind if I smoke?" he asked.

"Of course not, Lon. Oh, Lon! How could you make such a play as that? You won't get a single point this hand."

·31·

Dix sat looking out the window, his jaw grimly set, but saying nothing. Behind him the little doctor paced slowly up and down.

They were living very close to the river now, and all night

long they could hear the tugs moaning as they slid down-
stream pulling the big coal barges; and sometimes, when it
was exceptionally quiet, they could hear the waves, stirred
by the passage of the heavy-laden barges, washing and slapping against the old wharves at the foot of Front Street.
Through their one window they could see the Lackawanna
Street Bridge arching off toward the tall buildings of the
downtown area across the river. In the daytime the bridge
was huge, gray, and misty-looking; at night it was nothing
but a long, brilliant garland of yellow lights, duplicated
upside down in the black water.

Dix sat staring off at the distant lights of the Metropolitan
area strung endlessly along the east bank of the river. He
felt tense and irritable, and from time to time his wounded
side throbbed dully.

"If he don't produce in a day or so," snapped Dix, "I'm
for knocking him off. He's a no-good rat."

"How can he produce now?" Riemenschneider demanded mildly. "The town is as hot as a blast furnace.
Running that picture of mine in the papers did it. Somebody
in the Police Department has got brains."

"That's neither here nor there, Doc. That big phony got
us in all this trouble trying to gyp us. I say he ought to be
settled."

The little doctor sighed.

"Dix, I agree with you—he ought to be settled," he
said patiently. "But that's not our problem. It would be
a senseless thing to do now. Let's worry about us—not
him."

Dix grunted irritably and subsided.

Riemenschneider sighed again and, turning, began to pace
the floor slowly, his hands behind his back, his chin on his
chest. Dix stared out the window. A dimly lighted tug moved
laboriously upstream, leaving a widely fanned out wake that
rippled slowly toward shore, showing an oily sheen as it
moved through the lights reflected from the bridge.

"This is no good," said the German, turning suddenly.

"We're like rats in a trap. We can't afford to wait around any longer."

"What about Emmerich?" Dix persisted.

"Damn Emmerich! How much money have you got, Dix?"

"Plenty," said Dix. "Nearly five grand. What Cobby gave me before the job."

"It begins to look like we'd better give up as far as this town's concerned," said Riemenschneider. "Dix, let's go to New York. Maybe we can find some way to market the stuff there."

"No, Doc. I'm hitting south," said Dix. "I been telling you."

"Listen, Dix. You can always go home. And when you do, it's nothing. Believe me. I've done it. Nothing."

"I got a different idea about it."

"All right. But wouldn't you like to go home rich? So we have to take a big loss on this stuff! We're a certainty to get two hundred thousand dollars."

"I'll settle for the five grand more I got coming. The hell with percentage. Too tough."

The little doctor sighed and turned away. Dix raised his head and sat looking up at the sky, which was patterned with faintly glimmering stars. A meteor streaked down toward the tall buildings, then suddenly went out like a spent burst from a Roman candle. Shooting star! It reminded him of home and long summer nights ages ago. His resentment against Emmerich left him, and he sat thinking about the past, forgetful for a moment of the menacing present.

"Dix," said the German, breaking into his dreams, "if you won't go with me, will you finance me? I haven't got but four or five dollars."

"Sure," said Dix readily. "I'll finance you. But I got to keep some of this roll. I may need it."

"I can get along on a thousand dollars, thanks very much, and you can take your pick of the best stones. Say maybe fifty thousand dollars worth or so."

"What would I do with them, for Christ's sake? Can you

see me walking into a hock shop with stuff like that? First, they'd think it was phony. Then, they'd yell for the riot squad. No, Doc. You can have a grand, all right. But no rocks for me.''

There was a brief silence; then Dix turned his chair around and stared across the dimly lit room at Riemenschneider.

''And getting out of this place is not going to be any cinch for you, Doc.''

''Oh, I'll get out all right. I'll take a taxi and give the driver an address out at the edge of town; and when I get there, I'll have him drive me on to Cleveland.''

''Might work, except there's ten thousand out for you, Doc; and that's a lot of moo to a taxi-driver.''

They heard a sudden step in the hall, and Dix jumped up quickly, jerked his gun, and stood waiting.

Somebody scratched on the door, and Eddie's voice called softly: ''It's me.''

Dix put away his gun and opened the door. The little Sicilian stepped in quickly as if pursued, and glanced over his shoulder into the dingy, dark hallway as Dix closed the door behind him.

''They pulled Gus in again, my friends,'' he said, his voice uncertain with anxiety. ''I just talked to Mike Miklos. About his car . . . I don't exactly know what. I mean, Gus, he told the coppers the night of the dragnet he hadn't been no place; and some cop, he say the hood of his car was hot from driving. Anyway, they pulled him in.'' Now he looked toward Dix, and his eyeballs were china-white in the half darkness. ''Mike Miklos, he say to tell you the coppers give your apartment a working over, that's all he knows. Just a working over.''

Riemenschneider whistled softly to himself, and Dix stood thoughtfully rubbing his chin.

Now Eddie began to plead with them, tears in his voice.

''Look, my friends. Please. I'm a respectable man. I run nice little grocery. For Gus I do a favor all right! But, please . . . since this picture's in the paper, I can't wait on people or even sleep. I got fifteen-year-old boy working for me—very bright. He say who is living upstairs. How does he know!"

"You mean you want us to blow? Is that right, Eddie?" asked Dix.

Eddie shrank back from the big Southerner, but continued to plead.

"Please! I do all I can. For Gus I'm willing to do a favor. But how can I get mixed up in a thing like this—for a million dollars? I can't live . . . my friends! I can't live!"

Dix shut him off.

"Okay, Eddie." Then he turned to Riemenschneider. "This spot's no good now, and the sooner we blow, the better. Our friend Eddie's getting to the place where he'd talk with a little encouragement."

"Oh, my God, no!" cried Eddie. "I no talk. Gus cut my belly open." He looked wildly from Dix to the German; then he edged toward the door. "I go now, my friends. I'm sorry to bring you this bad news but . . ."

"You sit down," Dix broke in coldly. "You're not going any place till I say so."

Eddie stared at Dix in horror; then he made a quick dart for the door, but Dix grabbed him by the back of his shirt and heaved him across the room and onto the bed.

"Stay put, Eddie," he said. "Nobody's going to hurt you if you sit still and keep your mouth shut."

There was a long silence, broken only by Eddie's heavy breathing and his loud sighs demanding sympathy. Finally, Dix said: "This is your chance to blow, Doc—like you said. Maybe it's a good idea." Dix pulled out a roll, hurriedly counted off some bills, and handed them to the little doctor, who took them with a quick smile of gratitude.

"Thank you, Dix," he said. "But what about you?"

"I'll be okay," said Dix. Yesterday, while looking through his coat pockets for matches, he'd run across the card Doll had left for him with her address and phone number penciled on it. He'd put it carefully away in his wallet, just in case. "Come on. Let's get out of here."

Eddie watched them warily, cold with fear. Bad boys,

these fellows—like Gus, only worse; because, after all, Gus was an Italian, and how could you be as scared of another Italian as you were of this big, rough, farmer sort of guy? The little one was not so bad; only he looked at you funny through those thick glasses, like a fish in an aquarium!

Dix turned to him.

"Eddie," he said, "if you're a smart boy, you'll forget you ever seen us."

Eddie got up and gave a little bow, still not sure of Dix's intentions.

"I say nothing to nobody—don't you worry about that, mister."

Dix and the little doctor left without speaking again, closing the door softly behind them. Eddie hurried over on tiptoe and stood with his ear pressed to the door, listening to them descend; then he heaved a long sigh of relief as it gradually dawned on him that in spite of all his nerve-racking fears, he was safe.

There were very few people abroad in the Guerand Square district, and Dix and the little doctor made their way leisurely toward the Old Market, moving through narrow, dingy, ill-lit streets that climbed steeply from the river, leveled off, then climbed again. They passed hole-in-the-wall bars, Chinese laundries, poolrooms with a few loafers in front, battered diners on vacant lots, popcorn stands, hamburger joints, and dirty-looking, half-dark night clubs, from which came honky-tonk swing and loud laughter.

At the second level of Guerand Street, high above the river, they turned up Hollister Alley, actually a small winding, side street, where the poor Negroes lived. The one-story frame houses were old and unpainted, and leaned as if about to fall over. The window blinds were crooked and torn, the porches sagging. Somewhere an out-of-key piano was playing, and they heard Negro laughter. Through one window they could see a coal-oil lamp faintly lighting up a poverty-stricken interior, and beside it an old Negress with kinky, gray hair was bending over her sewing.

Beyond Hollister Alley they came to Parkway, a wide boulevard and through street, which they crossed cautiously. Traffic was heavy here, and there was always the chance of running into a prowl car or a harness bull. But they passed it safely, jay-walking, avoiding the intersection; and, ducking a few late private cars, the drivers of which yelled curses at them, they made the river entrance of the Old Market in safety and started through.

Years ago this had been the busiest place in the district; but, owing to its age, it had been condemned, and was now abandoned to the rats that swarmed through it. A huge, ponderous, arcade-like structure, it stretched for nearly three blocks, and was now partially open to the weather, as its big wooden doors and stall windows had been stolen for firewood by the Negroes of Hollister Alley.

A faint glow from the street lights outside showed in the arched, stall windows, but the corridor of the Old Market was as dark as the inside of a well.

Dix and the little doctor picked their way toward the Camden side in silence, aiding each other from time to time. The floor was littered with old newspapers, through which they could hear the rats scuttering as they approached. A tug moaned on the river, the sound echoing hollowly through the big, empty building.

Riemenschneider had decided that it would be wiser and safer to pick up a taxi on Camden West, which, though a through street, was narrow and dark, rather than risk detection on the spacious and brightly lighted Parkway.

They were ten or twelve feet from the Camden entrance when the beam of a torch sprang suddenly out of the darkness and fixed them in a circle of light. They both froze, turned.

"Where you guys think you're going?" a voice demanded out of the blackness beyond the torch—a gruff, authoritative voice, obviously that of a cop.

"We're on our way home," said Dix. "We always use the Old Market."

"Why?"

"Short cut. Besides, we don't have to dodge taxis, and when it rains we don't get wet."

"Where do you live?"

"South on Camden."

"Well . . ." drawled the cop, "you guys got no business in here—city property. You know that, don't you? Signs all over the front."

"Everybody uses it," said Dix mildly.

"You're telling me," said the cop. "Bunch of hoodlums been bringing young girls in here. Gang stuff!"

"Is that a fact?" asked the little doctor, interested at once.

"Yeah," said the cop. "It's already cost one of us boys his job on account of the beefs. If I was you guys I'd stay out of here, understand? It ain't healthy."

"Okay, officer," said Dix.

"All these young hoodlums!" said the cop, snorting his disapproval. "I don't know what this town's coming to."

He moved the torch beam from the little doctor to Dix and back again, then switched it off. They started for the door. Suddenly the torch was switched on again and played over the little doctor.

"Wait a minute!" cried the cop. "It seems to me . . ." He broke off momentarily, trying to remember something; then he said: "Come outside with me."

Dix heard the creak of holster leather and immediately leaped at the cop, straight down the beam from the torch. There was a violent shock of bodies, and the torch fell from the cop's hand, and one of them stepped on it, switching off the beam. Missing the gun hand with his first grab, Dix struck out blindly and landed two hard punches that thudded into the cop's stomach. But the gun swung down out of the darkness and clipped Dix a glancing blow on the side of the head, tearing his ear and making him cry out in pain as he lunged forward, swinging punches with his right and trying to grab the gun with his left.

Hearing Dix's cry of pain, the little doctor, grimacing with repugnance, jumped into the struggle just in time to

be struck by the second descent of the gun. He stumbled, staggered about, then fell headlong into a pile of
debris.

The struggle continued in the darkness, Dix and the
cop wrestling each other about, trying to get in the final
blow, grunting, cursing, groping for each other's throats.
But at last Dix landed a crippling blow into the cop's groin,
and as he sagged, Dix jerked the gun from his hand and
belted him with it. The cop fell groaning with a loud clatter. Dix tossed the gun away, then turned to find Riemenschneider.

Groping about, he stepped on the torch, picked it up,
switched it on, then ran its beam over the floor till he saw
the little doctor, lying full length, stirring weakly in a pile
of old newspapers.

Dix went over to him and jerked him roughly to his feet,
paying no attention to his groans of protest; then he switched
off the torch and threw it away from him.

"Come on, Doc," said Dix. "We better blow fast. Got
the stuff?"

Riemenschneider muttered unintelligibly, still groggy
and in great pain. Swearing impatiently, Dix frisked him
and found that he was still clutching the bag in his right
hand.

With Riemenschneider walking like a drunken man and
Dix steadying him, they emerged into Camden West.

Still supporting the little doctor, Dix found Doll's door
at the end of the dirty, half-dark hallway and knocked per-
emptorily. There was no answer. They waited for what
seemed like hours to both of them, knocking on the door
from time to time. There wasn't a sound inside.

"We got to get in there, Doc," said Dix. "Or we're
cooked."

Dix looked up and down the hallway cautiously; then,
satisfied that he was unobserved, he was just getting ready
to kick the door open when they heard a stirring inside. A

bed creaked, feet shuffled aimlessly across the floor, and a
hand fumbled with the lock. Finally the door was opened
a few inches.

Doll, with her coarse, multi-colored hair on end, stared
at them in an uncomprehending daze.

Dix pushed her roughly out of the way and, dragging the
little doctor inside, closed the door quickly.

Riemenschneider fell down into a chair, gasping, and,
taking off his hat, put his head in his hands and sat in a
stupor. Doll saw the blood dripping through his fingers and
shrank back; then she turned to look at Dix.

The big Southerner had sat down heavily on the edge of
the bed, and now, bending over and grasping his left side,
he was slowly wagging his head and gritting his teeth. As
he leaned over further his hat fell off and Doll saw his
bloody ear.

"Dix!" she cried as if waking out of a dream. "Honey!"
You got to excuse me, I . . ."

"Get some cold water and some towels, and don't stand
there yapping!" cried Dix.

"Sure, sure!" said Doll, her face brightening. "Dix . . .
honey, I took two sleeping-tablets. So I . . . I'm kind of
groggy. I haven't been able to sleep lately, worrying about
you and everything . . ."

"Okay, okay!" cried Dix. "For Christ's sake, will you
move?"

"You bet, honey! You bet!"

Doll ran for the bathroom, stumbling in her haste. This
was too good to be true; too good to believe. Just when she
needed him most—here was Dix!

A short while later the little doctor was lying on the bed
with his head wrapped in a cold towel. He looked very pale
and shaken, but he was able to smile now.

Doll did not like his looks and kept glancing at him with
distrust, hoping to get rid of him as soon as possible. Dix,
who had washed his wound and put a clean bandage on it,
and had also doctored his torn ear with iodine, and was now

feeling much better, sat on the edge of the bed, talking to Riemenschneider.

"Doc," he was saying, "soon as you feel like it, you've got to blow. That copper's got you pegged. All those damn pictures in the paper!"

Doll stared at the little doctor now as if seeing him for the first time, and her mouth dropped open and she gave a sudden start of recognition. "Arch international criminal; maybe the mastermind of a huge ring of jewel thieves," it had said in the yellow tabloid she read every night. In a way she was impressed; and yet the skimpy, fat little thing with the probing, wicked eyes didn't look like very much to her lying there in pain on her rumpled bed. Mastermind, eh? Compared with Dix he didn't exist!

"Can't persuade you to come along, I don't suppose," said the little doctor, sighing resignedly as if positive what Dix's answer would be.

"I'm going home," said Dix. "I told you ten times. But you'll be okay, Doc, if you move tonight."

Doll put her hand on Dix's arm.

"You really mean that, Dix? You're leaving?"

"Yeah," said Dix. "As soon as I can beg, borrow, or steal a car."

"But why, honey?"

Dix grimaced and said nothing. Riemenschneider looked from Dix to Doll, then shrugged slightly. An involvement— something he detested!

All of Doll's agitation had returned. Now that they were together again, she couldn't bear the thought of a separation.

"But you can't leave for quite a while yet, Dix," she said. "You're hurt. You need somebody to look after you."

"Stop yapping," said Dix, "and mind your own business! The little doc, here, is in real trouble!"

"Oh, don't worry about me," said Riemenschneider, smirking a little.

The Commissioner was sitting low in his swivel chair, his overcoat turned up to his ears, drinking coffee out of a paper carton. The heat was turned off in the Old City Building, a draft was blowing along the floor, and it was freezing cold. Several police officers and half a dozen detectives were lounging about his desk, smoking and drinking coffee.

"What about Gus Minisi?" snapped Hardy.

"Can't get nothing out of him, sir," said Andrews, a young homicide dick. "He's still locked up. Don't even yell for a lawyer."

"Ever get a line on that fellow—what's his name? The one we wanted for the club stick-ups."

"No, sir," said Andrews. "He just disappeared. He calls himself Handley. But the Camden boys frisked his apartment and found some old letters. Must have been his mother wrote them to him. His name is William Tuttle Jamieson. Quite a name for a cheap heister."

"Record?"

"Arrested in Youngstown as Handley and booked for assault with a deadly weapon. Beat the case. That was 1939. Arrested half a dozen times here for questioning. Couldn't pin anything on him. He was in the show-up once, about a year ago. No visible means of support. Benny the Fink told me one night he was a heister in town and was getting protected by Gus Minisi. We can't prove anything. He lives poor."

"How old would you say?"

"Middle forties, maybe. Though he don't look it."

"His record's longer than that, then."

"We sent his Youngstown prints on to the F.B.I. Nothing."

The Commissioner finished his coffee, grunted, then sat staring off across the room, lost in thought; finally he turned to Detective Sergeant Macklyn of Headquarters.

"Are you sure you sent your best men to keep that tail on Emmerich, Mac?"

"Yes, sir," said Macklyn. "Best men we got."

"I don't want him lost for a minute. He engineered this case if I know anything, and I'm going to prove it. What about Cully?"

"I got a telegram from the Chicago Chief of Police. They got a tail on him and they're going to keep it on."

The Commissioner nodded, then lit a cigar. He felt certain that he was gradually getting the pieces into his hands, but so far he hadn't the faintest idea how to fit them together. Well . . . it just had to be done, or good-bye, Administration! The impudent robbery of the biggest and oldest jewelry establishment in town had turned out to be the most sensational police case in twenty years. Murders didn't mean a thing any more—dime a dozen; people were fed up with them. But Pelletier's was an institution, and its looting gave people a feeling of insecurity. It also gave the newspapers, almost all hostile to the Administration, plenty of ammunition to fire at the city officials, from the Mayor down.

He turned suddenly to Andrews.

"This Brannom killing—pretty apropos, wasn't it?"

"That it was, sir. But Emmerich's alibi held. That red-haired girl's a silly little so-and-so, but . . . she gave it to me straight, and it would stand up in court." (And . . . "oh! what a dish!" Andrews was thinking; but you just didn't make observations like that around this hard-bitten, keen-eyed, puritanical Commissioner.)

The phone rang. Macklyn grabbed it up at once and answered it in a cold, offhand way; but at the first word from the other end his manner changed immediately and a broad pleasant grin showed on his tough cop's face.

"Macklyn. That's right. Tom Macklyn. Sure you remember me, ma'am." There was a brief pause as Macklyn listened, and Hardy sat eying him with open irritation. This was no time for irrelevant phone conversations. Macklyn laughed lightly. "Well, we do the best we can with him, ma'am. But he's a little hard to manage. Just a minute, ma'am." He turned and handed the receiver to the Commissioner. "It's Mrs. Hardy, sir."

Hardy jerked the receiver away from Macklyn with a brief show of childish petulance, and the men around him turned aside to hide their smiles.

"Now, listen, Martha . . ." Hardy began, and that was as far as he got.

"Theo Hardy," his wife broke in, "do you have any idea what time it is? And I'll bet you haven't had your dinner. Sitting around in that cold old barn of a place when you could just as well be sitting at home. There are such things as telephones, you know—you could handle your work from here! Besides, you don't have to run the Police Department singlehanded. After all, there is a Chief of Police, and . . ."

Hardy sat listening, his lips compressed into a thin, harsh line, and looking about him at the men in his office with his small, prying gray eyes, ready to detect and deal with any signs of amusement or levity. Finally he broke in: "Martha! I'm busy. Very important. I'll call you later. Or better still, go to bed. I'll be home when I can get there."

"Have you got your rubbers on?"

"Yes, yes!"

"And your overcoat?"

"I'm not in the habit of sitting in my office with my . . ." Hardy caught himself just in time and glanced down at his overcoat.

"Is the heat turned on?" his wife persisted.

"Yes," lied the Commissioner. "Of course it is."

"When you get home I want you to take a hot bath, rub some Mentholatum on your chest, and go right to bed. I'll fix some sandwiches and put them on your night table. You've got to take better care of yourself, Theo, and I'm going to pester you till you do. Understand? I don't care how much of a nuisance I make of myself; you're not going to work your way into an early grave . . ."

Hardy cleared his throat portentously and ran his eyes slowly over the men grouped near his desk. They were all looking at the floor, their faces blank.

". . . Edna and the baby are coming over to spend the week end," his wife was saying, "because Charles has to go to Cleveland on business. I certainly hope you get this case of yours settled by that time, because Edna was saying she never gets to talk to her father any more, and I'd think you would want to spend some time with your grandson."

"I *do* want to, Martha," said Hardy. "But you don't seem to understand what an important case this is. I can't just . . ."

"Plenty of important cases were handled by others before you were silly enough to give up your law practice to spend your days and nights at this thankless job; and there will be plenty more after we're all dead and gone. Don't forget the hot bath and the Mentholatum now, Theo. And good night . . . if I don't happen to wake up when you come home . . ."

A sudden warmth had come into his wife's voice now, and Hardy reacted to it by smiling in spite of himself. She'd be up waiting for him when he got home, no matter how late it was! An exceedingly irritating woman at times—but a damn fine one, nevertheless, and he was a very lucky man!

"Good night, Martha."

As he replaced the receiver he glanced up and found all the men smiling pleasantly at him. To them he had become for the moment just a human being like themselves, fallible, a little comic—a different person entirely from the harsh martinet they daily feared and obeyed. His face stiffened, and he turned away from them in his swivel chair and sat staring off across the dark, dingy office, pretending to be lost in thought but actually anticipating, with a good deal of pleasure, the hot bath, the late snack, the warm bed, and Martha's solicitude.

"She's a mighty nice woman—Mrs. Hardy," said Macklyn, bolder than the rest. "A mighty nice woman."

Hardy turned irritably and was about to hand Macklyn a stinging rebuke when the door opened and Hardy's secretary stepped in.

"Excuse me, Commissioner," he said, "but there's a taxi-driver out here who says he thinks he's got some important information. I tried to find out what . . ."

"Bring him in," cried Hardy impatiently.

The secretary went out hastily, and in a moment the door opened and a thin, spindly-looking man about forty entered the Commissioner's office. He was turning his battered and sweated taxi-driver's cap about idly in his hands and chewing on a frayed match. He recoiled slightly at the sight of all the big beefy policemen; then he recovered, but started again as his eyes met the Commissioner's harsh, unsympathetic gaze.

"What's this information you've got?" Hardy demanded, rising and standing behind his desk. "Something about the Pelletier case?"

"Yeah," said the taxi-driver; then he paused to get hold of himself. What's the idea—all these big meatheads staring at him like he'd come in to pick their pockets? He was only trying to do them a favor. Maybe he should have minded his own business, like his buddy had told him. "Don't meddle with them bastards," his buddy had said. "You'll just get yourself in a jam, Chuck. And if you're thinking about a reward, well . . . cops nab the rewards. You'll just get tossed out on your tail."

As the taxi-driver still stood tongue-tied, Hardy finally barked: "What's your name?"

"Charles Wright. Hackie number: 6456. Green Stripe Company."

"What's your information?"

"Well . . . Commissioner . . . You're him, ain't you?" Hardy nodded impatiently. "Well, I think that little doctor everybody's looking for . . . I think he was a fare . . ."

"You mean you drove him some place?"

"Well now . . . I wouldn't swear to it, but . . . you see, a few weeks ago I picked him up at the Lackawanna Bus Terminal—I think it was him, and . . ."

"Where did you take him?"

"Well, if it was him, you understand, I took him to a number on Camden West. I remember because I asked him if he wanted me to wait. The number was dark, see? And a guy can get his head knocked off on Camden West that time of night. I know a guy once, he got conked and a couple of young punks frisked him and he didn't have nothing so they stole his pants and shoes. . . ."

"Tom and Randy will be tickled to hear that," said Macklyn, but Hardy shut him up with a glance.

"Go ahead!" snapped Hardy.

"Well . . . he'd just got in, I guess, and he was carrying this keister, and he never said aye, yes, or no all time we was riding cross town. He was a kind of harmless-looking little bastard . . . excuse me, Commissioner . . . and I kind of felt guilty about leaving him at that dark number."

"Where did you take him—what number?"

"4717 Camden West—it was a kind of storeroom, dark . . ."

Hardy turned to Macklyn.

"Get Sergeant Dietrich. Right away. If he's in bed, roust him out."

"Yes, sir," said Macklyn; then he left at once.

Now the Commissioner reached into one of his desk drawers, took out half a dozen pictures, and spread them on the desk before the taxi-driver.

"Is that him?"

The taxi-driver's mouth dropped open; he stared, hesitated, then spoke with conviction: "That's him, Commissioner. Yeah. That's him, all right. But I just can't get over it. I was feeling maybe I was making a jerk out of myself coming down here. If that little man's an arch criminal—like it says in the papers—then I sure been going around in a fog all my life . . ."

"Yes, yes!" cried Hardy impatiently; then he turned to one of the harness bulls. "Take care of this man. Get all the details about him—everything." Then he turned to the driver. "Thank you for coming here, Mr. Wright. You are a public-spirited citizen, and I'm proud of you. Too bad there aren't more like you. You may be in for a reward. I hope so.''

The taxi-driver looked both bewildered and proud of himself. He expanded his puny chest and, grinning amiably, followed the big harness bull into the outer office. For the first time in his life he felt himself to be an important and looked-up-to member of society. Wait till he got hold of that buddy of his!

Macklyn came back into the Commissioner's office, showing some excitement.

"Did you find Dietrich?" Hardy demanded.

"Yes, sir. He'll be right over. And, Commissioner, I've got some good news. One of our patrolmen was on special duty at the Old Market. You know—about those rape cases . . ." Macklyn went on to explain what had happened, and Hardy's eyes began to flash with excitement.

"Good! Great!" he cried, interrupting Macklyn, who was getting a little wordy. "We'll block out the whole area—and no sirens! A sneak! Get busy, Mac."

Macklyn had a lot more to say, but, realizing suddenly that it was irrelevant, he turned and started out. Hardy called after him: "What about the patrolman—badly hurt?"

"Some nasty head wounds, they say, and he's kind of punchy; but the doc doesn't think he's got a fracture."

Macklyn went out. Hardy walked to the window and stood chewing on an unlighted cigar, looking out at the dark city. He had forgotten now about the hot bath, the warm bed, and the other comforts of pleasant domesticity.

The hunt was on!

· 33 ·

Cobby was playing poker in the middle cardroom when Timmons opened the door and motioned that he wanted to speak to him. Cobby was immediately worried, because Timmons never broke in on a big game unless there was something mighty important going on. Cobby felt his nerves beginning to jump. In fact they'd been jumping intermittently ever since the big deal blew up.

All the same, he had three jacks, which he was pretty sure was the winning hand, and he was anxious to play it out. He motioned for Timmons to wait. But Timmons shook his head warningly and showed some distress. Still Cobby couldn't give up. Turning to the players, he said: "Check!"

"It's not your bet, Cobby," cried one of the players. "What the Jesus kind of poker is this!"

"Okay, okay!" said the opener wearily. "Since it's all loused up now, I'll check."

Everybody checked, complaining, and the hands were laid down. Cobby ran third, much to his surprise; then he got up, laughing a little in spite of his apprehension. At least this interruption had saved him some money.

He left the cardroom, followed by sour looks. Timmons whispered in his ear: "Dietrich!"

"You mean they got the drag out again?"

"No," said Timmons. "That's what *I* thought. But he don't want me for nothing. He wants you. I put him in room one."

Cobby cleared his throat nervously, swallowed a couple of times; then, arranging his features into what he thought was a pleasant, easy smile, he opened the door of room one and went in. Big Dietrich looked up with a grin. He had a highball in front of him and he was smoking one of Cobby's best cigars. Cobby relaxed a little and sat down opposite the hulking Sergeant of Police.

"Crooked Ear fixed me up," said Dietrich. "I hope you don't mind, Cobby, my boy."

"No. Not at all, Monk," said Cobby, thawing more and more. "The place belongs to you. You know that."

"Thanks. Well, here's to you and yours." Dietrich drank, draining the glass; then he sat puffing for a moment on his cigar, eying Cobby, who began to fidget. "You know,

Cobby,'' he said finally, ''things were a little slow tonight; so I got to thinking about you, and I said to myself: 'I'll just drop down and talk to my old friend Cobby.' You see, I been worrying about you, Cobby. You're a nice little guy, with a nice big, semi-legitimate racket—doing all right. But sometimes guys get hungry, and they branch out, and then they get themselves in a lot of trouble.''

''What are you talking about, Monk? Me—I don't branch out.'' A nerve in Cobby's back began to twitch, and he shifted about nervously, trying to ease himself.

''Yes, sir,'' said Dietrich, ignoring what Cobby had said. ''They branch out—and then, wham! they get it. Every man should stick to his own racket. Why, Cobby—did you know for instance that a guy who helps to plan a robbery is as guilty as the guys who actually pull the job?''

''Never thought about it one way or another,'' mumbled Cobby. ''How about another drink, Monk?''

''No, thanks. Not tonight, Cobby. Take it another way. Suppose these guys who are pulling a robbery get themselves in a corner—you know—and they have to set a guy over. Well . . . the fellow sitting cozy at home who helped plan the robbery, he's equally guilty. They can burn him—in the chair. Now what do you think of that, Cobby?''

''Never thought about it at all. Why should I?''

The smile faded from Dietrich's big, fat, tough face, and, reaching a powerful paw across the table, he seized Cobby by the lapels and shook him violently.

''Well . . . you better think about it, and think about it hard and fast. If you don't, you're going to see what the death cells at the Walls look like!''

''Monk! Wait!'' cried Cobby. ''What goes here? Are you drunk, or pulling another one of your ribs—like the last time?''

Dietrich shouted in his face.

''Where's Riemenschneider?''

Cobby started violently, and his face began to turn deathly pale. Dietrich let go of him all of a sudden, and he fell back into his chair, limp. Nerves were twitching all over him now.

Leaning forward, Dietrich hit him a hard, sudden back-hand blow that spun him out of his chair and onto the floor, where he crouched, shaking his head, his mind void of all thought, his body quaking with fear.

Dietrich got up, walked over to him, and raised his huge, heavily shod foot as if to give him the boot. Cobby jumped to his feet immediately and tried to get behind the table, but Dietrich clouted him again and he fell over backwards, taking a chair with him this time.

Cobby began to plead with tears in his eyes as he crouched in front of Dietrich, torn with fear. If he stayed down, Dietrich might kick him and break his ribs. If he got up, Dietrich might knock him down again. Cobby was so sensitive to pain that he could scarcely bear the thought of it, let alone endure it.

"Monk! Monk! Have you gone crazy? Look. It's me. Cobby! For the love of God, Monk . . . !"

"Where's Riemenschneider?" cried Dietrich, staring down ferociously at Cobby. "I want answers, or I'm going to kick your teeth out."

Cobby jumped up in a panic, putting his hand over his mouth; and Dietrich belted him again, slamming him back against the wall, where his head knocked a sporting print to the floor, breaking the glass.

"He's gone," cried Cobby. "He holed up here. But now he's gone. I don't know where he is."

Dietrich had been using his open hand. He now doubled up his big, beefy fist and advanced on Cobby.

"Maybe you'd like to do a little talking," cried Dietrich. "Or should I fracture your skull?"

"Monk! For God's sake . . . !" gasped Cobby, hysterical with the fear of a beating. "What do you want me to talk about? I came clean on the doctor. He's gone. Swear to God, that's the truth!"

Dietrich stared at him, hard-eyed, menacing, for a long time, paying no attention to the fact that Cobby was wilting to such an extent that he had to grab the table for support and even so could barely stand upright.

Finally Dietrich spoke in a surprisingly gentle voice.

"Maybe it is, Cobby. Maybe it is. Now let's get down to the Pelletier business. How would you like to go down to Headquarters with me and make a statement in front of the Commissioner?"

"A statement . . . ?" stammered Cobby, hope beginning to show in his terrified eyes. "What . . . what about?"

"About who engineered the robbery, who pulled it off—who shot Brannom. Things like that."

Cobby nodded, unable to speak; then tears began to run down his cheeks, and, going to pieces completely, he fell into a chair and, putting his head on the card table, sobbed like a six-year-old kid.

Dietrich laid a heavy hand on his shoulder.

"That's my boy!" he said. "We'll make ourselves a little deal, Cobby. With the Commissioner, I mean. You turn state's—and maybe we can rig up a suspended sentence."

Without looking up, Cobby nodded again. Dietrich sat down at the table, picked up his cigar, and began to puff on it. Then he laughed coarsely.

"Remember what I told you, Cobby, about this case? Didn't I tell you some fink would blow it sky high?"

Cobby looked up at him with dead eyes; then he straightened in his chair and tried to get himself together.

"It . . . it's not that I'm a fink . . ." he began slowly and confusedly; then he broke off, turned away, and fumbled ineptly for a cigar.

"No, no; of course not!" said Dietrich, patting him on the shoulder. "It's just a manner of speaking."

· 34 ·

Doll stood looking on in awed silence as Dix helped the little doctor hide the jewels in the lower lining of his overcoat. Riemenschneider had decided that it would be too dangerous now to try to get away carrying the little bag.

"How's your head, Doc?" asked Dix, as they finished disposing of the jewels. "You okay?"

"I'll be able to make it, I think," said Riemenschneider. "If we hadn't run into that policeman, I'd stay in town for a while. But as it is . . ."

"Five Corners is your best bet, Doc. Always taxis around there—day and night."

"Five Corners, eh? How do I get there?"

"Go down the alley behind this place—toward the river. It'll take you right to it."

"All right," said Riemenschneider; then he shook hands with Dix slowly, looking up at him. "I wish you could see your way clear to coming along with me. We've got a fortune here if I can locate the right man in New York."

"No, thanks, Doc," said Dix. "It's not my way of doing things. Anyway, I'm going home."

"Give me that address," said the little doctor eagerly. "At least I can send you the five grand you've got coming."

Dix hesitated for a moment and rubbed his chin. Money had suddenly lost all importance to him. Five grand. Fifty grand. Five hundred grand. What did it matter? For years money in large amounts had run through his fingers like sand. To what purpose? Besides, once he got home, he didn't want to be bothered by communications from guys like the little doctor.

"Naw, Doc," he said. "Never mind. Maybe I'll see you around."

Riemenschneider gave up reluctantly. He'd never met a man like Dix before—one whose company gave him such a feeling of security. The thought of going it on his own now was excessively unpleasant.

"Well," he said, smiling sadly, "good-bye then."

"Good-bye, Doc," said Dix; then he remembered something. "Wait a minute. You haven't got any heater. I'd let you have mine, but . . ." He turned to Doll. "Got a gun, honey?"

"No, Dix. I used to have one around, but somebody stole it."

Dix showed impatience, but the German put a calming hand on his arm.

"Please forget it, Dix. I haven't carried a gun since my twenties. You carry a gun—you shoot a policeman. A bad rap. Hard to beat. You don't carry a gun—you give up when they hold one on you." Riemenschneider shrugged and laughed a little.

"Sure, Doc," said Dix. "But this time you got a killing rap hanging over you—if the law can prove it."

Riemenschneider shrugged again.

"I've had them before. Nobody's ever proved anything like that on me—only lesser charges."

"All right, Doc. You know best."

Riemenschneider smiled, looked from Doll to Dix, then went out without another word. For a moment they heard him moving cautiously through the dim-lit hallway; the stairs squeaked twice; then—silence.

Dix stood near the door, looking at it without seeing it, lost in thought. Doll watched him narrowly, wondering what was on his mind, afraid he might be deciding to go with the repulsive little German after all.

"How about some coffee, honey?" she asked with strained cheerfulness.

Dix ignored her.

"That squarehead, he's a funny little guy," mused Dix. "I don't get him at all. Maybe it's because he's a foreigner. Those guys, they don't think like us." He turned and stared at Doll but did not appear to see her. "Like when I was in Germany in the war. Even the Krauts who could talk English—well, I never knew what the hell they were talking about. Anyway, he's got plenty guts, foreigner or no foreigner!"

"How about some coffee, honey?" Doll persisted.

"Oh, for Christ's sake, stop bothering me about coffee, will you?" cried Dix. "Make it or shut up about it!"

Doll recoiled from his violence, turned and went out into

the tiny kitchenette, where he heard her moving about as she got ready to make the coffee.

He hesitated, then followed her, and stood in the doorway watching her in silence. All at once he grimaced, swore sharply, and grabbed his side. Violent, neuralgia-like pains stabbed upward across his chest; then his left shoulder and the back of his head began to ache.

"What's the matter, Dix?" cried Doll, turning toward him with startled eyes.

Dix groaned again, stumbled away from the doorway, fell down onto a straight chair in the bedroom, and sat doubled over, gasping. Doll followed him and knelt down beside him.

"It's that wound!" she cried.

"Bright girl!" gasped Dix, trying to laugh.

"I know! Aspirin. Take three or four of them. That'll stop it."

She jumped up and rushed into the bathroom, and in a moment came back carrying the aspirin bottle and a glass of water. Hope was rising within her. Maybe things would work out after all. Dix was in terrible pain—and it might get worse. How could he leave her and go on by himself when attacks of pain like this might overcome him at any time? She began to build up in her mind a rosy picture of the future. Dix ailing and docile; herself the angel of mercy, cooking for him, nursing him, sitting up all night with him!

"Here, honey!" she cried. "Better take four."

Dix straightened up to swallow the aspirin, groaning involuntarily; then he said: "I got to get out of this town. If I'm going to be laid up, it ain't going to be here."

He threw a worried glance at the bedroom window, beyond which sprawled the huge city with its clifflike buildings and its acres of hard cement. For a brief moment he felt a sort of terror—the terror of the exile abandoned to his fate far from home. He tried to rise, but sank back groaning.

"You can't go, feeling like this, Dix," cried Doll, kneeling beside him again. "You'd never make it—alone."

"Just the same I'm going," said Dix stubbornly. "If I have to walk!"

Doll was struck by a sudden thought.

"I can get you a car, Dix. Quigley's got an old, beat-up Ford he offered me for three hundred bucks one time when I was talking about getting a car."

Dix forgot his pain, straightened up, pulled a roll of crumpled bills out of his pocket and shoved it at Doll.

"Get the car."

"Jesus, Dix!" said Doll. "This is a lot of dough."

"Four grand," said Dix, indifferently. "Take four hundred just in case and give me back the rest."

Doll counted off what she needed; then she began to protest.

"But, Dix, honey . . . how're you going to drive all that way in the shape you're in?"

"I'll make it. I'll make it."

"No," said Doll with finality. "If I get the car, I'm going to drive you wherever you want to go."

Dix forgot his pain again and turned to stare at Doll.

"Are you crazy? I'm on the lam—wanted bad. You figuring on getting a stretch in some woman's prison?"

Doll hesitated, then spoke rapidly in a low, embarrassed voice, avoiding his eyes.

"I don't care, Dix—as long as I can be with you."

Dix gave her a puzzled glance.

"Well, I'm a son-of-a-bitch!" he said. "Okay. Get the car."

Doll jumped up, struggling hard to restrain a smile of triumph. She'd won! It was Dix and her now to the finish. How could he ever shake her after this?

· 35 ·

Two neighbor women were trying to restrain Maria Bellini, who was wild with grief and kept struggling to get up off the couch where they had placed her. She'd been given liquor, then sedatives—nothing seemed to do any good.

"How could it happen?" she cried. "My Louis! My handsome, wonderful Louis!"

"Maria," said one of the Italian women, "the Holy Mother knows best. Louis is happy now, and he's up there waiting for you . . ."

"Yes," said the other woman, "he's waiting. But he is not impatient. He wants you to raise the little Louis up to be a fine man, like himself."

"My little Louis!" cried Maria, starting up. "I forgot him. How could I forget him? Where is he?"

The women glanced at each other with relief. Maria was coming round now.

"He's sleeping like a little lamb, dear—not a worry in the world in his little head. Lie back, Maria. Rest."

Maria was quiet for a moment; then she turned and looked at them with her big, dark, beautiful eyes—the eyes that had weaned Louis away from the poolrooms, the dance halls, and the casual promiscuity of his former life.

"You think that Louis . . . he's really waiting up there, Mrs. Maggio?"

"Of course he is, my baby," said Mrs. Maggio. "He's waiting. My husband too. Maybe they already are talking together."

Maria burst into tears and flung herself into the older woman's arms.

"He'll always be near you, Maria dear. Like my Pete," said Mrs. Maggio. "I'm never worried. I'm never frightened. I know he's there, looking after us all—my kids, me!"

"Yes," cried Maria. "I believe you. Louis would wait forever. My wonderful Louis!"

Little by little she drifted into sleep. Mrs. Maggio watched her for a moment; then she sat down on the floor and began to cry. The other woman soothed her, talking quietly.

In a few minutes Father Sortino came out of the bedroom, and the women jumped up quickly and stood looking at him with awed respect. The priest glanced over at the couch,

then smiled sadly. He was a tall, dignified-looking Italian
with a handsome, ascetic face.

"Asleep finally, I see."

"Yes, Father," said Mrs. Maggio. "Poor child!"

"I'll be by early tomorrow. Will you stay with her?"

"We'll both stay, Father. Don't you worry."

"When she wakes, tell her I have all the papers, all of
Louis's records—the ones he was so insistent about before
he died. Also the keys. She'll understand."

"Yes, Father."

He patted the two middle-aged women gently.

"Thank you both. You are good neighbors, true Chris-
tians. Thank you."

Mrs. Maggio began to cry again, but managed to stifle
it and smile at the priest, who smiled back, then went out
closing the door softly.

He was halfway down the hall when he heard heavy
tramping on the stairs, and, compressing his lips grimly, he
hurried off to put a stop to it. Drunken men, no doubt.

But at the head of the stairs he was confronted by two
huge harness bulls and a Headquarters dick.

"Will you walk more quietly, please?" requested Father
Sortino. "There's been a death on this floor."

"Sure, Father," said one of the harness bulls, an Irishman.
"But with these shoes . . . well . . ." He grinned broadly.

They went on past him, and he was just starting down
the stairs when he noticed that they'd stopped in front of
the door of Maria Bellini's apartment. He hurried back before they could knock. The dick looked at Father Sortino
with some irritation. He was a Methodist himself and didn't
hold with long black skirts for preachers.

"You must have the wrong number, gentlemen," said
the priest.

"We're looking for Louis Bellini."

"Why, may I ask?"

The dick glanced at the priest in open irritation, angering
the big Irish harness bull, who could hardly keep his hands
from clenching themselves into fists.

"You got no right to ask," said the dick. "But I'm broad-minded. I'll tell you, anyway. He's wanted for robbery—and maybe murder."

Father Sortino recoiled slightly.

"There must be some mistake."

"Could be! But we've got our orders. Now do you mind if I go about my work?"

"I told you there was a death on this floor," said Father Sortino. "Louis Bellini died this evening."

The dick stared at the priest suspiciously and, pushing back his hat, carefully scratched his head.

"What did he die of?"

"Complications arising out of a bullet wound he received in a street fight."

"Street fight, eh? I got to take a look at the body."

The Irish harness bull stepped forward.

"If the Father says it's okay, Williams, it's okay."

The dick glanced at the big harness bull with resentment; then he took out a cigar and began to chew on it.

"I'd consider it a great favor," said Father Sortino, "if you didn't insist on going in. Mrs. Bellini is . . . well, I don't have to tell you."

The dick turned to the Irish cop and spoke harshly.

"Go call the Commissioner's office for instructions. And step on it."

"The Commissioner knows me," said the priest. "You may mention my name. Sortino."

"Thank you, Father," said the cop; then he turned and started back down the hallway, trying to walk quietly.

The dick lit his cigar, and he and the priest stood eying each other with mutual distrust.

· 36 ·

The little doctor had been extremely lucky—so lucky, in fact, that it had seemed almost like a direct intervention of providence. He sat in the swiftly moving cab, thinking about intangibles and remembering the cockeyed robbery with its atmosphere of farcical accident—the self-starting burglar alarms and the self-firing gun.

Leaving Doll's apartment, he had turned up the alley just in time to avoid a prowl car that was gliding along without lights, and in the alley he'd found a conveniently jutting shed to hide behind till the danger was past. At Five Corners, which was completely deserted, a cab had swung into the Square just as he was emerging from the alley. More miraculous still, the driver had turned out to be a middle-aged German from Stuttgart, an amiable fellow who was delighted to hear his native language spoken, and who went on and on about his experiences as a mechanic's helper in the big Mercedes-Benz factory, one of the landmarks of his home town. His name was Franz Schurz, although it said "Frank" on his hack license.

"You in the first big war?" he was asking.

"No," said the little doctor. "I was interned in England." He'd actually been serving a short stretch in a London jail on a swindling charge.

"You were a lucky fellow," said Schurz. "I was on the Western Front. Awful! Finally it's over, and I think: 'Thank God!' But then I go home. What do I find? Everybody hungry. Soldiers killing officers. A revolution! So I get out. I'm no fool. Now I'm a naturalized American citizen. I was drafted even in the second war. But I didn't have to fight—too old. They let me out pretty quick when my heart began to act up. It's been all right since, though." He leaned forward to laugh.

Riemenschneider puffed on his cigar in comfort and lounged back on the leather cushions. On top of everything, Schurz's cab was a fairly new one, unlike most of the crates banging around in the Camden Square area, and was actually comfortable to ride in.

"Franz," he said, "how would you like to drive me to Cleveland?"

"Cleveland!" cried the driver, twisting in his seat. "Why, that's a hell of a long ways from here, my friend."

"I know," said the little doctor. "I was going out to see these relatives of mine; then I intended to take the bus in the morning. But . . . I don't know. This cab of yours rides like a Pullman and it's private. Besides, the more I think about those relatives of mine, the less I want to see them."

Schurz laughed briefly.

"About the relatives, I understand," he said. "But, my friend, it's going to cost you quite a lot of money to go to Cleveland—and I'd have to check with the office. Anyway, what about your luggage?"

"I'll wire back. It can be sent on to me."

Schurz scratched his head, considering. They had left the downtown district far behind now and were traveling through an immense, flat suburban area where all the houses looked alike and all were dark. Street lights stretched off in all directions in diminishing perspective, looking wan and solitary as they cast their steady glow over nothing but acres of cement. There wasn't even a prowling cat in sight any place.

"I don't know," said Schurz. "I never did anything like that before."

Riemenschneider leaned forward and offered him a bill.

"If you're worrying about the money—here!"

Schurz took the bill and glanced at it in the dim light of the dash. It was a hundred-dollar bill. He whistled softly.

"When we run that out, let me know," said Riemenschneider.

"This bothers me," said Schurz. "I think I'd better call the office."

"And a big tip for you," said Riemenschneider. "Say, fifty dollars."

"Listen," said Schurz, "I'd drive you to the Arctic Circle for a fifty-dollar tip, only . . . if I don't call, I may get in real bad with the office. They might even have the police out looking for me. It's going to take me ten, twelve hours to drive to Cleveland and back."

The little doctor thought this over for a moment; then he said:

"I'll tell you what we'll do. When we get out to the far edge of town, you call."

"All right," said Schurz. "There's a diner out in Clark's Station. That's the last stop till we get to College City. Nothing but farm country in between."

They rode in silence for a while, and the little doctor sat staring out the window moodily, watching the dreary suburb slide past. Finally Schurz laughed and said: "You had me kind of worried for a while."

"Me? I had you worried?"

"Well, Five Corners is quite a place—awful tough. As a matter of fact, I'm getting ready to quit my job if they don't give me another beat. Nighthawking's bad enough any place. But around the Square a man's not safe. The police go in pairs all over the district. And here you come walking out of an alley."

Riemenschneider laughed good-naturedly and leaned forward to hand Schurz a cigar, then lit it for him.

"I know I can confide in you," he said. "I'm an importer, and I've got a big business in Cleveland. But I like to get away once in a while where I'm not known, and have a little fun gambling. There's a big game in the Square, and tonight I was very, very lucky. That's the reason I'm so free with my hundred-dollar bills."

They both laughed, and Schurz twisted around in his seat to take another look at Riemenschneider.

"I can't get over it," he said. "A harmless little man like you walking around the Camden district in the middle of the night carrying a roll! A German's a fool for luck. Why, they knock over a man in those alleys for the price of a cup of coffee."

"I've been in a lot of strange places in my life," said Riemenschneider quite truthfully, "and I've never had the slightest trouble. Ever been in Stamboul?"

"That's in Turkey, isn't it? No."

"They like to cut a stranger's throat in some districts of Stamboul just to test their knives. They especially like to chop up what they call the Franks. We're all Franks to them—Englishmen, Americans, Frenchmen, Germans. I went where I pleased at night—all over the native quarter. Nobody even looked at me."

"You've certainly been around, haven't you?"

"I have indeed," said the little doctor, sighing and puffing thoughtfully on his cigar.

They cleared the suburb at last, and huge factories and warehouses began to loom along their route. A light mist started to fall, making little pinkish haloes about the street lights. For a while they skirted a railroad embankment, and a freight train passed them going toward town, and they heard the lonely, off-key ringing of the crossing-bells.

At last they pulled clear of the giant warehouses, the factories, the big viaducts arching up out of the mists to nowhere, and came out into a wide, flat, sparsely settled area, with a few poor, frame houses grouped along cracked and weed-bordered sidewalks.

The mist turned to a drizzle, and the wet asphalt shone like black glass, palely reflecting the widely separated street lights. A cold wind began to blow, and Riemenschneider huddled down into his big overcoat.

He was beginning to feel a little weak. The cut on his head had been throbbing faintly for hours, but now he was becoming more and more conscious of it. Suddenly he realized that he was hungry, needed some good hot food to pick him up.

After what seemed like hours of darkness, drizzle, and cold wind, Schurz said: "There's the diner. See it up ahead?"

Riemenschneider roused himself and leaned forward to look through the front window. He saw the welcome glow of a yellow neon sign that read: EAT.

"What can you get there?" he asked. "I'm hungry."

"Hamburgers. Steak sandwiches—though they're not Kansas City beef. Almost anything. Barbecue stuff. You know."

A juke-box was playing in the diner when they entered. A tired-looking, fattish man in a dirty chef's cap was behind the counter, and a couple of loutish boys, their checked shirts hanging out and their corduroy pants rolled up, were lounging in a booth near by. With them was a blond young girl with a fat face and a pert manner. She was about fiteen or sixteen. Riemenschneider noticed her at once and sat down where he could look at her out of the corner of his eye.

"I'll call the office," said Schurz, "and give them a pitch—tell them it's an emergency."

"What will you have?" asked the little doctor. "Hungry?"

"I'm always hungry at night. Double hamburger and a glass of beer. The beer's terrible in this country, but it's better than no beer at all."

Schurz went back to the telephone booth, laughing. There was something very reassuring about him to Riemenschneider. German as sauerkraut. Complaining about the beer even. All over the world he'd heard exiled Germans complaining about the beer.

The little doctor gave his order to the limp-looking, fat counterman; then he turned sideways on his stool so he could watch the young girl. He found her very pleasant to look at. The boys were ribbing her about something, and she was tossing her head, laughing, and gabbing back at them in a high-pitched, rather petulant voice.

Finally the juke-box stopped.

"More, more!" cried the girl, clapping her hands at the boys as if they were lackeys.

But one of them said: "I'm fresh out of nickels, Jeannie. How about you, Red?"

"I'm always fresh out."

"Well, get some!" cried the girl impatiently.

"Say, you know you cost a guy a lot of money!"

"Nickels he's complaining about yet!" cried the girl. "What a spendthrift!"

"Anyway, I'm tired of all those numbers."

"I want to hear the King Cole one again. If I had a nickel, I'd play it myself."

"If you had a nickel! Dig down, baby, dig down."

The bickering went on for quite a while. In fact it was still going on when Schurz came back from the phone.

"It's okay," he said as he sat down beside Riemen-schneider at the counter.

"Good!" said the little doctor.

The counterman brought them their food, and they both began to eat in silence, Riemenschneider surreptitiously watching the girl.

"He wants a date," the girl was saying. "He always wants a date. But has he got a car? No! He's got to bring his chum Red along because chum Red's got a car—such as it is, and if you can call it a car! Where do we go? To a third-run movie where they've got three pictures for twenty-five cents. Then we take a ride and blow two tires. Not one—two! Then we come in here for what? Cokes! And I can't even listen to records in spite of the fact that my old man is going to whale me when I come in this time of night . . . but good . . . !"

"Stop!" cried one of the boys. "You're breaking my heart!"

The girl began to plead with them, but they jeered at her.

Schurz turned to the little doctor and said: "I'm ready whenever you are."

"I would like to have some more coffee," said Riemen-schneider with a certain sharpness in his voice, annoyed at the driver for interrupting his contemplation of the young girl.

"Sure, sure!" agreed the driver hurriedly.

"Well . . . take me home then!" the girl was saying. "You've stretched those Cokes out long enough."

The boys laughed and whispered to each other, then laughed again. The girl glared at them.

Leaning forward, the little doctor handed the counterman a dollar and told him to change it into nickels. Schurz glanced at him in some surprise but said nothing.

When the counterman came back with the change, the little doctor took it, then turned round on his stool and spoke in a very polite voice to the group in the booth.

"Excuse me, boys and girls," he said. "But I like music too. Miss, will you play a tune for me?"

The girl stared, then jumped up quickly, flushing, looking a little embarrassed.

"I sure will!" she said to the little doctor, smiling. "What do you like?"

"You pick them," he replied, smiling paternally and handing her all of the nickels.

"But . . . gee, gosh!" cried the girl. "How many nickels you got here?"

"Not very many. Play what you like."

"Gee! Okay."

She turned and looked in contemptuous triumph at the boys, who were a little bewildered and kept glancing at Riemenschneider; then she walked slowly and self-consciously up to the juke-box and dropped in a nickel. In a moment the music started—a lone guitar, playing a very sophisticated introduction; then King Cole began to sing a love song in his thin, intimate, expressive voice.

"That's for me!" cried the girl, hurrying back to the booth and sitting down. Then she turned to the little doctor and asked: "Do you like King Cole too?"

"Oh, yes! He's one of my favorites."

Schurz grew more and more restive as tune after tune was played. Riemenschneider ordered more coffee; then he bought Cokes and sandwiches for the boys, who had decided by now that he was okay. In a little while the girl came over and sat on a stool beside the little doctor, and they listened to the music in silence.

Puzzled, understanding nothing of what was going on, but feeling somewhat uneasy nevertheless, Schurz finally turned to Riemenschneider and said: "Mister, it's getting late. Don't you think we'd better be moving?"

The little doctor looked at the taxi-driver blankly, as if seeing him for the first time; then he glanced at the girl beside him, who was listening to the music with artificial raptness, acting a part. He could hardly tear himself away, and yet Schurz was right. He should have left long ago and not presumed on his luck. He turned. The girl was looking at him, smirking a little, showing her childish white teeth.

Smiling at her, he nodded to the music; but finally, as the number concluded, he sighed, shrugged, and got up.

"I'm extremely sorry," he said, "but I've got to be on my way. Business, you know. Important business."

The young girl had been basking in Riemenschneider's obviously abject worship, well aware of the fact that his interest in her was far from paternal—though the loutish boys had noticed nothing out of the way. A fat little four-eyed guy like that? Oh, please!

"But we haven't used all the nickels," the girl protested, showing her childish white teeth again in what she hoped was a seductive smile—like in the movies.

"*You* use them," said the little doctor, with a slavish smile.

"Gee, thanks! It was sure nice of you, playing all those numbers just for me."

"Just for you—that's right," said Riemenschneider, sighing; then he rose reluctantly, paid the bill, and turned to Schurz. "All right, my friend. I'm ready to go."

They started out. The boys called exuberant thanks after the funny little guy, but the girl, wanting to enjoy as long as possible the uncritical worship she'd sensed in Riemen-schneider's gaze, and reluctant for the moment to return to the company of the wise-cracking, too-familiar boys, accompanied him to the door.

"Good-bye," she said softly, shaking hands with him. "And thanks. Thanks ever so much."

"The pleasure was all mine," said the little doctor.

When the door closed behind them, Schurz exclaimed with a certain amount of distaste: "Damn fresh kid, if you ask me! Running around this time of night! She should have been home in bed hours ago."

Riemenschneider smiled to himself. The respectable German speaking! Schurz—he was typical.

"It's awful," Schurz went on as they walked toward the taxi through the drizzle, "the way the Americans let their young girls run around at night. No wonder things are always happening to them—like those Old Market cases. It gives me the shivers."

"Yes," Riemenschneider agreed, "it's very disturbing."

Just as they reached the cab two motorcycle policemen stepped out from the deep shadows of the darkened filling-station next to the diner. Schurz gave a start, but the little doctor turned and looked at them with mild interest.

One of them switched a torch on Riemenschneider, and then both of them studied him in silence for quite a long time. The one without the torch had a heavy police revolver in his right hand.

"You men want something?" asked Riemenschneider quietly.

"What do *you* think, Ed? Soon as I saw him through the window sitting at the counter, I had an idea maybe we'd run up on something," said the cop with the torch.

"Say, what is this, boys?" Schurz demanded. "My fare's a respectable man—nice fellow. He's got an importing business in Cleveland, Ohio."

"Keep out of this, hackie!"

"We better frisk him."

"I have no objection," said the little doctor, calmly taking off his overcoat and handing it to Schurz. "Go right ahead."

The two cops worked him over carefully and found nothing except a roll of bills, which they counted and handed back to him.

"Give me that coat, hackie," said the cop with the torch.

Schurz handed it to him. The cop searched all the pockets, trying them again and again. Finally he handed the coat back to Schurz.

"I tell you you're making a big mistake," cried the taxi-driver.

One of the cops turned on Riemenschneider.

"What have you got to say for yourself?"

"Not a thing," said the little doctor mildly. "Why should I? I haven't the faintest idea what this is all about. I'm baffled." As he spoke he took the overcoat from Schurz and put it back on.

"What do *you* think, Ed?"

"Looks like the number-one boy to me." Then he turned to Schurz. "Where did you pick this guy up?"

Riemenschneider's stomach muscles tightened, and his head began to throb worse than before. This was it, then!

"Why . . . Five Corners," said Schurz, stammering a little. "But . . ."

"Five Corners, eh?" The cop with the torch laughed triumphantly. "Got anything to say, doctor?"

"Doctor?" Riemenschneider spoke as if bewildered. "Now I *know* you have me mixed up with somebody else. My name's Klemperer. I'm from Cleveland. And I'm no doctor."

"I'm going inside and phone the Commissioner," said the cop called Ed. "He'll tell us what to do with this character." Turning, he walked away rapidly across the tamped gravel.

The other cop said: "Don't move, fellow. Just stay where you are, with your back to me."

"Of course," said the little doctor, shrugging slightly.

They waited in silence for quite a while; then the diner door opened and the kids came out, talking and laughing, the boys ribbing Jeannie as before.

None of them saw the little doctor standing in the shadow of the taxi, or the big, broad-shouldered motor cop behind him. They leaped into a cut-down Ford, yelling and punching each other, and drove off with a loud banging of the exhaust, trailing a thick cloud of stinking smoke.

Even after they had turned off on the side road beyond the little diner, Riemenschneider could still hear Jeannie's exciting laughter drifting through the night across the empty fields.

"Excuse me, officer," said the little doctor, turning his head, "but will you tell me something?"

"Maybe. But just keep the eyes front."

"How long have you been out here?"

"That's a damn funny question. But I don't see why I shouldn't answer it. I'd say about two, three minutes."

"Thank you."

Long enough for the playing of only one record, Riemenschneider told himself; and he'd listened to a dozen or so!

"Why don't we get out of this drizzle?" he asked the
cop without turning.

"We won't melt," said the cop. "Just stand still."

"How about me?" asked Schurz, thoroughly intimidated now.

"Go sit in the cab if you want to."

Schurz glanced at his fare, who neither spoke nor looked
up; then he turned, walked to the cab, and got in.

Riemenschneider stood shivering a little in the dampness,
lost in thought. The future did not look as hopeless to him
as it would have to most men in his position. If disaster
couldn't be circumvented, it could at least be moderated
and minimized; there were ways and means, and he was
familiar with all of them through long experience. Trials
could be delayed, witnesses frightened or bought—for a
man of the little doctor's standing, money was always to
be found; juries could be maneuvered into disagreement,
judges forced, through the manipulation of technicalities,
to declare a mistrial. At worst, it was possible to make deals
with district attorneys, afraid of acquittals. When they were
not actually venal, they were at least politically ambitious
and willing to accept pleas of guilt to lesser offenses in order
to insure the publicity of a conviction.

As for prison itself, the little doctor neither feared nor
dreaded it. To him the procedure was very simple. Prisons
were full of stupid, emotional men who kept getting themselves into easily avoidable jams. He always breezed along,
liked, and even respected, by all, and was soon working at
a cushy job with plenty of leisure and privileges. He pre-
sented no problem at all to the authorities, and for this they
were grateful and rewarded him.

Three qualities were necessary for successful living in
prison (or out of it, for that matter), and he had them all:
intelligence, patience, and equanimity. And yet, he had a
great weakness too. A weakness that at times cancelled out

all his virtues, and tonight had caught him in a trap as cheese catches a mouse.

All men had these weaknesses in one form or another . . . and their derelictions and failures were invariably the result of them. In other words, men were only rational by fits and starts. That was what was meant by human, all too human; and that was why the prisons were full—even of cold-blooded professionals like himself. Theoretically, a plan could be perfect; but plans—whether for a robbery, like the Pelletier affair, or a military campaign, or a big business coup (professional crime being only a left-handed intensification of normal forms of endeavor)—had to be executed; and not by well-oiled, soulless machines, but by men, the best and most efficient of whom suffered from unpredictable aberrations of the ego and the emotions.

He thought about Cobby. Cagey and cunning, and able to prosper in an environment where most men would have gone under—yet, for all that, a vain silly fool, flattered into flagrant bad judgment by the shrewd and patronizing attentions of Mr. Alonzo Emmerich.

And as for Emmerich himself . . . his folly was unbelievable! He had survived for thirty years by a system of masterly evasions, bewildering about-faces and changes of front; his opponents were always at a disadvantage because they could never predict what he would do next. He grew to have a contempt for the intelligence of others—all others; and for this reason he neglected all the weapons in his arsenal but one—duplicity. And although desperation had gradually warped his judgment, duplicity had served him well until the Pelletier affair. By that time he was completely unable to see that its use in this business was a certain guarantee of disaster.

And Dix . . . what about him? Big and tough as he was, the little doctor mused, he suffered from a simple and universal form of romanticism: the desire to return to a former mode of life. Home after twenty-five years . . . the light in the window . . . the happy faces of the loved ones. All nonsense, as Riemenschneider knew through experience, though he himself had gone home only for a breather and not because of any mistaken idea that the worries and responsibilities of adult life would cease once he got there.

The little doctor sighed. You plan and you plan, and if blind chance doesn't upset you, you find yourself at the mercy of the vagaries of your associates. To operate alone was perhaps best. At least then you had to wrestle only with your own irrationality . . . ! He sighed again, then turned slowly toward the cop behind him.

"Officer," he said, "do you mind if I smoke a cigar?"

"Just stand still, mister," said the cop. "Keep your face front. We'll talk about smoking a cigar later."

"Certainly, officer," said the little doctor, "certainly."

· 37 ·

Angela just couldn't settle down she was so excited. She moved about the room, talking at the top of her voice, kneeling in a chair for a moment, then leaping up and dashing over to the coffee table for a cigarette, which she lit hurriedly, puffed on briefly, then put down and forgot.

Her animation brought a pearly glow to her fair complexion, which at times appeared too white, too marred by freckles; and her thick red hair seemed to have a life of its own tonight, as if charged with electricity—it bushed out, coarse and flaming, casting pale, pinkish reflections over her face.

She was wearing tight white silk slacks and a bright-green sweater, and even to Emmerich, who was heartily sick and tired of her, she looked extremely attractive, even beautiful; and he sat in a big easy chair, an English antique that had cost him over six hundred dollars, with his legs comfortably crossed, smoking one of his Cuban cigars, a highball beside him, thinking about the day he'd seen Angela for the first time in that little restaurant whose name for the moment escaped him.

All his troubles dated from that portentous day. Or did they? Silly to blame Angela for a disaster that had been hovering over him ever since his graduation from law school. Born for trouble, as his father had always said. Unable to run with the pack and yet with no desire whatever to be the fox, he had oscillated from side to side, and had finally brought himself into a sort of no man's land where danger threatened from every direction and from which the cleverest man in the world couldn't hope to escape unscathed.

Sighing and sipping his drink, he watched Angela's ex-aggerated antics with a mixture of amusement and envy. Angus McDonald had already been able to raise a little money for him, and he'd given Angela three thousand dollars so she could go to Miami Beach for the winter. It seemed to him like a cheap and painless way of getting rid of her. When she returned, the cottage on the river, with all its elaborate furniture, would be in other hands, and he'd be . . . well, God knows where; but at least he'd have this excessively expensive, and now completely purposeless, ménage off his neck.

But her reaction amazed him. All this wild celebration over a little trip to Florida! She was always surprising him by her simplicity of outlook, and yet he never learned.

Talking rapidly, she rushed out of the living-room and came back with a travel magazine, which she insisted on showing him—white beach, palm trees, tremendous luxury hotels, well-upholstered girls in scanty bathing-suits, aqua-planing—all the worn-out clichés of a big tourist resort—the works!

"Imagine me on this beach here in my new green bathing-suit—yipe!" cried Angela. "Or maybe the salmon-pink one would look better. I almost bought one of those French suits—but, oh, my God! I'd need a bodyguard. What do you think, Uncle Lon—the green one or the pink one . . . ?"

The lawyer seemed to be giving considerable thought to this important matter as he puffed gravely on his cigar. Angela rushed on.

"You've got to tell me now, Uncle Lon. Because when you come down to Florida . . ."

"If I can get away. I'm pretty busy right now—lots of cases coming up."

"Oh, you'll get away all right!" cried Angela. "Don't be silly. What was I saying? My God, I'm so excited I don't even know what I'm talking about. Oh, yes. I want to know which one you like best—or maybe you'd prefer a white one. I saw a beauty at Martine's the other day, but it wasn't quite extreme enough. I mean . . . don't get me wrong. If I really went in for the *extreme* extreme, I'd have got that French suit—but run for your lives, girls; the fleet's in! No, really. I mean it. I don't mind nakedness, but I don't want to have to worry myself to death every time I sit down or lean over. You think you like the green one best?"

Earlier in the evening Angela had modeled her "Miami Beach" wardrobe for him, strutting about and trying to imitate the mannikins she'd seen in the swank department stores.

"Yes," said Emmerich at last, pursing his lips judiciously, "I think, all things considered, that I like the green one best."

"Good! The green one, then—I won't wear it till you get there . . ."

". . . however, on the other hand," Emmerich went on, beginning to enjoy himself a little, "while the green one may be the more attractive of the two I've seen, I must say I'm rather curious about that French affair you've been talking about."

Angela burst out laughing.

"Why, Uncle Lon! I'm surprised at you. I simply couldn't wear it on a public beach. I'd feel . . . well, indecent. Now you wouldn't want me to feel indecent, would you, Uncle Lon? Of course, if we had a private swimming-pool and you were the only one there . . ."

"Well, maybe you're right," said Emmerich. "Naturally, I wouldn't want you to outrage your sense of modesty for the sake of a bathing-suit."

"You see?" cried Angela. "That's what I mean."

A sudden thought struck her, and she jumped up and ran out to her bedroom to get a fashion magazine that had just arrived that afternoon.

Emmerich got up and poured himself another drink; then he glanced at his watch. It was later than he'd thought. Maybe his wife was worrying about his absence tonight—as she'd done in the old days. Maybe not. A whole new batch of current books had been sent over to her that afternoon by her bookseller, and she'd seemed very much absorbed in them.

"Maybe I ought to do a little reading myself," said Emmerich, thoughtfully. "I'll have to put in my old age some way—if I get that far."

Angela came running back with the fashion magazine just as the front-door buzzer sounded.

"Oh, bother!" she cried. "Look, Uncle Lon. Here's a French bathing-suit. You see? Doesn't she look indecent!"

"Well," said Emmerich, "in a sort of attractive way."

"Lon! Really, I'm surprised at you. No, I mean it. A man of your education and . . . and taste and all. Nevertheless, if you want me to . . ." But she broke off and turned, somewhat startled by a sound of loud knocking. "It's awfully late, isn't it?" she asked, turning to Emmerich.

The lawyer had a premonition and hesitated for a moment. Should he make a rush for it? But, no; if Hardy, by some great stroke of luck, had finally broken the case and had come to arrest him, the place was surrounded. On the other hand, it might only be a messenger boy or a special-delivery letter from Angela's mother—asking none too politely for a "small, temporary" loan; or it might be a motorist who had lost his way in the darkness of the River Road.

The knocking continued.

"Lonnie, I'm scared," said Angela in a babyish voice. "Why are they pounding so?"

Emmerich shrugged and went out to open the door. Angela followed him as far as the living-room archway, where she stood peering fearfully down the pleasantly lit, luxurious entrance hall.

Emmerich opened the door abruptly, irritated by the pounding, and caught Andrews, the homicide dick, with hand raised and a look of dogged determination on his tough, handsome, young face. Commissioner Hardy was standing just beyond him with his overcoat collar turned up and his hat down almost to his eyes. He seemed to be shivering. Some distance behind Hardy stood two hulking harness bulls.

Emmerich stared at Andrews before he spoke, smiling ironically.

"What—no hammer?" he exclaimed. "You must be a very hardfisted young man." He looked beyond Andrews contemptuously, and the young dick flushed. "Hello, Hardy. Come on in. I've got a fire. You look cold. Forget your rubbers?"

The two harness bulls cleared their throats uneasily and glanced at each other sideways. They were mortally afraid of the Commissioner and couldn't understand Emmerich's temerity.

Hardy and Andrews followed Emmerich into the entrance hall, leaving the two policemen outside. Emmerich shut the door in their faces with a feeling of pleasure and led the way to the living-room.

Angela had disappeared. Andrews, taking off his hat and walking carefully over the luxurious carpets, looked about for her hopefully.

Hardy went at once to the fireplace and held his benumbed hands out to the blaze.

"I don't know why we're all being so polite," he said gruffly. "I came here to arrest you, Emmerich."

"I'm not being polite," said Emmerich. "And if beating the front door down is politeness . . ."

"Andrews doesn't know his own strength," said Hardy, and the young dick flushed painfully again, and then, in order to assert himself, put his hat back on.

Emmerich sat down and made himself comfortable, lit a fresh cigar, crossed his legs, and picked up his highball glass.

"So you've come to arrest me, eh, Hardy? What is it this time?"

"All-around complicity," said Hardy. "Robbery—murder. Want any more?"

Emmerich laughed. Silly little stick of a man, who should be superintending a Sunday-school class for backward boys!

"No," said Emmerich, "that's enough. However, if I were you, I'd dig up a few more charges, because that way you might be able to make one of them stand up—providing you had an imbecile jury and the right judge."

"It won't be Dickerson," said Hardy. "I started impeachment proceedings against him today." He turned to Andrews. "Find the young lady."

"Yes, *sir!*" cried Andrews with such an unnecessary burst of enthusiasm that both Hardy and Emmerich turned to look at him as he whirled and hurried out.

"Ah, youth!" said Emmerich mockingly.

At first Angela wouldn't pay any attention to Andrews's gentle taps at her bedroom door, nor to his embarrassed voice pleading with her to open up.

Finally he lost his temper.

"Okay, miss," he said harshly. "It's a shame to bust this pretty door in, but here goes!"

The door was unlocked and opened at once, and Andrews found himself looking into blazing yellow eyes as beautiful and as merciless as those of an infuriated cat. He recoiled, snatched off his hat.

"Haven't you bothered me enough?" cried Angela. "You big . . . bananahead!"

As she groped for an epithet, Andrews had winced inwardly, expecting the worst and not wanting to hear it. He had romantic feelings about pretty young women, and these feelings were always being outraged. He felt such marked relief that he burst out laughing.

Angela slammed the door in his face, but opened it again in a moment, her anger considerably diminished. After all,

this young cop was quite a spectacle. Big, roughly handsome, and with shoulders like a football-player. Besides . . . who knows? She might need him. But to give in
too fast was never very wise; so she narrowed her eyes again.

"Go ahead, laugh!" she cried. "But bananahead it is!
Talking about breaking my door in! Mr. Emmerich will
have you thrown out of your job."

"I'm afraid not," said Andrews calmly.

Angela glanced at him with a certain amount of apprehension now, his tone warning her that this time things were
very serious. The time before, the whole business had seemed
like one big joke. Lon had called her and told her exactly
what to say. She'd written it down and learned it practically
by heart. Lon had explained that Commissioner Hardy was
a political enemy of long standing and was out to ruin him
by any means possible. Angela had always had the greatest
contempt for politics—a lot of silly men running around
yelling. About what? But maybe Lon hadn't told her the
truth. Maybe there *was* something serious. Anyway, why
had he needed *her* for an alibi? What was wrong with that
stupid wife of his?

"You mean," she began, speaking in her most seductive
and babyish voice, "that Mr. Emmerich is really in some
bad trouble?"

Andrews drew back a little—not liking the baby-talk approach. The first time, she'd been somewhat harsh with
him—harsh and straightforward—or so it had seemed.

"Well," he said, "murder's kind of serious."

"Murder!" cried Angela, badly startled for a moment.
Then she began to laugh. "You policemen—bothering Mr.
Emmerich about a murder! As if he'd kill anybody! Why
waste my time with such stuff?"

"All I know is we've got a warrant for him. And the
Commissioner wants to see you—right now."

"Me? Why?"

"He wants to ask you about that nice little alibi you set
up for Emmerich. You'd better tell him the truth or he'll
put you in jail."

Now Angela was really startled. Jail! At this point? When she was all ready to leave for Miami Beach for the winter? Impossible! It couldn't be. Why, she had all of her clothes bought—a wonderful new wardrobe: bathing-suits, play clothes, sports dresses, two new evening gowns, gorgeous accessories. How could a thing like this happen to her!

Andrews noticed her distress and began to feel romantic about her again. The hell with the baby talk! The kid was in a spot. And all on account of that big, arrogant, plausible, curly-headed phony in the next room. The kid had probably been very poor, and then this louse had come along and . . . Andrews suddenly pulled himself up short, thinking: "What the hell kind of fairy story is this I'm making up as I go along!"

"But suppose I told the truth the first time!" cried Angela, very upset and nervous and beginning to bite her nails.

"The Commissioner knows you didn't. And he's a very tough guy—hates perjurers worse than anything in the world."

"What's a perjurer?" asked Angela.

Andrews stared at her for a moment, wondering if she was kidding him; then, feeling sure at last that she was not, he explained: "Somebody, for instance, who sets up a false alibi to keep somebody else from being punished for a crime he committed."

"But Mr. Emmerich—do you think he goes around committing crimes?"

"Yes," said Andrews.

A loud voice began calling from the front room: "Hey! Andrews! What the blazes are you doing out there? Bring that young lady in here."

Angela began to tremble at the sound of the harsh, thin, unsympathetic voice.

"That's the Commissioner," said Andrews. "And sounds like he's about to blow a fuse."

"Oh, God!" cried Angela. "Do I have to talk to him? Why can't I just talk to you?"

She looked genuinely distressed now, and Andrews couldn't control himself any longer. He took her hand awkwardly and squeezed it so hard in his big paw that it became numb.

"Listen, honey," he said; "forget I'm a copper. I just don't want to see anything happen to you. You're a doll, baby—the best-looking doll I ever saw in my life—and I've been thinking about you ever since that last time. I'm going to see that nothing happens to you. Emmerich's a dead duck. Take my word for it. Be smart now. Tell the Commissioner the truth."

He felt her trembling, and wanted to hold and comfort her and tell her not to be scared. "Okay," he told himself, "so I'm a goddamn fool!"

"Andrews!" shouted the Commissioner.

"Come on, baby," said the young dick. "Get it over with. That's the only thing to do."

When they entered the living-room, Hardy was standing with his back to the fire, staring into space. Emmerich was sitting in a big easy chair with his feet up on an ottoman. Much to Andrews's surprise, he looked completely unconcerned. What a guy!

"Sit down, young lady," said Hardy; then he turned to Andrews. "Read her that transcript."

Angela sat huddled on the edge of a straight chair like a small girl who feels she isn't wanted. She glanced up apprehensively from time to time at Emmerich, but he paid no attention to her, seemed absorbed in his highball and cigar.

Andrews read the transcript of Angela's testimony in a shaky, self-conscious voice, with his head carefully averted from her. When he had finished, the Commissioner turned to Angela and asked: "Is that the statement you signed, Miss Finlay?"

"Yes, sir," said Angela in such a low voice that they could scarcely hear her.

"Is it true?" Hardy shouted at her, his little gray eyes flashing in an ominous manner behind his spectacles.

Angela stammered unintelligibly for a moment; then she looked to Emmerich for guidance, forgetting all about the big young cop, whose hands were now cold and clammy and whose brow was beaded with sweat.

Emmerich rose and tossed his cigar into the fireplace; then he finished off his highball. For a moment there was dead silence in the room, and two clocks could be heard ticking in staggered time.

Hardy continued to stare at the red-haired girl, his eyes coldly unsympathetic. Her lovely exterior meant nothing to him. A sink of iniquity was a sink of iniquity, no matter how delicate or polished or bedizened. Right and wrong were very simple things to him—and from this he drew his strength.

Emmerich spoke at last.

"Angela," he said, "tell them the truth."

She glanced up at him completely bewildered. What did he mean—the truth? Was he referring to what he'd told her to say? Or did he really mean . . . ?

"Uncle Lon . . ." she began, stammering, then broke off, unable to go on.

Andrews grimaced as if somebody had stuck a knife in between his ribs. *Uncle Lon*—for Christ's sake! Hardy's pinched face showed deep disgust.

"There's nothing to do but tell the truth," he snapped, "unless you want to be indicted for obstructing justice."

She glanced at Hardy in bewilderment. What was he talking about? Obstructing justice—indicted? The words meant nothing to her. But his cold, inquisitorial gaze terrified her. Was he really a man? And if so, how could he look at her that way? Hating her, not to be fooled, making her conscious of all the flabbiness and uncertainty of her character masked from other men by her outward lusciousness!

"That statement I signed," she said, unable any longer to bear the silence, which seemed to be drawing out indefinitely, "it . . . well, it's not exactly . . . I mean, it's not really . . ."

"Is it the whole truth?" shouted Hardy.

"No, sir," stammered Angela.

"Emmerich wasn't here at all, was he?"

"No, sir."

"He told you exactly what to say, didn't he? Made you learn it by heart?"

Angela was becoming hysterical now. She doubled over, put her head on her knees, and began to cry bitterly.

"Answer me!" cried Hardy.

"No, sir. I mean yes, sir," sobbed Angela. "I mean . . . I learned it by heart."

Hardy sighed and looked at Emmerich thoughtfully for a moment; then he turned to Andrews.

"Take a new statement from her. And this time, young lady, I want the truth."

Andrews's face was shiny with sweat now, and his heart was pounding. He stood there bitterly hating the Commissioner and all his mean, eccentric ways.

"Commissioner Hardy," he said, "couldn't we give her a little time to . . ."

"Get the statement now," snapped Hardy, turning away.

"There's a sun room right out there," said Emmerich calmly, indicating the way to the badly befuddled Andrews. "Just switch the lights on. You'll find a writing-table, pens, ink—everything you need."

As they passed Emmerich on the way to the sun room, Angela looked up at him with anguished eyes and said: "I . . . I tried . . . I'm sorry, Lon."

Emmerich smiled and nodded.

"You did pretty well—considering."

She hesitated, then spoke to him in a very low voice.

"My trip, Lon! What about my trip?"

"You'll be able to make it all right. Don't worry about it," said Emmerich, soothingly, in spite of himself feeling a little sorry for Angela and her naïve selfishness. She was young, had many years ahead of her, and as she was poorly equipped for dealing with life, except for her looks and a crude sort of cunning, the sledding would get progressively rougher.

As far as he himself was concerned, Emmerich felt a growing sense of relief. Maybe he was cooked at last. Maybe the rat race was finally over. Maybe Hardy had woven a web around him so strong and clinging that he would never be able to break through it to freedom.

He paused in his reflections, struck by a sudden thought. Was he still considering the possibility of fighting on?

All at once he recalled the violent, nightmarish episode with that hard-faced, Southern brute Dix, when he'd knelt on the floor in abject abasement, pleading for his life—willing, for a few horrible moments, to do anything on God's earth to save himself from annihilation . . . !

Nothing like that must ever happen to him again!

When Angela and Andrews had disappeared into the sun room, Hardy turned and said: "Seems to be all wrapped up, Emmerich. I want you to come along with me as soon as we get this statement."

Emmerich smiled slightly.

"I will admit, Commissioner," he said, "that this is the toughest case I've ever had to fight. But I'm pretty sure that I've already figured a way to beat it."

"I doubt it very much," said Hardy. "But time will tell."

There was a brief silence, both men thoughtful; then Emmerich offered Hardy one of his big Cuban cigars, but the Commissioner refused it.

"A little rich for my blood, thanks," he said. "Like the rest of this place—and the red-haired girl. I'm a hick at heart, Emmerich."

"Stop bragging," said the lawyer; then he bit off the end of a fresh cigar and lit up. "By the way," he said, "do you mind if I call my wife? She might be worrying about me. It's getting late."

"No. Help yourself."

"I'd prefer to call her in the cardroom. It's more private—but come along if you like."

"No need for me to go along, Emmerich. But don't try to run. You won't get far."

Emmerich laughed.

"Can you picture me on the lam—dodging big-bellied cops?"

Hardy threw an irritated but triumphant glance after Emmerich as he went out through the living-room archway; then he went back to the fire. Damn, it was a cold night!

The cardroom was chilly, and Emmerich shivered slightly as he sat down at his desk. Through the window at his elbow he could see a couple of harness bulls standing on the lawn. They were faintly illumined by the glow from the eaves lights. Dialing his home number, he watched them idly. They began to stamp up and down to warm their feet. He could imagine what they were thinking about the Commissioner, who had left them out in the cold.

His wife answered almost at once on her bedroom extension.

"Hello. Lon? Somehow . . . I've been expecting you to call. It's late, isn't it?"

"Sort of late, May. What are you doing?"

"Reading. Bracy sent me over a new book about Russia. Very interesting. When are you coming home?"

"That's what I called you about. May, I've managed to get myself into somewhat of a jam, and Commissioner Hardy has just arrested me."

There was a brief silence; then he heard his wife laughing at the other end.

"Lon! Stop joking."

"I'm not joking. I'm serious. Quit laughing, May, and listen to me. I don't know whether I'll be able to beat this case or not. I tell you this so you will see how serious it is."

"Oh, I'm not worried about you, Lon. There isn't a case you can't beat. You're the smartest lawyer in the United States. You should have been Attorney General. In fact, you would have been if you'd gone into politics."

Emmerich felt a sudden rush of emotion. What a revelation! Had she felt like this about him all along—and not just at first?

"This one," he said, trying to make his voice sound steady, "would take Blackstone himself."

"Don't exaggerate, Lon. When will you be home?"

"I'm trying to tell you, May; I don't know. You must get used to that thought and not worry."

"I won't worry for a minute. Didn't I just say . . ."

"All right, May. That's fine. Now you'd better get some sleep."

"But, Lon . . . I don't understand. How could you have done anything they could possibly arrest you for?"

Emmerich hesitated, bit his lips, wanting suddenly to tell her everything—all his errors, weaknesses, and follies; wanting above all to justify the erratic course of his life, and maybe even to gain a little sympathy. But it was no use. How could he make her understand? She might just as well have one more night of peace of mind.

"It's too complicated, May; I can't explain over the phone. A terrible legal tangle. All a misunderstanding, of course," he added, not thinking what he was saying, and then suddenly realizing that it was useless for him to think of trying to tell the truth; lying and evasion and deviousness were basic in his nature—perhaps always had been.

"Well, I knew it must be something like that," she broke in.

"So now you get some sleep, May. And don't worry. Everything's for the best."

"Lon! Wait. You don't sound like yourself. I never heard you say anything like 'everything's for the best' before. You don't talk that way—in clichés. What *is* it, Lon?"

"May—please do me a favor. I can't talk any longer. They're waiting for me. Get yourself a good night's sleep. Good-bye, dear. Good-bye."

He hung up quickly, then sat staring at the floor for a moment. An awful weariness had settled over him now, and suddenly he admitted to himself with unaccustomed candor that he'd been tired for years, bored with everything, moving through his life with automatic soullessness, like a clockwork robot.

Suddenly Emmerich experienced an overpowering sensation of release, as if the weight of all his years had at once been lifted from his shoulders. No more evasion; no more lies and devious twists and turns. He had faced the truth at last, and he knew now that it would set him free.

With tears in his eyes, he took out a memo pad and swiftly wrote on it a note that read:

HARDY:
Don't disturb my wife till noon tomorrow. She is not well and needs her sleep.
							ALONZO EMMERICH

He read the note over twice; then he took a small automatic from the bottom desk drawer, pressed it against the left side of his chest, and pulled the trigger.

It seemed to Emmerich as if there had been a terrific explosion of some kind; then a sledge hammer hit him a crushing blow in the chest . . . and red-and-white lights burst up through the darkness like fireworks at the old Lake Pavilion . . .

. . . at the Pavilion it was nice at night, the sky full of stars, and the dance-hall lights reflected in the placid dark water of the lake . . . but in the daytime it was nicer, with waltz music floating out over the water, where brightly painted rowboats were bobbing in the small swells from the sightseeing launch . . .

. . . along the bank the grass trampled by the Sunday crowd smelled wonderfully sweet. A big bunch of balloons got away from an excitable Italian vendor; and May, her face pink from the sunlight filtering through her pink silk parasol, burst out laughing as the balloons sailed off over the Pavilion into the hazy blue of a summer day . . .

. . . the hazy blue of a summer day!

Doll was very much worried about Dix and kept glancing at him as they drove along through the waking countryside. His face was gaunt and pale in the grayish, pre-dawn light, and at times his big, powerful, capable-looking hands trembled on the wheel. If only he wouldn't insist on driving! But she had given up arguing with him about it. He didn't get angry or shout suddenly at her as had been his habit. No, he answered all her arguments by saying in a mild voice: "You don't know the way. I'd just have to keep telling you."

They were passing through beautiful farm country now, with wide, gently rolling fields enclosed by stout, well-cared-for fences, pleasant white frame houses, and huge red barns dominated by their tall and massive silos. Harvest time was past, and the corn stood in thick, golden-brown shocks, flanked by big, orange-colored pumpkins, fat, ripe, and ready to be cut from the vine.

In the woods the leaves had turned from green to red, to russet, rich dark brown, and gold. Flocks of migratory birds were flying south over the trees, and crows were cawing hoarsely in the empty stubble fields.

A faint pink glow showed in the east now, and Doll sighed with relief. The sun would soon be up. For hours she'd despaired of ever seeing another day. The night had dragged on interminably, as if the clock of the universe had run down.

She sat thinking about their almost miraculous escape from the city. She had been stopped twice by prowl cars before she could get back to the apartment with Quigley's Ford. After that it had seemed hopeless to try to break out of the mobile police ring encircling the Camden Square district. But Dix wouldn't listen to reason. He kept insisting that he was going home—and damn the police! She tried to make him see that all they had to do was hole up for a few days until the heat was off. But she was wasting her breath.

At the last minute Dix decided to drive; nothing she could
say would dissuade him. He got in behind the wheel, and
they moved off through the city as if they were two tame
citizens going downtown to a late show. Dix made no at-
tempt to dodge about the side streets or take short cuts
through the twisting alleys. He drove straight to Parkway
and headed for the business district by way of the big, well-
lighted Erie Street Bridge. They passed through the sleeping
downtown area without one challenge, though they saw
many motorcycle policemen. Dix ignored them—didn't even
seem to realize that they were there.

The rest of the ride through the city had taken on the
quality of a nightmare for Doll, who sat in silence, hunched
up against the cold, as Dix drove at a moderate pace through
miles and miles of unfamiliar streets; past huge, dark mysterious buildings; through endless, flat suburbs; past warehouses, labyrinthine railroad yards, tall, ominous viaducts,
angular cement causeways; through slums where the frame
houses leaned and little all-night eating joints stabbed the
misty darkness with red, green, and yellow neon signs;
through factory districts, silent as a cemetery, where faint,
lonely lights showed beyond the high fences in the deserted
yards.

Doll, who hadn't left the Camden Square district all the
time she'd been in the city, was appalled and intimidated
by the monstrous, sprawling immensity of what she had
once considered a familiar place.

Groggy from weariness, and dozing from time to time in
spite of herself, she began to feel that somebody had succeeded in putting a hex on them and that they were condemned to go round and round the inside of a huge, inescapable
ring till they collapsed from exhaustion or died.

More suburban districts slid by; more warehouses, more
factories, more deserted shopping centers, shuttered against
the night . . . till finally they saw a little diner at the far
end of no place, a diner with a small yellow neon sign that
read: EAT. Then suddenly they were in the open country
passing darkened farmhouses.

At this point Dix, without a word, turned and shook a big fist at the city, which lay behind them now, harmless, inert, nothing but a wide faint glow on the horizon. . . .

Doll sat watching the sun come up, big and red, over the brown fields. They crossed a little stone bridge, and the creek flowing under it showed a delicate glaze of pink and opal in the dawn light. Cattle were standing knee-deep in the water drinking slowly.

"Won't be long now," said Dix, turning to smile at her.

Doll felt a sudden pang. Dix's smile, a very unusual expression for his gaunt, hard face, showed happiness and hope, but also pain and extreme exhaustion.

"Dix," cried Doll, "your wound's bothering you again, isn't it? And you're about worn out. Please . . . let me drive."

"I'm okay," said Dix. "Anyway, we'll be there in a little while—soon as we cross the big river."

He laughed suddenly, a pleasant chortling sound; and Doll stared at him in surprise. She had never heard him laugh like that before. He sounded like a different person entirely—young, happy, carefree!

Doll gasped when she saw the huge, lake-like river spreading before them, and immediately felt a sharp fear of it. *And the bridge!*—a gigantic structure, making the many bridges of the city they'd left behind look like toys.

It was toward evening now, and the far shore was hidden by a gauzy autumn mist. They started across the bridge. Hundreds of feet below them was a tremendous sheet of dark water, glimmering dully, like oil, in the descending dusk. To Doll, huddled down in her seat, cold, tired, and nervous from long, incessant strain, it seemed to have all the vastness of an ocean—as if they had reached land's end and were now heading off into nowhere.

It grew steadily darker on the bridge; but in a few moments lights began to appear on the far shore, tiny little yellow pinpricks in the hazy blue twilight, faintly and softly reflected in the deeper twilight of the water. Doll felt an overwhelming surge of relief at the appearance of the lights. At least, somewhere in the distance there was land.

The man seemed both puzzled and unfriendly, Doll thought, as he stood in the flood of light from the open farmhouse door, looking up at Dix. He was short, chunky, and bald, and dressed in neat overalls and a worn leather jacket. He looked like an East German or a Pole and spoke with a slight foreign accent.

". . . but, look here, mister," he was saying, "the Jamiesons haven't owned this place for ten, twelve years. I know because my father bought it from them. He's dead. I work it now. It's all mine. You're a little mixed up, aren't you, mister?"

Dix's face was shadowed by his wide hat brim, and the chunky little man kept peering up, trying to get a good look at him so maybe he could figure him out.

Dix stood staring about him in blank bewilderment. There were the trees the bats used to fly out of on summer evenings, hunting their dinner. There was the trampled dooryard and the big oak whose trunk he used to try to span with his outstretched arms. Not so far away through the darkness was the pond where the frogs used to sing at nightfall, and where the bluish will-o'-the-wisp used to dart along the tops of the tall cattails. And there, just above him, its window brightly lit, was the room where he'd been born, November 15, 1895.

All this belonged to him as nothing else in the whole world since had ever belonged to him. And yet . . . it wasn't his at all. This fat little Polack fellow standing before him, suspicious and unfriendly, had just said: "It's all mine."

Doll noticed that Dix was beginning to sag like an old tire with a slow leak. He turned away and leaned on the car for support.

"You all right, mister?" asked the foreign farmer, a note of grudging anxiety in his voice. Then, as he got no reply, he went on: "If you're looking for the Jamiesons, the old missus is living in town on Elm Street, next to the A. and P. She's living with her son Wolfert . . ."

"Woodford," Dix corrected him with a faint note of contempt in his voice; then he raised his head and spoke to

Doll. "I guess you better drive the rest of the way. I'll show you."

Doll moved over behind the wheel, and Dix stumbled around the car, finally managed to get the door open after several fumbling tries, and fell down into the other seat with a groan.

"Straight on in," said the farmer, wanting to be more helpful now, feeling sure that the big lanky man was either sick or in trouble of some kind—or both. "Just follow the main highway."

"I know," said Dix morosely.

The man stared, annoyed at the way his helpfulness was being received.

"Thanks," said Doll hurriedly as she started the car. "Sorry we had to bother you. Thanks very much."

The man thawed immediately.

"Oh, that's all right, lady. Always glad to help."

Doll drove out of the dooryard and turned off onto the main highway. After a moment she could see across the flat, open country the lights of a little town strung along the horizon.

"Mighty funny," Dix mumbled as if talking to himself. "We been there five, six generations. Now this Polack fellow's got it."

"You all right, honey?" asked Doll, trying to sound calm, but half hysterical with exhaustion and worry.

"Little weak. I'm okay."

The main street of the little town was bordered by tall oak and elm trees, and men were busy at the curbs burning huge piles of dead leaves, the yellowish flames leaping in the blue darkness, filling the air with a pleasant, pungent aroma.

Dix stared at the fires uncomprehendingly. Doll had to speak to him several times before he answered her.

"This is Elm Street, Dix. Where's the A. and P.?"

Dix roused himself, then sat up and looked around him.

"Ain't changed much," he said. "Always was a one-horse town. Never liked it. They had a big parade for us

here—right down this street—when we come back from
France. Woodford got drunk and stole Judge Meredith's
chestnut gelding and rode him to hell and gone—damn near
killed him! But the Judge just laughed about it. You see,
we whipped the Germans. So we had the town. That is, for
a short while . . ."

"Where's the A. and P., Dix?"

"Right there," said Dix, suddenly speaking in his natural
voice. "It's dark—but there it is. Same as ever. Old man
Beaufort's son Alan used to work there in the summer. But
he stole too much. They wouldn't put up with that, even
from a Beaufort . . ." Dix laughed, then shouted impatiently: "Right there, I told you—for Christ's sake!"

Next door to the A. and P. was a run-down-looking little
frame house with a light in the window. Doll stopped in
front of it; then she hurried around to help Dix out of the
car. He rested his hand on her shoulder so heavily that she
staggered and would have fallen if she hadn't taken hold of
the car door in time.

As she was helping him across the sidewalk, he said:
"Funny for us to be living here. This is where an old girl
friend of mine used to live when I was going to high school.
She was no beauty, but she was cute and smart. She married
Judge Meredith's no-good son Lafe . . . she could have
married me and not done any worse . . ."

Doll knocked at the door softly, and they stood waiting
in the shadows of the little wooden porch. She was so
exhausted and nervous and worried about Dix that she could
just barely restrain herself from bursting into hysterical tears.
Dix leaned against the house front for support, but went on
talking.

". . . used to be a porch swing here. One night Woodford
and me horsed around with it till we got some of the links
sprung, and when Lou Sally's old man sat down in it, the
chains broke and you could hear him yelling and swearing
clear out to Harter's Creek . . ." Dix laughed weakly.

But Doll was paying no attention to what he was saying.
Dix was about ready to fall, and she could feel her own

strength ebbing. What was she going to do if there was nobody at home? She knocked frantically, then kicked at the door.

"Getting cold out," said Dix, shivering and looking about him dazedly. "Didn't used to be so cold here in the fall."

"Oh, God!" cried Doll. "What are we going to do?"

"Why . . . wait," said Dix, laughing. "Woodford always was slow as molasses in January. How do you like that Polack fellow calling him Wolfert?"

Dix lurched forward suddenly, and Doll caught him just in time and by a great straining effort managed to move him back against the wall.

"Dix!" she cried. "Do you hear me?"

"Hear you? Christ! Course I hear you. No need shouting at me. I'm not deaf."

He straightened up a little and took some of his weight off Doll, who was almost ready to fall. Now she heard movement in the house, and in a moment the door was opened by a big gaunt man in his shirt sleeves, wearing a battered, old-fashioned star badge on his unbuttoned vest. A tall, thin old woman, with bold dark eyes and thick iron-gray hair skinned back over her ears, came hurrying up behind him.

"Whoever is it, Woodford," she asked in a mild voice, "kicking at the door?"

Woodford peered out with unfriendly, narrowed eyes.

"A drunk man," he said. "And a strange woman."

"Woodford!" cried Dix. "I was just telling Doll about the porch-swing chain . . ."

"Glory!" cried the old woman, her face calm but her voice startled. "It's William Tuttle . . . !"

Dix stumbled into the room, staggered wildly for a moment, then pitched forward into his brother's arms. Doll stood staring, utterly alien, not knowing what to do or say, feeling completely excluded.

Woodford and the old woman pulled and tugged at Dix till they got him across the room; then little by little they lowered him to a battered old couch, where he lay gasping and looking up at them, trying to smile.

"I was at the farm," he said between gasps, "and a Polack fellow said it was all his."

"We sold it, Tuttle," said his brother. "We had to. Bad times and all."

Doll moved back against the wall so she'd be out of the way, and kept looking about her at the poor, bare room with its hundred-year-old furniture, its faded pictures in ancient walnut frames, its family Bible on the old walnut gate-leg table—its spotlessness! She wanted to run—leave this place which made her feel like a badly soiled outsider from another world.

She began to cry, and the old woman glanced at her in irritation.

"That badge there, Woodford," said Dix. "Since when?"

"Since things went to hell in the thirties. It's a living."

Dix stared at his brother for a long time, breathing heavily as if he'd just climbed a steep hill. Finally he laughed.

"You chasing kids out of the apple orchard! I'd like to see that—biggest apple thief in the county when we was kids!" He laughed again; then he started up. "Where's that girl who came with me? Where's Doll?"

"I'm here, Dix," called Doll, biting her lips to keep back the sobs. "You want me?"

"Her name's Dorothy Pelky," Dix explained. "And she's all right."

Dix's mother and brother turned to look at her. Their faces were harsh and unfriendly.

Doll looked timidly from one to the other; then she spoke in nervous haste, trying to placate them, trying to justify her existence.

"If it hadn't been for me, Dix . . . I mean, him . . . William Tuttle would . . . would never have got back home. I bought the car for him. I . . . " Suddenly she noticed the color of Dix's face and stopped, then broke out: "He . . . he's hurt bad. He was shot. Don't you think you'd better call a doctor?"

Waiting for the doctor, they all sat in uneasy silence, listening to Dix, who was rambling from one subject to another like a man under the influence of a powerful drug. All pain seemed to have left him. He was no longer turning and twisting as he had been a short while back, but was lying comfortably on the couch, hardly moving at all, his big feet hanging over the edge. Just as the clock was striking ten, he stirred, his eyes opened, and he sat up slowly and looked about him. His gaze, vacant at first, gradually cleared, and his eyes traveled from his mother to his brother, then to Doll. Finally he reached into his pocket and took out a crumpled roll of bills and handed it to his brother.

"Over three thousand bucks there," he said in his natural voice. "I want you to hang onto it for me. This time . . . I might not make it. Doll's got nothing. No people. No place to go. You look after her, Woodford. Now mind what I say. You look after her—you and your badge. No matter what I did, she didn't know anything about it. Law's got nothing on her—except she was with me. Maybe that's a crime, but I don't think so, and you don't either, badge and all . . ."

Exhausted, Dix lay back and drifted away from them into another world . . . the pleasant world of the past. He could plainly see the old walnut gate-leg table, but it wasn't in Lou Sally's living-room now. It was by the big north window that looked out over the dooryard toward the stable and the white-fenced paddock, where a couple of weanlings were kicking up their heels, as weanlings always did when the weather was fine. His old man was looking up a date in the family Bible. There had been a discussion at breakfast about one of the old man's uncles: Titus, the one who'd gone west in the eighties and had never been heard of again. "There it is, right there, goddamn it!—right in the Bible. He was born in '43. That's what I said." William Tuttle wanted to talk about the weanlings, but his father was so preoccupied with the Uncle Titus argument that he wouldn't listen. William Tuttle liked the black weanling best and wanted to give his reasons. Even Woodford wouldn't listen . . .

But later the black weanling, now a big colt, sixteen hands

two, won the Governor's Cup at the county fair, and even
managed to win a race or so at Latonia in the overnights.
Best horse the Jamiesons had ever owned except for the
Irish thoroughbred Tuttle's great-grandfather had imported
from the old country—and maybe that was all just a lot of
talk . . . !

Damn foolishness, or just pure greed, as his mother had
said, when the old man sold the big black colt to a horseman
from Lexington. Tuttle couldn't stand to see him led away.
He went out to the barn and found Woodford alone in the
tackroom, pretending to mend some harness. Woodford didn't
want to see the colt led away either. Tuttle joshed him about
it, and they got into a fight and Woodford split his lip . . .

He'd never forget that day. Sunlight was warm in the
dooryard, and the hoarse cawing of crows sounded from
the cornfield . . .

Suddenly a voice broke in on Dix's dreams, a vaguely
familiar voice that seemed to come from a long distance
away—an old, irritable, masculine voice.

"Not much use, Woodford. Do the best I can, but . . ."

Dix opened his eyes. A face was near to his—a lined,
leathery face with flashing spectacles. Why, Christ! It was
old Doc Carmichael. Was he still living? Must be pushing
eighty.

Someone was holding his hand in a tight grip. He turned
his head with a great effort. Some woman or other—some
stranger—was sitting there staring at him with tears in her
eyes. Now where the hell did she come from? And who the
hell was she?

Dix wanted to be back with the black colt. He turned his
head slowly on the hard pillow of the couch.

"He's trying to say something," said the doctor.

They all watched Dix in anxious silence.

". . . always said . . . best of the lot," gasped Dix. "The
bay was all right. Nice little horse. But the black one . . ."

Woodford stared.

"He's talking about Jett Prince. God! I haven't thought
of that horse for over forty years . . ."

Doll began to sob, and Mrs. Jamieson glanced at her with irritation, then her harsh face softened a little.

Dix died shortly after midnight.

"I bring 'em into the world, and I bury 'em. The same ones," thought old Doctor Carmichael. "It's getting a little trying."

· 39 ·

It was nearly two o'clock in the morning when the phone began ringing at the Commissioner's house. Not long before, Mrs. Hardy had finally managed to get her husband to go to sleep. She was worried about him. He was a nervous man, with more courage than strength, and he'd been pushing himself to the limit the past few weeks—ever since those horrible gorillas from the Camden Square slums had broken into Pelletier's and stolen all those jewels. Imagine—over a million dollars worth!

Swearing under her breath (what a shock Theo would get if he knew that she swore!), she lifted the receiver and spoke into it in a whisper.

"Commissioner Hardy's residence."

An operator spoke to her. There was a long-distance call for the Commissioner.

"I'll take it. This is Mrs. Hardy."

"It's the Commissioner who's wanted, ma'am."

"I don't care who's wanted, miss. Either I take it or you can forget it."

"Hold on please."

There was a long delay; then a harsh masculine voice began to speak.

"Mrs. Hardy? Detective Lieutenant LeMoyne. May I speak to the Commissioner?"

"You may not, Lieutenant. I just got him to sleep."

"Well . . . I guess it will keep, Mrs. Hardy. Meanwhile

I'll call the Chief of Police. Anyway, you can tell him tomorrow that the case is wrapped up.''

Mrs. Hardy felt a great sense of relief, and now she spoke more amiably.

"Thank you, Lieutenant. Thank you very much.''

"Not at all, Mrs. Hardy. I hope the Commissioner gets a good sleep. He can use it. Good night.''

Mrs. Hardy hung up and tiptoed down the hall to the bedroom, opening the door with extreme care, inch by inch. A dim night light was burning on a little stand. The Commissioner seemed lost in the huge double bed. He was on his side, with his face turned away from the light, sleeping peacefully.

His wife smiled, then inch by inch, closed the door and tiptoed down to the kitchen to make Theo a couple of sandwiches in case he might wake up hungry before dawn, as he often did.

· 40 ·

Farbstein, a little the worse for bourbon, was sitting in the city room with his feet on the desk, reading an early edition of a rival newspaper when the word came through.

Young Bryan told him about it. Farbstein sat lost in meditation for a long time; then he began to speak slowly and in a rather impressive voice.

"What though the field be lost?'' Farbstein intoned. " 'All is not lost; th' unconquerable will, and study of revenge, immortal hate, and courage never to submit or yield, and what is else not to be overcome; that glory never shall his wrath or might extort from me.' ''

Young Bryan stared in half-amused wonder. If it had been written, Farbstein had read it.

"Shakespeare?'' he inquired.

"Ill-read fellow,'' cried Farbstein. "Not the Bard. Milton.'' He rose slowly and uncertainly, and struggled in silence till he got his hat on straight and his overcoat buttoned. Then he said, "*You* know. My cousin—Milton Farbstein.''

Bryan snickered appreciatively. Farbstein yawned widely, leaning against the desk to support himself; then he turned and walked with slow and careful dignity across the long, dim-lit city room and out the door.

As the door fanned, a chill, numbing blast blew in from the cold, dark streets of the sleeping city.